RECKONING

KERRY WILKINSON was one of two things as a child. If you ask him, he was a well-meaning, slightly hyperactive young man with an active imagination. If you ask his mother or teachers, he was a bit of a pain in the bum.

Before the age of flat screen televisions, laptops, mobile phones, hover boards and the internet, there were BBC B Microcomputers and there were real books with actual paper pages. Really! Kerry grew up playing ropey-looking computer games that you needed a keyboard for, being rubbish at football, and reading science fiction and fantasy novels.

The Silver Blackthorn trilogy is Kerry's first fantasy work. His other series, the Jessica Daniel crime books, are also published by Pan Macmillan.

He is also definitely not a pain in the bum.

For more information about Kerry and his books visit:
Website: www.kerrywilkinson.com or
www.panmacmillan.com
Twitter: http://twitter.com/kerrywk
Or you can email Kerry at
kerryawilkinson@googlemail.com

Kerry Wilkinson

RECKONING

PAN BOOKS

First published 2014 by Pan Books
an imprint of Pan Macmillan Ltd, a division of Macmillan Publishers Limited
Pan Macmillan, 20 New Wharf Road, London N1 9RR
Basingstoke and Oxford
Associated companies throughout the world
www.panmacmillan.com

ISBN 978-1-4472-3530-9

3 5 7 9 8 6 4

A CIP catalogue record for this book is available from the British Library.

Printed and bound by CPI Group (UK) Ltd, Croydon, CR0 4YY

RECKONING

1

It's difficult to describe the sensation when you walk out of your front door and there are thousands of people there. I have lived here all of my sixteen years and know almost every part of the cobbled streets that criss-cross Martindale. All the years of playing hide and seek, rushing in between the houses, exploring and generally getting into trouble means that I could close my eyes and still find my way from one side of the village to the other.

Not today though. Now the streets feel as if they belong to other people.

I'm not sure what it is that unnerves me the most: the sheer number of bodies I can see, or the noise. It vibrates everywhere around me, footsteps clipping loose stones along the crumbling paths and excited chattering voices bouncing around our usually quiet streets. There is a nervous hum too – an indefinable energy that you can feel in the air.

In the murky, dirtied window of our house, I catch my own reflection and push the light streak of long silver hair hanging across my face over the top of my head, where it settles with the rest of my straight, dark locks.

I look more tired than I feel, the weight of the day already upon me.

My family left a little while ago, wanting to give me time to think and get ready for my big day. My mother kissed me on the forehead, telling me to do my best and that she believed in me. Now they are somewhere among the crowd; individual parts of a single throbbing mass of humanity. Sat alone in my room, staring at my own reflection in the mirror, I could hear the atmosphere building but it didn't prepare me for this. It is almost overwhelming.

I find myself glancing down at the dull white-grey thinkwatch on my wrist. It is almost like a morning reflex, to check my alerts. Today, there is only one word – 'RECKONING' – followed by the time and place. On so many occasions, I have scrolled forward through the days to stare at that one word that now it feels a tiny bit under-whelming to see it there. Reckoning day and the Offering that follows only comes once a year and everyone has been waiting twelve months for this. For me, the Reckoning is something I have spent my whole life anticipating as each year's has become a progressively larger event. Even though we will only spend a few hours inside the village hall, the build-up has grown into a whole morning for everyone – a time for people to celebrate the end of war, although it isn't as if we have prosperity to enjoy. Perhaps that is why this is something to look forward to?

The time when us children become adults and go out to help rebuild the nation.

Our battered school with its leaking roof and mouldy, damp corners is too small to be suitable for the enormity of the day. Others may talk of the repairs that need to be done to the old building but I like the fact we get to use an item as modern as a thinkpad against the backdrop of something that comes from a different age. I am fond of my creaky, slightly soft wooden chair too. I suppose that is somebody else's now that I will no longer be going back.

I turn and step into the crowd, heading in the vague direction of the hall but not wanting to get there too quickly. The atmosphere is friendly, parents holding onto their children's hands as we all bob through the streets, unable to move too fast because of the sheer weight of people.

Most of the residents of Martindale know me by name. They have seen me grow up; many of them have told me off at various times for not looking where I am going when I am running through the streets. As I look from person to person, I cannot see a face that I recognise. Feeling a stranger in my own village, I manage to reach the edge of the street, out of everyone's way, where I stand on tiptoes and glance towards the far reaches of the village.

Over the tops of the bobbing heads, I see a train with a long row of carriages behind it, stretching into the distance, rusty and battered. It becomes apparent where all the people have come from. Although some sixteen-year-olds would have been brought in for their Reckoning anyway, it seems like everyone they've ever known has come too.

I'm still not sure why – it wasn't like this last year.

After another glance at my thinkwatch, I slide into the crowd again. At first it is easy to move between the people but the numbers soon thicken. By the time I am within sight of the hall, people are standing four or five deep along the edge of the road, packed tightly, buzzing with excitement.

When I finally reach the main square, it isn't simply the number of people disorientating me. There is colour everywhere, baskets of flowers hanging from buildings – scattering yellows, pinks, reds, purples and everything in between as far as I can see. Decorations which have sprung up overnight.

Around me, every other person seems to be waving a flag with the cross of St George on it, the white corners glowing bright in the morning sun against the blazing blue sky.

I try to think where they might have come from but then I see a man walking along a space that has been cleared at the back of the square, handing them out from a box. It's not hard to realise he is different to us. His suit fits perfectly and his shoes are shinier than most of the coins we use. We make do with items of clothing which have been passed down that don't fit, are ripped and permanently stained. He walks tall and without pain, a clear sign he has not had to undergo the manual labour most of the people in Martindale endure.

The man disappears out of sight along an alleyway and then returns moments later with another box of flags. I wonder what it is all for, then I see heads turning to look behind me. I spin to see a man with a camera pointing in my direction and realise why there are so many people here. Ours is one of the villages that will be featured on this evening's Reckoning round-up. I suppose it is our turn. The cheers of the crowd suddenly increase and I turn to see the flag-man waving his arms around encouragingly.

Now I am closer to the centre, I notice a handful of familiar faces among the sea of bodies, neighbours and parents of people I go to school with. Then I look up to see the other teenagers taking the Reckoning standing on the steps of the hall. I am early for the test itself, but somehow late to the celebrations. I want to stay away from the attention, so sink into the crowd, a few rows back from the steps.

Behind me, the man in the suit is urging everyone forward towards the base of the stone steps that lead up to the hall. My friend Opie is in the centre at the top, bouncing awkwardly from one foot to the other and probably wondering where I am. I want to stop to watch them for a few moments but, behind me, I feel hands on my back as a woman who lives on our street pushes me towards the stage. 'Go on, love,' she says with a friendly grin, 'it's your day.'

Given the number of other people who seem to be enjoying themselves, I'm not sure the day is much to do with me any longer.

As I stumble forward, others notice and urge me on, delighted someone who is taking the Reckoning is actually among them.

Gradually, I nudge my way through, avoiding the stamping feet and manic, flailing arms. Over the voices and footsteps, I can hear the sound of someone playing a flute towards the back of the square. The beautiful melody catches on the breeze, carrying over the crowd before somebody else joins in. Within moments, it sounds as if there is a whole band playing: trumpets, recorders, a drum, perhaps even a violin? I have only ever seen one once, when a travelling show came through the village. I want to stand on tiptoes again to see if I can find out where the music is coming from but the crowd is too tight and I am being pressed forwards.

I have never seen or heard anything like this.

As I get to the front, I edge up the steps, trying not to attract too much attention. Kingsmen stand at either end of the line, their black uniforms in stark contrast to the white of the flags being waved around them. They aren't exactly unknown on the streets of Martindale but as I reach the top, I can see more of the dark colours that signify the country's combined army and police force massing along the back of the crowd, out of sight of the cameras.

Everything they wear is made of a thin, flexible metal called borodron that no one else seems to have access to. They have black tunics, matching trousers and shiny boots, as well as helmets that arch over their head and ears. Even their thinkwatches are made of the same black material, in contrast to the silver metal everyone else's is created from. Two of the Kingsmen at the top of the stairs stand motionless, their slick appearance somewhat jarring with the solid shining metal swords that are wedged into their belts.

I slide behind one of the people I don't know and glance sideways towards Opie, who hasn't noticed me yet. It looks as if his mum has made an effort to tidy his hair, as the blonde tufts that would usually be naturally tousled have been flattened. He has a bristle of dark hair on his chin. I remember the day two years ago when he excitedly showed me the first few wisps under his mouth, telling me he was on the road to becoming a man. I laughed then but he seems like one now with his larger, stronger shoulders.

He is looking at his own thinkwatch, a constant reminder of how different we can be. The devices remind us of what we need to do each day and when each night's curfew is. He accepts everyone has to use their thinkwatches to enter and exit buildings and pick up the weekly rations; I think about who decides what those limits are. He accepts that they work; I wonder why nobody can take the lifetime batteries inside and use them to make sure no one has to freeze to death during the winter.

Opie glances away from his wrist and, although I don't think he means to, he is so pleased to see a familiar face that he says my name. I smile awkwardly, attempting to ignore the camera now skimming along the line.

It is only from the top of the steps that I am able to take in the true scale of how different the square looks. Bunting, flags and the flower baskets are attached to every roof and the layer of grime which would usually greet us has been washed from the bricks and stone. It is so unfamiliar and I wonder how much it has all cost – probably enough to feed everyone who actually lives here for weeks. The effort to make this happen overnight is beyond my comprehension.

I try to look for the band but they have gone silent. The Kingsmen have now spread out, encircling everyone. From ground level, where another camera is, nothing is visible except for excited villagers waving their flags. It's not hard to picture how it is going to appear on everyone's screens at home tonight but then this is the biggest day of the year. Now I am a child but after a few hours in the hall, I will be expected to leave an adult.

It is a reckoning in every sense of the word.

2

As the hall doors open, the crowd cheers on cue. Then it's a whirlwind of action, the Kingsmen springing to life, ushering us into the main part of the building. I have only been inside once before, when we had to register my brother Colt for school two years ago. The grim, yellowing brickwork is as I remember and my footsteps clatter on the hard surface. I look up to see a full-length painting of King Victor hanging on the wall directly ahead, dwarfing everything else. His short ginger hair and regal crimson gown are instantly recognisable from the images of him on our screens but he seems utterly unnatural due to the sheer size of the canvas he has been depicted on. I am towards the back of a queue that has bottlenecked as people stop to stare in awe.

I manage to squeeze myself through the crowds until I am close to Opie. I can see the nerves rattling through him.

'I don't want to be a Trog,' he whispers to me.

I try to speak reassuringly but he isn't listening. 'You won't be.'

After the Reckoning, we will all end up in one of the

four categories. An Elite is just that. I should probably be a Member, the next level down. Most end up as Intermediates but no one wants to be a Trog. They get the worst jobs and the lowest credit on their thinkwatches. They are assigned everything no one else can be bothered to do. For Opie, being graded as an Inter is something he aspires to; for me – for my mother – it would be a disappointment. Wanting to be an Elite is perhaps aiming too high; hardly any come from our village.

I say his name but his eyes are as blank as I've seen them. Eventually, he faces me, nodding towards my wrist. 'Did you change your mind?'

My eyes flicker sideways but there is only a nervous bustle of teenagers and no one around us to overhear. He is wondering if I have done anything to my thinkwatch to try to cheat the Reckoning but he knows we shouldn't talk about that here.

'I've not touched it,' I reply.

Opie is one of the few people who knows how good I am with technology; I've been doing it for so long that it is natural. But altering your thinkwatch is an offence punishable by either banishment or death. It is never for anything noticeable; an extra bit of food when my brother Colt was poorly, or a few more minutes of electricity when our house is unbearably cold in the winter. Opie is the only person I can trust to keep these secrets to himself.

The lake outside Martindale has long since run dry. It is filled with old computers and circuit boards, keyboards, screens, primitive thinkpads and watches. In the distance, there are mountains of old fridges and freezers, piles of rusting vehicles, metal, plastic, rotting wood; all different shapes and materials. Some of the areas I know well but there is more here than could ever be explored in a lifetime; a collection that spans decades of innovation, before the war and the shortage of electricity and power that followed. At some point these items would have filled people's homes and lives but they have long since been thrown away. I began to naturally drift there, playing with the objects as if they were toys and figuring out how everything worked – then creating my own versions. Opie and I have spent so much time there that we have our own nickname for the place – the gully. Even before the Reckoning tells me what I should be doing, everyone expects me to end up working in research and electronics, trying to find practical answers to the nation's problems. It sounds too easy, as if there aren't already people trying to do the same thing.

'I've heard Paul Fisher is going to try to trick it,' Opie adds quietly, nodding to a boy on the far side of the room who is standing by himself.

I'm not entirely surprised. Anyone who is aged sixteen on the first of July has to take the Reckoning. Opie and myself only just qualify this year but Paul is almost a year older than us and has had all those extra months of worry and anticipation. Opie is concerned too but no one in our village expects him to perform that well. He is a practical person and the Reckoning is an academic test, or so everyone assumes. No one really knows how it works. I'm expected to do what I always do – get by. For Paul, there is more to it than that. His family were rich before the war and, although they have the same rations as the rest of us, there is a belief that someone such as Paul should perform strongly. This could be the worst day of his life.

'What is he expected to get?' I whisper.

'He should be a Member but he wants to be an Elite.'

It's all guesswork anyway; some say you end up with the rank you want, others that you have to work for it. Some say it is all about what happens on the day but there are those who insist it is about the things you have studied over the years in school.

If Paul is going to interfere, I hope he knows what he's doing, even though I doubt it. There isn't enough power for any of us to go to school for more than two days a week and I know he wouldn't be able to rival me when it comes to assembling and reassembling a thinkwatch – not that he would be aware of my talents as I hide the extent of what I can do well enough.

Before Opie can say anything else, more Kingsmen appear, motioning for us to stand in single file.

For the first time, I begin to feel something at the bottom of my stomach, nerves I am not used to, reminding me that the next few hours will define who I am to be. I near the front. One of the Kingsmen is holding a flat screen that looks like a slightly larger version of a thinkpad, on which I scan my thinkwatch. After it acknowledges me with an authoritative-sounding beep, the Kingsman says one word: 'Thumb'.

I press my thumb onto the pad as a red light scans underneath. At first nothing happens and, just for a moment, I feel a panic that something is wrong. Then, as quickly as the feeling arrived, it disappears as the machine emits another satisfied beep. The cameras are there again as we troop one by one through to a large room. Rows of tables are laid out and a tall bank of windows allows the sun to stream through. I blink rapidly to adjust to the light before I feel a hand on my arm. A Kingsman is pushing me towards an empty seat on the far side of the room.

I stumble slightly from his shove and try to look for Opie as I move. He is at the front and though I will him to turn and look at me, he doesn't move.

Waiting on the desk is a thinkpad but not like the ones we usually have at school. Those are thick, scratched and heavy, but this is silvery, thin and soft. When I touch the screen, it leaves a small indentation. In the bottom corner is the communication port which I press my finger into. I feel a prickling at the base of my skull, as it scans my thoughts. I feel something in my head, asking my name and date of birth, and no sooner have they come to the front of my mind than I feel it telling me the answers have been accepted. A page of text appears on the screen, cataloguing so many things about me that I had forgotten most of them, a complete listing of everything I have ever successfully remembered at school. When you first start using one, it takes a while to figure out which thoughts you should be giving it. It doesn't read your mind, it simply stores what you tell it. Where the information is kept, no one seems to know, but this new thinkpad has all the data from our school ones, so it must be somewhere externally.

I look up from the device but, apart from the back of Paul's head in front of me, there is little to see. His thumb is pressed to his thinkpad and I wonder how he might try to cheat. My only guess is by tampering with his thinkwatch. The thinkpads connect to your thoughts but we've all felt the tingling under the metal of our thinkwatches as it does so. On its own, a thinkwatch acts as a way for us to communicate with each other, for our days to be planned, to receive alerts, and to tell us the time. With the thinkpads we use at school – and this new one in particular – the two seem to work in tandem.

The thinkwatches are complicated devices but logical at least. You are not supposed to remove the underside panel but, if you do, there is a trick I found through years of playing at the gully which allows you to get into programming mode. With a mixture of guesswork and experimentation, I worked out that you can use that to take advantage of almost anything you want. The only problem is that I am almost certain everything is fed back to some sort of central server. You can get away with cheating on your rations or altering your schedule – but only if you do so in small amounts. The first time I tried, I doubled my rations but after a week, the Kingsmen refused to let me leave the allocations carriage of the supplies train. I was terrified as they scanned my thinkwatch but then, after an hour or so, they released me. The next day, my rations were back to normal. It took me another six months before I was brave enough to try again and only by using it sparingly have I stayed undetected. Or at least this is what I assume.

I wonder if Paul is somehow aware of the things I am. Perhaps he has gone further and has been able to manipulate the way our thinkwatches communicate with the thinkpad? As my eyes begin to peer towards the light of the windows, I feel the device tugging at my thumb, letting me know it is time to begin.

The strangest thing is that no two people have the same story to tell about what the Reckoning is. After each year's is over, the younger children ask the older ones what happens but all I have ever heard is that it is a new kind of experience. Some say it is a conversation, some a test. Others seem scarred by it, almost bullied, while the mother of one of Martindale's few Elites once told me her son said it was the best few hours he had ever had.

Not knowing what to expect, I feel a question drifting into the front of my mind, wondering how my day is going. I try not to smile but respond that I thought the Reckoning would be a little harder than this. I can feel the itching under my watch as a tickle goes down my spine. For me, this feels like a conversation, as the thinkpad starts painting scenarios into my mind and asking me what I think. For the most part, it is a pleasurable experience. It makes me feel like I am flying, then judges whether I am happy. Suddenly, I feel as if I am falling rapidly. I breathe deeply and calm myself and the device seems pleased. It asks me what grade I would like, telling me I could be a Trog and not replying when I tell it I would not be that concerned. Broadly it is the truth. It shows me images of death and asks what I think, then instantly flicks to an infant child. I can feel it trying to manipulate me, searching for who I am as a person.

It asks me if there's something I'd rather not tell it. I fight to keep Paul away from my thoughts but I can tell that's not what it's searching for. Instead the pressure is building in my ears, starting with a gentle squeal and increasing quickly until the sound is everywhere, squashing and squeezing me like the most brutal of hugs. In the moment it takes for me to breathe in, I feel as if I am falling again and suddenly the Reckoning is tugging a memory from my mind.

3

YESTERDAY

I feel the goosebumps rise on my arm as the chilled rush of the breeze skims across the remains of the gully, a reminder the warmth of summer is almost over for another year. I can hear my mother in my head, telling me it's time to go in, that tomorrow is a big day and the last thing I need is a cold to go with the nerves, even if most of the anxiety is hers. The truth is, I am sat here gazing at the pile of shattered electrical goods for a reason, waiting for the snap of a broken screen or the crunch of an old piece of plastic to disturb me. Maybe Opie believes the gentle howl of the wind will be enough to cover his footsteps or, more likely, he still has no control over how much noise he makes as he blunders through the mounds of other people's rubbish. It's not as if I haven't told him to be quiet enough times when we've been out. But there it is, a brush of broken glass against boot that makes me want to grin, although I remain sitting against the dirt bank, facing the other way.

If I wasn't trying to pretend I didn't know he was there, I would probably laugh at the fact Opie thinks he can sneak up on me. We have known each other for most of the sixteen years since we were born a day apart and, although he has those few extra hours, he has rarely been able to get anything over on me.

But today is different because tomorrow's Reckoning will change both of our lives, almost certainly dividing us. That is why I came out to our spot to wait, pressed up against the gentle incline of the dry lake facing away from the forest, away from our village. I knew he would show up at some point: he has a question to ask.

As I feel him approaching, I decide to let Opie have his moment, keeping my eyes steady on the wreck of plastic and glass filling the space that once brimmed with water, fish and any number of creatures we hear stories about. I never knew my grandparents, but Opie's grandmother never seemed happier than the evenings she spent telling us stories of how things were before the war; when the gully held water, not the waste and memories of a different generation.

As he touches my shoulder and grunts a 'raargh' of happiness, I jolt my body in mock surprise, turning around, grabbing his legs and pushing him to the ground. I roll on top, peering down at the sandy soil which has caked his hair. He tries to grab me but I wriggle from his grasp and elbow him under the ribs in the way I know will make him giggle with ticklish enjoyment. He writhes involuntarily and kicks me upwards until we are both lying in the dust, staring at the grey skies, hooting to ourselves as if this won't be the last time we do this. Around us is the sea of technology that no longer works.

'You knew I was there, didn't you?' he says in a voice that seems to get deeper each day.

'It wasn't hard with those big feet of yours scaring everything that is still alive out there.'

Opie doesn't reply but I feel his hand rubbing the back of mine and allow him to lock our fingers together as we listen to the draught of air scuttling around us.

'You do know those parts belong to the King,' he eventually says.

I knew he would say that; he always does. Technically he is right – the piles of unwanted, unusable electronics that fill our abandoned lake certainly aren't mine.

'Everything belongs to the King,' I remind him.

'What are you looking for anyway?' he says, ignoring my point. I know he is hoping I will answer the question he has come to ask before he even gets to it.

'The usual,' I reply, pushing myself up onto my elbows, still holding his hand and acting as if I don't know what he is up to.

Opie raises himself up too and we lean into each other, back-to-back. 'How are you so good with this stuff?' he asks.

I'm not sure I know why myself. I have grown up with all of this around me and, for whatever reason, I find technology easy.

When it's clear I don't have an answer, Opie lets my hand go and shows me his thinkwatch. 'What do you think it was like before these?' he asks.

It's hard to imagine life without them and as an adult they will define who we are. Before you take the Reckoning, the face of everyone's thinkwatch is a dull white-grey, in contrast to the silver metal circle around it. Once your place in society has been decided your thinkwatch becomes coloured and branded. If you are an Elite, the face turns black with the faint symbol of a crown to show that you belong to the top section of society. If you are a Member, the front becomes orange with a lightning bolt to symbolise industry and productivity. Inters have blue watch faces marked with a sword, while those in the lowest band of society – the Trogs – have yellow watches inscribed with a small sickle. I look at the piles of orphaned electrical items in front of us. 'Probably not that different,' I say. 'They just used other things then.'

'I can't imagine one of those on my wrist,' Opie replies, nodding towards an old screen, but he has missed the point. Perhaps that's why I'm good with this type of thing and he isn't.

I stand and walk towards where he indicated, picking

up the remains of an old thinkpad. It is light as the back has been pulled off, the battery removed. The screen is scratched, although I can still see fingerprints from where someone would have typed and swished their fingers across. Opie joins me, running his hands through his hair in an effort to clear the muck from the ground.

He still hasn't asked me what he came to.

The panel comes apart easily as I reach into where the battery would have once been and pull. It exposes a near see-through board that is wedged underneath the screen. I sit on the floor and hand it to Opie.

'Can you pull that out?' I ask.

He sits beside me and easily wrenches it free, even though he struggles to fit his grimy nail in between the layers. Handing it back, he asks if I'm nervous, although he knows the Reckoning is far more of a worry for him than it is for me.

'Who isn't?' I reply, trying to make him feel better.

Gently balancing the screen, I reach in and pull out the tiny springs that hold it together. I feel Opie watching me, his blue eyes absorbing the movements of my fingers, before I put them in my pocket.

'What are they for?' he asks.

I hold out my white-grey thinkwatch for him to see. 'The last time I opened mine up, I broke one of the springs. It's always useful to have a backup.'

His eyebrows angle downwards in disapproval. They are thicker than I remember, one of them caked in a smattering of sand from where we were play-fighting.

'You know you shouldn't be messing with it,' he scolds, although he doesn't mean it. He pauses, before adding: 'You're not trying to cheat, are you?'

His tone is suddenly nervous and I know he is close to getting to the point.

I turn to face him but he can't meet my eyes; instead he stares out over the rest of the gully, where the deepest depths of the lake would have once been. It stretches as far as I can see, rusting old vehicles, engines, and many things I don't recognise. Miles and miles of rubbish.

'No one in their right mind would try to fix something as big as tomorrow,' I say as delicately as I can, deciding to give him the answer before he is forced to ask. Extra rations now and again is one thing but someone's entire future is too big to go unnoticed.

Opie nods an acceptance as I rest my head on his shoulder, watching the clouds drift slowly overhead and trying to see shapes that don't exist. The air smells of rain, although it remains dry for now. Soon, Opie sits, scratching at his scalp, trying to remove the dust but making it worse as he doesn't realise how dirty his hands are. I can see his shoulders twitching as they always do when there's something on his mind. Perhaps he is more nervous about tomorrow than I thought? Or maybe he is worried that this will be our last afternoon together? I stare straight at him, waiting for him to ask the other question he has been holding back.

'What if you're chosen?' he asks.

We both know our lives are going to be different whatever happens after the Reckoning but being an Elite or a Member has risks as well as benefits. The King requires that each of the four Realms offer him four Elites – two boys and two girls – and two Members, one from each gender, every year as an Offering. Your remaining family are showered with credits, rations and gifts in exchange, but you never see them again as you spend the rest of your life in service to the King. He only takes one Inter from each area and two Trogs in total, alternating between the districts. No one wants to be a Trog though, even if it reduces your probability of becoming an Offering.

'If I'm chosen, I'd have no choice,' I say, although that isn't what he is really asking. Because it is the North's turn to send a male Inter this year, I could have my way out if I could fix it.

'It's a great honour,' he adds, sounding the way his grandmother used to speak before she died. She was always a big supporter of the King, although most people who lived through the war are.

All of a sudden, I am wondering if that's why he wants

to be an Inter so badly – because it will give him a chance of becoming an Offering. Both of our families could certainly do with the riches it would bring, despite the price. The fact none of us knows what being an Offering entails is seemingly lost on everyone. It's one of the things people never talk about. When I asked my mother, she told me not to ask questions. That is always her reply when you mention something she doesn't know the answer to, or feels uncomfortable speaking about. Even when we are at home, she will look around as if someone else is watching, then tell me to hush.

Perhaps it is just because of the age she grew up in: war, famine, mistrust and death.

I hear the gentle pitter-patter of rain before I feel it, the slow drizzle licking the leaves of the trees behind us as I lift myself up before the dirt becomes mud. I haul Opie to his feet, although he doesn't need my help. He continues to hold my hand as we run up the muddying bank from the gully. His grip is strong, although he allows me to lead. The rain grows stronger but I pick my way along a different route to usual, telling Opie it is because the branches are thicker and will keep us drier. If he suspects it is because I don't want to let him go quite yet then he plays along without saying anything.

All too soon we reach the edge of the trees. I can feel the looser strands of hair sticking to my face and it is genuinely soothing as Opie reaches towards me, stroking them away from my eyes. He laughs as he tells me he has accidentally left a smear of dirt across my forehead and I playfully slap his hand away before scrubbing at my skin. We stand together, his arm around me, my head on his shoulder. Our hair sticks together but neither of us minds.

We each stare out towards Martindale, watching the thin wafts of smoke beginning to drift upwards as people light the logs in their fireplaces to try to warm their houses. I can just about see the roof of my house through the thin mist which is descending, although Opie's is obscured, even though it is only across the road. I squint to look at the patch next to our chimney stack which Opie helped to fix last winter, using his hands to seal the gap with a skill that can't be measured by tests.

I go to speak but he pulls me tighter and gets in first. 'I'm going to miss you, Silver Blackthorn,' he says, and I can't tell if he is trying to hold back tears.

I have spent months, maybe years, thinking the day wouldn't come but now there is no avoiding it. As the water drips from my forehead, I realise we could be sent our separate ways in a matter of hours.

*   *   *

I gasp as the memory flutters out of my mind but I can still feel the thinkpad holding me. That spot on the banks of the gully is something that should belong only to Opie and me. At first it feels like a violation but then I realise the Reckoning isn't interested anyway – it only wanted to examine my feelings, not know the exact memory. No sooner can I catch my breath than I feel it pulling at me again. I want to fight back, to deny it access to my most private memories, but I cannot stop it.

4

I have never understood how something can seem close and yet it ends up being such a long way away. I have lived in Martindale for my entire life, waking each morning and walking onto the streets to stare up at the hill in the distance. I have always believed I could walk there one day. When I was very young, I remember asking my father about it and he always promised we would make the trip when I was older. I asked how long it would take and he grinned in the way only my daddy could, telling me it would take as long as it needed to.

As I walk towards the hill now, I know I am not going to get close. My legs feel sluggish and I know I have slowed down. If anything, the destination seems to be retreating further, the hazy sunshine making it shimmer in the distance.

Opie has dropped his pace to stay by my side. We have been walking all morning. At first we chatted and laughed, speaking about when we were younger and telling stories about the people we know. Now I can feel a slight shortness of breath, knowing I am going to have to rest soon. We got up as the sun was rising, sitting on the grassy banks outside of Martindale and watching the gentle orange glow fill the sky until a beautiful blue enveloped everything above us. We have been looking forward to this day for months now, telling ourselves we would do something different for our fifteenth birthdays.

For at least an hour, all we have seen are endless lush grassy fields, trees, squirrels scurrying in and out of the hedgerows, pheasants and pigeons chirping to each other and, of course, that hill towering on the horizon – as far away as it ever was.

The sun is at its highest and I know I cannot continue. We could walk for the rest of the afternoon and not reach our target but even if we turn around, we are still hours from home.

Opie is a few steps past me when he realises I have stopped. He turns around, his blonde hair ruffling in the breeze, but, if anything, its untidiness makes him more appealing. His head is tilted as he grins lopsidedly.

I love it when he looks at me like that.

He scratches the back of his neck, unsure what to say, but I sit on the ground, relaxing into the luxurious grass and taking a breath.

'I could just leave you here,' Opie says, half-turning away as if heading back to our village. He must have known for as long as I have that we were not going to get to the hill.

'Go on then, Opie Cotton,' I dare him, knowing he won't.

He takes two steps away but I don't budge. 'Are you coming?'

'No.'

'You can't stay here forever.'

'I can.'

Opie sighs. 'What about your mum?'

'She'll blame you for leaving me.'

He snorts at the suggestion. 'Don't you want to see Colt again?'

'He'll blame you too. He'll say, "Why, Opie? Why? Why would you leave my only sister out in the open?" His little face will be all upset and it will be your fault.'

Opie shakes his head. 'You can't blackmail me.'

'Want to bet?'

He smiles again and it is magical – he makes me like being me. 'What do you want?'

'A piggyback. You're all big and strong and male. I'm a little girl. Look at me.'

I can feel the breeze in my hair too, whipping it across

my face as the silver streak at the front that gave me my name separates from the longer, darker strands at the back.

'I'm not carrying you all the way home,' he says.

I smile, knowing I am winning. 'You don't have to take me all the way back – just most of it. I need a rest.'

'It's too far.'

'Think of poor Imp. He might be your brother but he looks at me like a sister. Who's he going to fight with if you leave me here?'

Opie shakes his head and starts walking away. I run the grass between my fingers, plucking individual blades and counting under my breath. I get to eight before he turns and screams my name. It disappears into the vast open space as he runs back towards me, throwing himself onto the ground as we roll around, giggling uncontrollably. His big arms are wrapped around me as I cradle my head into his neck.

'You're a menace, Silver Blackthorn,' he says.

'I'm *your* menace,' I correct him, knowing today is a day I will never forget.

* * *

The experience feels so real that it takes me a few seconds to realise where I am. I start to count in my head, reminding myself that this is the fifteenth annual Reckoning. Many sixteen-year-olds have gone through this before. Now I can understand why no two people have the same story to tell about it – I'm not sure what it is myself, even when I'm in the middle of taking it. Its mystery is the biggest reason why the day is so fearsome for us, that and the fact that our results are pooled together across the country. Our Northern Realm is ranked against the East, South and West to determine who gets the most supplies for the next twelve months. We are taking part not just for ourselves but for everyone around us too. I can feel it skimming through my memories, but it doesn't seem particularly focused on the exact contents, more on how I respond to things. Am I emotional? Impulsive? Strong?

I can sense it stretching further, delving deeper, wanting to know more about me. My throat is dry and I am desperate for a drink but before I can even think about doing anything, it has taken me again.

5

SEVEN YEARS AGO

It has just begun to rain as I creep around the hedge, peering into the murky distance. I can hear my mother's voice in my head, telling me not to venture out into the woods, telling me it's not safe and making up stories about mystery animals she thinks should scare me. I smile as I somehow know she only says these things to try to make me stay close to home. I keep moving, even as the patter of rain increases, bouncing from the plants and hitting the floor.

I don't even remember the first time I came to the woods on my own but I must have only been six or seven, walking to the edge of the village and staring towards the trees before dashing home again. My mother was always happy to let me play in the streets as long as I didn't go too far. Even then, I knew her definition of 'too far' would not be the same as mine. Month by month, I would venture further until today, where I promised myself I would keep walking until I found the old lake people around the village talk about. It is officially out of bounds, with people saying Kingsmen used to patrol nearby to make sure no one ever went there. Either that was a myth, or they don't bother now as I see nothing but scurrying small animals, apparently terrified of me.

I continue moving through the trees, quicker now as if the accelerating rhythm of the rain is keeping time for me. Soon I am running, giggling to myself as I know how naughty I am being. I cannot stop myself; I know every corner of the streets around Martindale and have a craving that is hard to describe, a need to find somewhere new.

It isn't long before I end up sliding across a mossy patch of land, stumbling and covering my trousers in grass and mud. It won't be the first time I return home looking like this and my failed promise to stay in the village is going to get me into trouble again . . . if my mother isn't too busy looking after Colt, of course. He's so young and she only has time for him at the moment. She lets me get away with things now because her attention has mainly been focused on him since my dad died. At first I pushed because I wanted attention, now I do it because I cannot stop.

As I pull myself to my feet, I emerge through a final row of trees and stand open-mouthed staring at the sight. I have seen images of lakes on the screen at home and know they should be full of water. In front of me must be the lake people around the village have spoken of but instead of the rain rippling the surface of water, it is clanging off pile after pile of metal and plastic objects. On and on the sea of discarded items goes, as far as I can see.

Crucially, there are no Kingsmen either.

I know I should turn and race home – I have seen what I came to – but somehow I feel drawn to the sight in front of me, stepping carefully across the sopping ground until I am at the rim of the rubbish. On the edge, wedged into the mud, is what looks like a cross between the thinkwatch strapped to my wrist and the thinkpads we use in school. I crouch and pick it up, running my fingers across a cracked screen and fumbling around its hard metallic edges for anything that might make it work. I don't know what it is about it but I feel some sort of spark as I weigh it in my hands. I know instinctively that this object comes from before I was born, probably from before the war. I feel an uncontrollable urge to find out what it does.

As the rain starts to ease, I notice three more of the items and pick them all up, hurrying back towards a large tree that offers a degree of shelter. Each of the devices has a button at the top which pushes in but nothing happens when I try it. I twist each of them around in my hands, knowing they must have done something at one point. I compare them to my thinkwatch.

Grabbing a fallen branch, I whittle it on a tree stump,

rubbing as hard as I can until I have filed it to a point. When it feels sharp enough, I use the wood to dig into the side of the device, pushing as hard as I can until it pops open. One by one, I open the other three too.

I am not the best reader in my class but I make out the word 'phone' written on a label inside one of the devices. I have no idea what it means but think I'll memorise it and perhaps ask my mother at some point. I can pretend I heard someone in the streets talking about one.

I pull out all of the pieces inside, laying them on the ground next to each other, choosing the shiniest from each of the four sets and rebuilding one of the phones as best I can. My thin fingers dig easily into the corners behind the glass, pressing everything back together until I am convinced it will show me whatever it is that it does.

I press the button on the top, holding my breath, waiting for something to happen.

Nothing does.

The rain has gone by now but I check my thinkwatch and know I have to head home. Colt will have had his tea by now and Mum will start to get worried if I'm not back soon. Standing, I brush all of the parts underneath a bush with my feet and start to plan when I might be able to come here next. I glance at my watch again, wondering if the parts underneath are anything like the ones I have just taken out of the phone.

Somehow I know I will return here many times in the future.

*   *   *

I gasp again as I finally manage to shut down the memory. I had forgotten that day, the time where I first started exploring the items around the gully, taking them apart and putting them together again, trying to figure out how they worked. It wasn't long after that when I first risked opening up my thinkwatch. I shake with shock at the fact the Reckoning has taken these thoughts from me, but that only makes me want to fight back.

I wonder if the Reckoning is going to keep pushing me, if it is trying to catch me out for all the things I have done wrong in the past, but somehow it doesn't feel as if that's what it was after. Perhaps my resistance was what it wanted all along?

I sense that the thinkpad wants my emotions, not my memories, so I don't hold back, embracing the anger it has made me feel. Suddenly I am full of confidence as it continues to probe my mind. Words are drifting into my head but I push them away, instead forcing my questions towards it, wondering where the information goes, who invented it, how exactly it works. Each of my thoughts is resisted as a dull pain creeps through my forehead. When it shows me a crinkled black ball and asks me what I see, I respond that it is a crinkled black ball. When it says it has nearly finished and allows me to see myself standing and walking away, I think of myself in the spot I am now. The thoughts evaporate in a grey haze before I feel the tingling in my thumb again. This time, instead of drawing me in, it is pushing me away.

I stop touching the thinkpad and look up to see everyone else turning to face each other. Some are smiling, others frowning. Some seem confused, others as if they have woken from a long sleep. The only noise is a scraping of chairs, no one daring – or trusting themselves – to speak. I stand and turn towards the exit where lines of Kingsmen are standing close to the door. One by one people begin to file out, ruffling their hair, or touching their faces. I suddenly notice I am doing it too, my fingers scratching the back of my neck, as if rubbing away the memories.

I can see why no one really has an answer for what the Reckoning is. It is all the things people have told us it is: a conversation, a threat, a dream, a laugh, enjoyable, hateful, challenging, and so much more. Some people clearly have a life-changing experience but I feel the same as I did when I walked in.

Opie appears at my side but there is something not quite right about his eyelids. They are drooping more than they would usually and his pupils are larger. He smiles at me, asking if I am all right. I want to reply to say that it is him who looks strange but then we hear the commotion ahead.

The slow line of people leaving has stopped as we bunch forward into a semi-circle around the exit. Two Kingsmen are standing between us and the way out and I know instantly something is wrong. I have never seen a Kingsman with his sword unsheathed, but the two ahead are holding weapons at their sides. People are beginning to step backwards slowly as I see Paul isolated in the centre. He is glancing from one Kingsman to the other, panic on his face.

There is a moment of silence before he says: 'You've got it all wrong.' Neither of the guards reply, instead they reach forward at the same time. Paul sidesteps one of them but the other grips him by the throat, backing him towards a wall. Everyone seems to breathe in at the same time and we all know something bad is going to happen. I will Paul to go limp and not fight but instead his legs flail in resistance. They pin him to the floor, the second Kingsman wrenching Paul's arm free and pressing his thumb onto one of the thinkpads. We all see the red line scanning downwards and then a momentary pause before it emits a crunching noise and flashes white.

There is no hesitation as the second Kingsman raises his sword and plunges it deep into Paul's thigh, skewering him like a snared rabbit.

6

None of us moves. We all know the rules of Reckoning day; don't miss it and don't cheat. Or, I suppose, don't get caught. Paul screams in agony as dark, black-looking blood spews from his leg, pooling on the floor. We have all seen far worse on our screens, where people are punished and killed routinely as a warning for their transgressions. It feels different to witness it in person, the anguish uncomfortably real, Paul's cries of pain rippling through my ears. I feel like covering them but, within seconds, more Kingsmen pour through the door, lifting Paul and carrying him away as he drips spots of blood behind them.

Everything has happened in a matter of seconds.

Behind me, a voice breaks the stunned silence: 'I guess that's what happens when you cheat.'

They are stating the obvious, although their tone makes it sound as if this is something perfectly normal. I have never been friends with Paul, yet it didn't feel right watching him writhing on the ground.

Before I can begin to process what has happened, some- one steps forward and walks through the door and within moments we are all following. I feel Opie's hand at the bottom of my back guiding me but only for a second.

Outside, there is another wave of celebration. From the top of the steps I can't see anything other than streamers, confetti and people waving and cheering. There are more faces than before and the sun is higher and brighter. At the entrance are two cameras but I avoid them, hiding behind Opie's imposing figure before sliding through a gap between people and disappearing into the crowd.

It is hard to move because everyone is so tightly packed but I squeeze in and out of the masses before the numbers eventually thin. Kingsmen are still circling as I reach the back but, as one of their hands edge towards his sword, I say that I have just finished, holding up my thinkwatch. He could choose to scan it to make sure I'm telling the truth but instead he stands to one side, letting me through. Colt and my mother are in the crowd somewhere and Opie will wonder where I have gone but I need this moment for myself.

On the outskirts of the village, the only other people I can see are lone Trogs sweeping the confetti in the space between the Kingsmen and the buildings. One of them has his shirt sleeves rolled up, exposing the thinkwatch on his wrist and the gentle yellow face. I don't bother going home, instead dashing through the deserted streets, heading towards the gully.

Past the village border, over the ridge, through the trees until I am sitting in the same spot as I did yesterday, lying on the dry-again ground and listening. When I was a child, Mum would tell me bedtime stories of how things used to be. She would talk about birds chirping to christen a new day but, as I close my eyes, there isn't even a rustle of the wind to comfort me. I try to picture what the lake might once have looked like but can't think of anything other than the piles of unusable glass, silicon and plastic that litter the hollow bowl in the ground.

My thinkwatch begins to beep and I know it is time. For a moment I do nothing except open my eyes, squinting at the bright blue of the sky. I hold my wrist in front of my face but it takes a second or two for my eyes to adjust to the crisp dark words on the screen.

'Silver Blackthorn: Member'

It is hard to know exactly how the decision is arrived at. No one has a definitive explanation. The phrase 'Await further instruction' drifts into view and I know I will be given my role in society at some point tomorrow. The circular white-grey portion in the centre of the metal begins to swirl yellow and red until it settles into an orange colour. Initially, it burns bright before fading into the more gentle hint I have seen on other people's thinkwatches. In the centre is the outline of a lightning bolt, etched in a slightly lighter orange shade.

I should share the news with my mother and Colt; they will both be excited and disappointed at the same time. My status will reflect on the pair of them and they will gain greater credits because of it – but it is still likely I will have to leave Martindale to fulfil whatever role I am assigned. Most Members are sent to the bigger cities, where there are the bigger industries and they can be of more use.

I lie thinking for a while, drinking in the air, and then take my time returning to the village, allowing myself to enjoy the trees for one final time, even if they don't feel quite like they belong to me when it is sunny. As I stand on the bank that overlooks our houses, I see lines of citizens ready to get back onto the train. Pockets of people are drifting through the streets but, as I look towards the hall in the distance, I can't see anything other than the black dots of the Kingsmen.

At the house, Colt and my mother are both waiting for me. People around the village say we all look alike but I have never seen it. My mother's hair is lighter than mine and nature has lined her face with wrinkled reminders of what it is to bring up two children. I cannot ever imagine a time where she would have been able to chase around avoiding trouble in the way I somehow manage to. Colt is excited but Mum says something about wondering where I went. I don't mention the gully, or Paul, instead flicking through the message screen on my watch and showing her the colour and the news. Her smile is a mix of pride and sadness. Colt bounces on the spot in happiness. He has short brown hair cut into a bowl shape, almost as if Mum has done it with a pair of scissors and a dish. Perhaps she did?

The rest of the day is a haze of congratulations, with messages arriving on my thinkwatch from friends every few minutes until I know what everyone else has been selected as. The village has produced no Elites but only one Trog – a relatively good year. Opie's fears were not realised as he comes around to tell me he is an Intermediate, proudly showing off the pale blue on the face of his thinkwatch with the imprinted sword. Although I don't understand how the grades are arrived at, I know Opie well enough to realise that he would not have fought back against his Reckoning in the way I did.

As the sun sets, the sharpness of the season returns, the moisture in the air sticking to my throat and a frost appearing underfoot. This is one night no one will go cold, the one evening a year where everyone has electricity to heat their houses and watch the Offering. Despite that, it has been an annual tradition for Opie and his family to come to our house. Although that doesn't mean things are the same every year. For one, his family grows rapidly. He has four younger brothers: Samuel, Felix, Eli and the youngest, Imp, who is six. They each look like smaller versions of

Opie, as if he has been captured at various points in his life. Imp is the only one who differs slightly; his grin is more lopsided and his eyes are a different colour, though they all have the same distinctive mess of blonde hair and sense of adventure.

My mother sits with Opie's parents on the sofa as Colt plays with Eli at the back of the room. I lean next to Opie on the floor, playing thumb wars with Imp, who cheats by pinching my knee and then pinning me. I tell him he should sleep with one eye open but he tells me he does anyway. Seeing as he has four older brothers, I am inclined to believe him. There is a small smear of dirt along his knuckles and under his chin, as there always seems to be. I try to lock that image in my mind as a way to remember him. He spoils it by whacking the back of my hands and asking if I want to play slapsies. Usually I would say no but, as a final hurrah, I decide to teach him I can hit hard for a girl.

As I have him shrieking in gleeful pain, the screen switches itself on. We all stop talking and shuffle ourselves around to face it. It is small and the colours are too bright but it functions when there is power. Many of my early memories involve huddling around the screen underneath blankets. Tonight, the radiator in the corner, brown through age, is plugged in and spewing warmth into the room, although I still think it would be nice to have the comfort of a blanket. We rarely light an actual fire.

The national anthem plays as a St George's cross flutters on screen before fading to an image of King Victor. The orange of his hair is amplified by the colours on our screen, distorting his face. It is the same introduction that opens the public floggings and hangings, which are shown automatically on our screens once a month.

The screen fades until it reveals the outside of Windsor Castle. More trumpets, more flags and then it is time to get serious. Imp shuffles uncomfortably on the floor but I put my arm around him and he snuggles into me, nestling his head under my armpit.

The screen changes to a much dimmer scene. A caption at the bottom tells us it is the Tower of London and there is a row of seven people against a wall – a lot fewer than any other year I remember. I gasp and turn to Opie as the camera pans past Paul. His face is swollen, purple and bloody as he hangs limply from cuffs attached to the wall. Opie seems unmoving, which I can't blame him for. These are the circumstances we have all grown up in. Although we have watched the parade of cheats each year, to actually see someone we know still comes as a shock.

The Minister Prime is on the screen, a face which, if anything, is more familiar than the King's. He is our monarch's right-hand man and is always there for the televised punishments and executions. Aside from the annual State of the Nation speech, it is always the Minister Prime who addresses us – even when the King is sitting next to him. He has short black hair and a square, solid-looking jaw with wide, broad shoulders. His eyes are as dark as his hair and, as he strides along the line, I find myself focusing on how big he is, his heavy boots thumping off the floor with every step.

The Minister Prime walks along the line, allowing the camera to showcase everyone. Some of the cheats have been beaten more than others; Paul is among the worst. There is a cut along the side of his face, his eyelids are black. He can barely open them as he says: 'My name is Paul Fisher and I tried to cheat the Reckoning.'

'Is that him?' Opie's father asks.

'Yes,' Opie replies.

'Good.'

Opie doesn't take after him but his father, Evan Cotton, has always been the most patriotic person I know.

After everyone has confessed, a Kingsman strides along the length of the line, cutting the thinkwatches from each of their wrists. There is only one thing worse than being a Trog – Paul has been condemned to life as an Outcast. He will be sent to the mines and have to live on whatever food or water they choose to give him, as well as having no status. It is a far worse punishment than death. To further enforce the point, we are told that all of the cheats' families have had their status downgraded to Trog.

The King knows how to send a message.

After that, we switch back to an electronic map which has England and Wales divided into the Realms we know. We all know there was once a 'Scotland' but we are no longer supposed to speak of it.

A man wearing a Kingsman's uniform runs through a list of overall statistics: the percentage of Elites is marginally up this year but so is the amount of Trogs. Members are a little down but Inters are steady. Because of the increased number of people taking the Reckoning, however, the projected figures show a sharp upsurge in the predicted productivity of the country. Opie's father gives an approving whoop at the news.

We then get the results for the Realms. The South has again produced the most Elites, which has everyone, including Opie, bristling in annoyance. We are third, with the East behind us. We are also third for the number of Members produced but second for Intermediates. Even I feel myself holding my breath as we reach the final figure and cannot stop myself cheering as we find out we have produced the fewest number of Trogs. I give Imp a squeeze and feel Opie rubbing my back. I am nowhere near as nationalist as some are but even I like the idea of winning at something. Even though I am not convinced being a Trog holds as much shame as people seem to think.

In the final results, the South has won the Reckoning and we have come a distant second. The West is third, narrowly behind us, and the East fourth. We are reminded that these results determine how much rations each area gets and it is hard not to get drawn into the excitement of the moment. All of the people around me should be able to eat more next year, even if it is only a slight increase. Last time, we were fourth – so it is an incredible turnaround.

Next, we get the same speech we hear every year. Only the numbers change. 'Twenty-five years ago, this country was destroyed by selfishness, incompetence and lies. Eight years on, King Victor united this nation in peace, showing us the light where there was none. Tonight we show our gratitude.'

A Kingsman turns, pressing a button on the screen behind him that displays a list of names. 'This year, for the thirteenth time, the South was victorious in the Reckoning. These are the names of every young boy and girl who will become Elite men and women.'

I squint but the words are too small to see. He presses another number and one zooms into focus, reading 'Hoyle Brent', before they all begin scrolling sideways. They whizz across the screen far too quickly for any of us to be able to read.

The Kingsman reminds us that each Realm has to provide four Elites, not that any of us could have forgotten. One by one the names on the screen freeze, revealing the Offerings from the South who will be going to serve the King. Then the two Members, a boy Inter and a girl Trog are confirmed. He says there will be partying on the streets tonight and maybe there will be.

The West is next, names scrolling along the screen until there are four more Elites, two Members and a female Inter. No Trog is required from the West this year.

It feels as if everyone breathes in together as we are told it is time for the North. Eli and Colt join the rest of us in front of the screen as we all huddle together, not because we're cold but simply as we are so used to doing it. One by one our Elite Offerings are named, although they all come from the bigger cities.

The last Elite to come from Martindale was named Hart and he is the village's only Offering too. I remember sitting in this spot two years ago when his name appeared on screen and the ripple of satisfaction and excitement which went through us. It gave our community a feeling of purpose, that we were a part of the Realm and could contribute the same as everyone else. The morning after that Reckoning, we all went onto the streets to wave Hart goodbye and wish him well, everyone grabbing his wrist to stare at the strange grey-black colour on his thinkwatch that we had only previously seen on screen. I still remember him telling his mother that he loved her and the tears that came. Most of all, she was proud of him, as we all were. I can't think of anything that has brought us together quite like that did. This morning's celebrations felt forced and mechanical in some ways, prompted by cameras and flags. That moment was spontaneous, an eruption of pride in ourselves and respect for Hart.

None of us has seen or heard from him since.

After the Elites, it is time for the Members. The boys are always chosen first and a full list of names appears on the screen, although the words are barely dots before the first one zooms into place and everyone starts scrolling side-ways. I can feel the sweat on my hands as I clutch Imp tighter, using him as the blanket I don't have, before the screen halts on a name from one of the cities I don't recog-nise. Opie is next to me and I can almost feel what he no doubt does at this moment – the excitement, fear, pride and realisation.

Then it is time for a female Member to be chosen. I see the dots of names on the screen and know mine is there somewhere. Imp wraps his arms around me and I feel Opie's reassuring hand on my spine. One name comes into focus and then they are all scrolling at speed. I think I see mine a few times but it is just a jumble of letters blurring into one. As they begin to slow, I find myself holding my breath and as the carousel slides slowly from one name to its final selection, I realise it has been inevitable this whole time. Everyone seems to gasp together but somehow I already knew what was going to happen. My thinkwatch beeps and buzzes at the same time as my eyes focus on the screen and the name that has been selected: 'Silver Blackthorn, Member, Martindale, North'.

7

People start knocking on our door almost immediately, many bringing offerings of food: buns, bread and fruit. I eat nothing, leaving everything for my mother and Colt to have. There are pats on the back and words of encouragement but, most of all, smiles of pride from villagers who see me as someone their own children can aspire to be. It feels strange as I am just me, the same person I have always been. I wonder if I really have done something worthy of the adulation; did my Reckoning have something special about it which prompted my choosing or is it really a random lottery?

Opie's mum hugs me and says well done. Imp clings to me, only letting go when his mother says it is time to go home. She kisses me on the head and says she'll see me tomorrow as she shivers her way out onto the street. Opie doesn't seem to know what to say, offering a half-shrug, half-wave which is about as emotional as I would expect him to be in front of others. The bewilderment in his eyes is enough to tell me how he feels.

And then it is just me, Colt and Mum. My brother

doesn't seem to know whether he should be happy or sad but then neither do I. Pride and fear, confusion and exhilaration, loss and anticipation; I feel it all and more. I was expecting to leave to go to the city for work but there would always have been the opportunity to return home on odd occasions. This is final.

Soon my mother sends Colt off to bed, saying he needs his sleep before tomorrow's big day. Then she holds me and I feel as if I'm a child again, being cradled by my mummy after she has told me I won't be seeing my father again.

'I'm so proud of you,' she whispers in my ear but I don't know what to say as I haven't done anything out of the ordinary, I have simply been chosen. Even if I wanted to reply, there is a lump in my throat that stops me from saying anything.

She sends me to bed with a final kiss on my head and says she will wake me in the morning, although we both know the chances of me sleeping through the night are non-existent. I lie awake and think of the extra provisions and status she and Colt will have and realise the good it will do for everyone. I try to think of what I may have to do as an Offering and wonder if this has already been decided.

I drift in and out of consciousness and, as the sun begins to rise, Mum joins me in my room, sitting behind me in front of the mirror, combing my hair. I don't mind, even though I can't remember the last time I allowed her to help.

She runs a damp sponge through it, gently easing the teeth of the comb through as she does so, removing the last bits of dirt and grime from my trip to the woods yesterday. She doesn't ask if I was out with Opie, although she probably knows.

The position of the mirror forces me to look at us both and I can see what everyone has spent a lifetime telling me: we share the same eyes. There are a few more crinkles around the corners of hers but we each have a matching deep, dark brown colour that almost makes it look as if we don't have pupils. She looks into mine briefly, before returning to what she is doing, pulling my dark locks back tightly, leaving the strand of light, silver-white hair at the front to fall loose. I tuck it behind my ear and then ask her to tell me the story of how I got my name. She has told me many times before but I always find it comforting and we both know this will be the last time she tells it.

She looks into my eyes for a moment and hers narrow slightly, a small smile spreading across her lips. I think she enjoys telling it.

Her voice is soft as her fingers gently knead the bottom of my neck. 'There was such relief after the war ended,' she begins. 'It had gone on for all those years and so many people had died. I didn't even know your father had survived until he knocked on the door.'

'Go back further,' I urge, wanting to hear as much of her voice as I can.

She checks her thinkwatch, the face that same dull-white colour that all adults who haven't taken the Reckoning are branded by, and then starts again. 'The war had gone on for so long that no one knew if it was ever going to end. Almost all of the men had gone to fight – some of the younger, fitter women went too. As soon as the boys turned fourteen, they went as well. Everyone else had to help.'

'What did you do?' I ask, playing along as if she had never told me in the past.

'I helped with the uniforms and the armour. Before the war we used to live in Manchester, further south, but the rebels moved out anyone they considered useful, bringing us up here to the lakes where they thought the nationalists wouldn't think about targeting anyone.'

Her fingers move their way onto my shoulders and she massages me delicately. I can't remember the last time she did this. Whether that's her fault or mine, I'm not sure.

'After the war ended, everyone was so confused,' she continues. 'There was a small community of us refugees around here and we didn't know where we should be going. The cities were damaged quite badly and then everything was divided into the Realms we have now. At first we were worried about being in someone else's house but there were so few people that we could choose between staying here and returning to the city. Everyone was given somewhere to live relative to their needs.'

That is likely what would have happened to me if I had not been chosen as an Offering. When you get your Reckoning results, you are given two days to move to wherever you need to be to best serve the country. For some, like Opie, that means staying in the same place to work, for others it means moving to a city, very occasionally another Realm.

Her fingers skim lower on my back, rubbing steadily through my shirt. 'We were all struggling for food up here and some of the others who stayed were talking about going to one of the cities anyway, even though we didn't know if they had any more food than we did. No one knew if their partners were still alive and it was almost impossible to get information from anyone because the power rarely worked for long enough. Our old phones had long since stopped functioning.'

I shudder, remembering the Reckoning skimming through my first memory of the phones that sit in the gully. Much of the technology is the same as in our thinkwatches, although I have never managed to get a phone to come to life because I can't find batteries that work.

'So you were cut off from everything?' I ask, knowing this is so much more than just the story of my name.

'Yes, every now and then the Kingsmen would bring

supplies or we would hear something on the radio or through our screens. Then, one day there was a knock on the door. I thought it was someone bringing news, or food, but it was your father standing there, looking almost as he had the last time I had seen him eight years before.'

She has never told me this part before and rarely speaks of my father. I feel her fingers tensing slightly as she grips me around my hips and pulls me towards her. 'He can't have looked that similar,' I say, trying to picture him in my head.

'His hair was a bit greyer and his face had more wrinkles but his eyes and mouth were the same,' she says, her words kind and deliberate. 'I suppose he had lost weight but we all had. He limped through the doorway, saying "Aren't you going to invite me in?" with that grin of his.'

'What did you do?'

Mum winks at me in the mirror and smiles with her eyes, something I'm not sure she's done in a while. 'Well, you came along not long after,' she replies, her fingers gently tickling my sides. I wriggle in annoyance but can't avoid laughing. 'Everyone was having children at the same time,' she continues.

I remember an early Reckoning, with just a handful of teenagers. It has grown steadily through the years until reaching the size it is now. Suddenly I realise why this was the biggest event the village has had in my lifetime: because so many of us were born at the same time. Somehow it had escaped me until now. For me this was always going to be a part of life, but for the adults, this is new. Next year's will surely be even larger?

She stumbles over her words and then remembers what she was supposed to be telling me. 'Anyway,' she says, her voice cracking with emotion, 'when you arrived you already had hair on your little head – tufts of that dark stuff you have now, but there was a lighter strand sticking up in the middle. I said it was white but your father replied straight away that it was silver, so that's what we named you.'

She finishes with a sigh and then wraps her arms around me. 'Wait there,' she says, and then moves quickly into the living room before returning moments later holding a large paper bag with a hook poking out. 'I was wearing this when I met your father,' she says, pulling the paper over the top.

I have seen it hanging in the cupboard at the back of the living room but never known what was underneath the paper. Mum always told me it was special and, though I was as curious as any child would be, the paper always seemed so fragile that there was no way of me discovering what was underneath without revealing what I had done.

The layers of wrapping soon reveal a flowing purple gown, jewels zigzagging beautifully around it. I know it will fit perfectly, hugging me where it should and stretching to the floor. My mother knows full well I don't usually wear this type of thing but then Offerings can only take what they are wearing with them. Not only will this be the last thing I ever take from home, this will also be the one thing I have that's actually mine.

'I want you to have this,' she says, smiling wearily. I start to protest but she says it was always going to be mine one day, so it may as well be now.

She leaves me to try it on while she wakes Colt. As I slide into the soft sheen of the material, I try to picture my mother in it, younger and happier, but I can't see her as anything other than what she has become now. The dress is perfect, reaching my ankles but not below and enveloping my body. With my clean hair left to hang loose and the strange, almost alien material wrapped around me, I see myself in the mirror but I am almost unrecognisable; I look like the girl I am, instead of the woman I am supposed to be.

It is only then that the enormity of everything hits me – this is the last time I will see the room I have grown up in. I take a little time to remember the details; my pillow that sags in the middle, the dresser with the top drawer that sticks. It is goodbye to everything I have known.

When I am ready, I open the door into our living room and yawn, playing up to it as my mother fusses over me, telling me how pretty I look. Usually I would hate it but today it feels nice. Even Colt is quiet, apparently awestruck by the enormity of what is happening. Well, either that or by seeing his sister in a dress. His Reckoning is seven years away, when he turns sixteen, and although he has experienced everything in previous years, it has always been other people from other families involved.

Mum has used her own rations to get a little extra food and is seemingly determined to give me the fullest stomach possible. I told her not to, although there was never any doubt she would. I try to pass some of the extra bread and paste to Colt, but he refuses, pointing and smiling behind her back to indicate he will tell Mum if I don't eat it myself. It tells me everything I need to know about the type of person he will grow into, but both me and my mother know the Reckoning will be simple for him – he could even be one of Martindale's rare Elites if he tries.

I lick my thumb and rub a smear of dirt from his chin as he slaps me away, making an 'ugh' sound until Mum turns around and tells him to stop disturbing me on my big day. I wink, just to remind him who's boss. He sticks his tongue out but his forced grin says it all. He will miss me.

Our main room doubles up as a living room and kitchen, with just the two bedrooms at the rear of the one-storey house. Colt has his own room and I have mine. Mum refuses to sleep anywhere other than the battered, uncomfortable sofa we've had for as long as I can remember.

Sometimes, on the coldest nights, we all sleep in the same room together, huddled under blankets.

I finish the last of the bread when my mother turns and asks me to name one thing I would most like to eat on my final morning here. It reminds me of my seventh birthday, with us all sitting in our living room. My dad was still alive then, although I can barely recall his face. Now, I just remember him being in pain, a survivor of the war in body but not mind. My mother had saved their rations to get me a currant bun from the bakery and we sat on the sofa as I insisted they each had a bite.

At first I refuse to play along, telling her she should not waste rations. When Colt joins in, I persuade myself this is their day as much as it is mine and start to name everything I've ever tried. I talk about the hog everyone in our road chipped in for and sticky fruit buns. When they say no but keep grinning, I begin to get more worried that they've spent a lot on me. It isn't that I don't appreciate it; just that I would rather they looked after themselves.

Eventually, my mother tells me to look in the cupboard above the cooker. I know it is usually empty of anything other than a pot of meat paste and, occasionally, a jar of vegetable soup. My mother helps make and mend clothes for local families and they often return the favour by bartering with food, even though I get the feeling she would do it for free if she didn't have us to feed. I never see her happier than when she is on the sofa with thread, cloth and a smile.

Colt's anticipation fills the room as I stand and walk towards the cupboard before my mum steps behind me, covering my eyes. She whispers in my ear that I'm worth it but that's not really the point. I fumble around, trying not to knock anything over, although there is little danger of that as the space seems to be empty.

'At the back,' Mum says softly, her breath brushing across my ear and tickling. I reach further until my fingers clasp a small glass jar. Instantly I know what it is and, even though I know what it must have cost, I can't stop myself grinning. I blink as my eyes are released and focus on the purple-red mixture inside the pot.

'It's all for you,' Mum adds and I can feel Colt nearby, excitedly waiting for my response.

I pull the cloth from the top and dip my finger into the velvety fruity jam, digging deep before licking every spot from my skin and nail. I've only tried it once before, when Opie's mother won a basket of food on the lottery a couple of years ago. Everyone over the age of twelve has the opportunity to enter by trading in part of their rations. When he was alive, Dad always reckoned it was a waste of time, although he said that about most things. I suppose he was right considering that's the only time I have ever known anyone to win. When word went around the village that Iris Cotton's name had been chosen, people didn't know whether to congratulate or curse her. As it was, they did what people always do: said 'well done' to her face and called her a lucky so-and-so behind her back. That said, the prize was amazing: breads, meats and sweets – most of which I had never heard of.

After a week or so, we were invited over to share what was left, although Opie had already smuggled me out bits and pieces, including a small square of chocolate and a shaving of pineapple. They were unlike anything I had ever tasted but Mum said they used to have food like that regularly before the war broke out twenty-five years ago. Probably because they'd had so many new things to try, a jar of jam had gone largely ignored, so Opie's mother said I could have it. As everyone else tried veal, turkey and salmon, plus various cheeses, fruits, teas and coffees, and many other things, I sat happily in the corner eating my jam.

I have to resort to digging my tongue into the cracks between my teeth in an effort to free the stickiest bits, making sure I don't touch the dress with my gooey fingers. Colt laughs at the face I am pulling, so I offer him the jar.

'That's your sister's,' Mum chides, but I tell her I will refuse to eat any more unless they each try some.

She stands with her hands disapprovingly on her hips but it's not long before her resistance breaks and she too wipes her finger around the inside of the rim, smiling gently as she tastes it. Although she won't say what it cost, she tells me she had to pay someone on the market upfront, and they managed to trade for it from someone in the West. She was planning on giving it to me as a gift for getting through the Reckoning; now it is a going-away present.

I leave almost half of it, telling Mum I'm full, although it is really because I want to leave it for them. Reluctantly, she puts it back in the cupboard and tells Colt to get ready. It would usually be a school day for him but no one will be going now that someone from Martindale has been chosen as an Offering.

I hear more footsteps gathering outside and glance at my thinkwatch to see that it is nearly time. 'Come on,' Mum calls from the living room. 'You can't be late.'

As we leave the house, there are again people on the streets but this time the atmosphere feels more authentic. I recognise face after face, adults and children, friends and foes, all of whom I have grown up with. More smiles, more pats on the back, compliments on my dress, my hair and everything else. Everyone wants a piece of me and I let them, returning the smiles, showing them the orange of my thinkwatch face, and accepting their sentiments with as much grace as I can.

The people of Martindale have lined the streets again but this time they are leading me towards the train station.

The morning is bright and crisp but the arms around me keep me warm as I see the dark uniforms of the Kingsmen at the end of the street. It hadn't crossed my mind before, but I wonder what would happen if I turned and ran, heading towards the gully and keeping going until my legs couldn't move any longer. It's not a rational thought, I know. This is a moment of pride and achievement but something about the Kingsmen's presence doesn't feel right. They are unmoving as I approach, simply waiting by one of the carriages at a small set of steps leading up to the open door.

I turn to my mother and thank her for everything she has done for me. After that, I crouch, making sure not to get the dress dirty, and tell Colt to be good. I say that I hope I'll be able to return at some point but we both know it won't happen. I don't belong to them any longer. Our words will never be enough because what can you say?

I look around for Opie and Imp but they are not there. Before I can peer deeper into the swarm of people, someone in a suit grips my upper arm. He asks how I am, as if I can say anything other than excited, then he turns to the crowd and asks them if they're proud of me. Their cheering is appreciated and, as I look out over the sea of faces, I see the blonde heads of Opie and his brothers. He's not looking at me, instead staring sideways along the length of the train, holding Imp's hand. It is Imp's eyes that make me crack, giving everyone else what they want. He stares at me full of sadness that we will no longer torment each other with our childish games. Colt is my brother but Imp may as well be too. He catches my eye for a moment and then I feel the lump in my throat again. The man asks something about my dress but I'm not even listening, instead I'm blinking quickly, trying to suppress the tears that feel so close. I turn away from the crowds and walk into the train without answering.

Inside, I don't even look at the surroundings, instead resting my hands on the cool glass on the far side, swallowing, blinking, and trying to tell myself I'm an adult now. A Kingsman tells me it is going to be a long day – we are the furthest north so have to stop through the Realm to pick up everyone else but I am not really listening. I almost ask if I can go back for my pot of jam but he says there will be food and drink for the journey. Then he tells me there are five minutes before we leave and that I can spend that time with whoever I wish.

The obvious choice is my mum but we've said everything we have to and I don't want to see her cry again. I tell him Opie's name and start to describe him but he already knows. 'That tall blonde kid, yes?' he asks and I realise how distinctive Opie is, even among a crowd.

A moment later and he is in front of me. The compartment is large with rows of seats lining the sides but we stand, watching each other. He seems taller and thicker, his large arms by his side, his hair messy as if he has just got up.

'Hello,' I say as I feel myself smiling.

'Hello.'

We continue to stare at each other before his arms twitch and suddenly I am within them, feeling them around me, the bristle of his chin rubbing the top of my head. We don't speak but I feel a tingle along my spine as his fingers cup my head and slide along the curves of my back.

It feels like mere seconds before people are in the carriage, telling us it is time, that there is a schedule and a long day.

Before we move apart I whisper in Opie's ear, telling him to look after Colt and my mother, even though I already know he will. He nods, smiles and winks – and then, as quickly as he arrived, he is gone.

The compartment door slides shut and the train begins to move as everyone files out again. The green of Martindale is soon the grey of wilderness and then I realise, finally, that my childhood is over.

8

Once every two weeks, a steam train chugs through Martindale dropping off supplies. It carries a limited number of passengers to the city and back as well but people are not encouraged to move around. It is an expensive and rare privilege. I have only travelled by train twice, only once officially. On the other occasion Opie and I sneaked aboard, hiding among the bags of grain and piles of fruit in one of the cabins at the back. We were young and silly and luckily didn't get caught; the potential penalty for being found is something not worth thinking about.

Both journeys were uncomfortable, yet somehow thrilling too. The ability to be somewhere so different to my village, within such a short space of time, was something almost too hard to get my head around. Mum said travelling was something she took for granted as a child. For those my age, unless we walk, it is the only way of getting outside Martindale. Perhaps that's why the gully became so important to me?

This train is completely different to the service ones that go through Martindale. Instead of the noise and the heat, it glides effortlessly and silently along the tracks to a degree that, if it wasn't for the windows, I wouldn't even know we were moving. We have the other Offerings to pick up and stop at a town a little further south to collect an Elite. The crowds are thicker than they were in Martindale; masses of people are pointing, waving and cheering.

After the Elite says his goodbyes, we sit together in silence. I try to stop myself peering at the grey-black hue of his thinkwatch, with the faint outline of a crown on it. He takes some fruit from the selection of food left for us but neither of us knows what to say to the other. He stares longingly out of the window and I wonder if he has left someone behind. I realise we are perhaps the only people who can understand each other, the mixed feelings of being chosen to serve our King, leaving behind everything and everyone we have ever known.

Although we never hear anything official about what happens to our Offerings, there are always rumours. Some-one's cousin knows somebody who lives in a city who heard from a Kingsman and so on. Of course there is no way of knowing for sure but it is sometimes fun to speculate. I've heard about an Offering who is supposedly now captain of the King's army and another who is in charge of research and technology. Some have apparently been sent abroad to marry, to help rebuild the alliances smashed down by years of war. I wonder if that is to be my fate and begin to feel self-conscious in my dress.

We zigzag across the Realm but most of our pick-ups come from the cities where the crowds are beyond anything I have ever seen. Thousands have gathered to wave their Offerings goodbye as the carriage begins to fill up.

The two Elite girls come from the same place. One is wearing a beautiful silver dress and seems friendly, introducing herself as Jela. She has long, straight blonde hair and is naturally pretty, her high cheekbones framing large brown eyes that almost stare through you. The other, Pietra, says hello, but goes to sit at the back of the carriage. Her brown hair is pinned up and she is wearing a blue velvet dress covered with glittering jewels. She sits watching me with her arms crossed, as if weighing me up, but she says little else. Jela goes to sit with her.

Soon after, two boys – a Member and an Inter, dressed in a blue that matches his thinkwatch – step on together at another point. This is our year to provide a male Trog, who we collect from our final stop along with the last male Elite. These last two Offerings could not be more different. The Elite reminds me of Opie because of his build and hair colour – he is tall and handsome with a square, solid jaw and huge broad shoulders but his eyes lack the kindness that Opie's have. Our Trog is thin and short, his thighs barely as wide as the Elite's arms. His hair is brown and patchy and, despite us being the same age, he reminds me of Imp because of the dimples in his cheeks and the way he smiles.

They step onto the train together and instantly separate. The Elite heads towards the food, as the Trog, rubbing the front of his yellow thinkwatch, looks around at us all, before shuffling into the corner and sitting by himself. I notice a few of the others glancing in his direction but nobody says anything. The four Elites have drifted towards each other and are standing near the food table, eating and smiling.

We are all here now and ready to head to Windsor: four Elites, myself and another Member, an Inter and the Trog. Three girls and five boys. By the time we get to the castle and join with the Offerings from the other Realms, there will be thirty of us; fifteen boys and fifteen girls.

As I am adding up the numbers in my head, I catch the Trog's eye and he smiles nervously before looking away. I glance towards the Elites and the newest one, who looks a little like Opie, stares me up and down before indicating for me to come over with a flick of his head.

For me there is no decision to make as I cross the carriage and sit next to the Trog instead. I feel the eyes of the others on me as I shake his hand and ask his name.

'Wray,' he tells me with the same nervous smile as before, still playing with his watch front. He doesn't want to meet my eyes but I don't mind as I tell him my name.

'Is that like your hair?' he asks, pointing to my silver streak.

'Exactly.'

Wray asks where I come from but has, perhaps not surprisingly, never heard of Martindale. He tells me about life in the city, where he and his mother live in a partially rebuilt tower block. He tells me his mum lost the use of her legs a few years ago and never leaves the flat, which left him to look after her. Although school is held more often in the city, Wray has not been in years. He doesn't say it but, from what I can tell, it looks as if he gives most of his rations to his mother. He says his younger sister will now be looking after her and that although he is sad and worried to be leaving, his mum told him the previous evening that his selection was the proudest moment of her life. He gulps hard, his throat bobbing as he speaks.

I ask if he wants some food but he says no, even though I can see the hunger in his eyes. I tell him I'll get him something anyway and cross to the food table.

The bigger male Elite is eyeing me again. He is talking with the others and I overhear one of them calling him 'Rush'. As I look across the food, I try to ignore him until he actually speaks, his voice deep and gravelly and any similarity to Opie immediately lost.

'What are you doing hanging around with *him*?' Rush asks, loudly enough for everyone to hear.

'His name is Wray,' I say, choosing two fruit buns from a tray. They are still slightly warm and I greedily smear butter across them.

'He's a Trog,' Rush replies firmly, as the girl in the blue dress sniggers.

I spot a small plate of jam at the back and smile, thinking of my mother and Colt and the half-pot I've left for them at the back of the cupboard.

'He comes from the same place you do,' I reply, not looking behind me.

As I spread a generous helping of jam, I hear more laughing. 'He's nothing to do with me,' Rush sneers. 'He's nothing at all.'

'We're all Offerings,' I say, putting the buns on a plate and turning around to face him. 'We've all been chosen and we're all the same. You're no better or worse than any of us.'

I see Rush's face contort in anger, his top lip curling into a snarl. His eyebrow is twitching as he glances to Pietra, who is standing next to him, as if to confirm he has heard correctly. 'All the same?' he asks disbelievingly. 'What are you? A Member? Why are you wasting your time with the likes of him? You should be with us.'

Pietra nods approvingly, her eyes flickering beyond me towards Wray.

I ignore them and return to the corner of the carriage,

sitting next to Wray and handing him the bun. He must have heard what was being said but doesn't rise to it, taking the food and biting into it hungrily.

'Have you ever had one of these?' I ask.

His reply is muffled as he tries to speak with his mouth full but he shakes his head. We both laugh as we eat. Wray gets through his entire bun before I am halfway done, so I let him finish mine off.

We watch the scenery flashing past the window; factories with smoke belching from the chimneys are interspersed with patches of grass and small towns, villages and hamlets. Most of all, we see rubble: piles of bricks, tiles, wood and masonry – all abandoned years before and never returned to.

'I never realised there was so much carnage out here,' I say as Wray points to what looks as if it was once a village that has been destroyed.

'It's a lot like this where I live,' he replies. 'Some places have been patched together but mainly we live in what's left.'

I think about the house I won't be returning to and, although it's small, it is complete and provides adequate shelter. 'Why don't they rebuild these places properly?' I ask.

Wray doesn't reply instantly, instead we both focus on the final, flattened remnants of the village. 'If they don't repair things, it keeps us all remembering what might happen if we go to war again,' he eventually says.

I think about his words and realise he is right. What better way to stop people rising up than by leaving them a permanent reminder of what happened the last time they did? For now, the King is popular but perhaps that won't always be the case.

I want to ask Wray what happened at his Reckoning but it feels too personal a question. Maybe the Reckoning sensed that he wasn't ready to leave home and wanted to continue looking after his mother, which is why it made him a Trog? It is hard to know exactly how it works, but he certainly isn't stupid.

As we continue to watch through the window, I hear Rush's voice behind us, shouting and sneering. 'Oi, Trog-boy, come over here.'

Wray's body tenses slightly but neither of us turns. Aside from the air swishing past the train, there is silence for a few seconds before his voice sounds again. 'I'm talking to you, Trog-boy.'

I catch Wray's eyes as he glances sideways at me. They are full of fright and I know this is the life he has led for years: intimidation and fear. I take his hand in mine and he is shaking. Remnants of some fruit fizzes past our heads and crashes into the window, the pulp and juice running down the glass as I realise it was meant for Wray's head.

'Don't move,' I whisper as I turn. I try to release his hand but his fingers are clasping at mine before he finally lets me go.

Rush is standing with more fruit in his hands ready to throw. When he realises he has my attention, he grins and puts the food down. 'You may as well be Troggy filth like him if you're going to spend all your time over there,' he says, taking another moment to look me up and down.

At first I couldn't figure it out but now I understand why he wants my attention. He thinks the gorgeous flowing dress is who I am; that I'm a naive child from the middle of nowhere and this is how I live. I struggle not to smile as he stands cockily. Pietra is at his side, staring at me.

'His name is Wray,' I say again. 'My name is Silver. We've not done anything to you so why won't you leave us alone?'

Rush's eyes narrow. 'Because I'm an Elite and he's a Trog. I'll do what I want.'

I nod gently as a smile spreads across his face. He thinks I am accepting that he can do what he wants, when really there is only one solution.

I stride towards Rush, who doesn't move until I am within a metre or two. He glances sideways at Pietra, suddenly nervous, as if to ask what's going on. By the time he fixes his attention back on me, it is too late. The dress and the hair are all well and good but the real me is the one who has grown up fighting and wrestling with Opie.

Rush doesn't know what's happening as I duck sideways and then hammer my elbow up under his ribs. With Opie, I would do this playfully and gently but now I do it as hard as I can. He doubles over automatically but I don't give him a second, thudding the side of my hand into his windpipe as he lurches forward. I wince in pain but it's nothing compared to what he feels. He doesn't know if he should be crumbling forwards or backwards as he struggles to find his balance, thrusting his hands out and trying to grab me. If it was Opie, we would be rolling in the dirt by now, laughing and joking, but this is different. Pietra has cowered away, as I thought she would. I step to the side and smash my fist as hard as I can into Rush's ear, once and then twice. Everything has happened in a matter of seconds and he falls to the ground, cradling the various body parts he won't be using any time soon.

I step away and watch him rolling on the floor. Aside from his groans, there is silence around the cabin. I look down at my unmarked, uncreased dress and think of how Opie would probably be grinning at me right now in that lopsided way of his.

Without a word, I cross to the other side of the carriage and sit next to Wray, taking his hand in mine. He is still shaking but it is in disbelief, not fear.

'You did that for me?' he whispers, stumbling over his words.

I don't reply, gripping his hand reassuringly tighter and watching as Rush slowly gets back to his feet.

9

The rest of the train journey is unsurprisingly quiet. None of the Kingsmen bother to check on us, although the doors and windows are all sealed, so it's not as if they have any need. Rush brushes away any offers of sympathy or help, refusing to do anything other than skulk to a corner and act as if none of it happened. I try to feel bad about everything – it's not often I've hurt anyone on purpose – but then I remember the way poor Wray was shaking with fear.

Wray doesn't talk quite as much through the rest of the journey and I wonder if perhaps he is a little scared of me too. Certainly none of the others bother to approach us.

Now we are travelling south, I feel my first real moment of excitement as the train begins to slow. We have all heard of Middle England, and seen it on our screens and think-pads, but none of us will have ever visited here. I push myself against the window and stare upwards, trying to peer around an impossible angle to take in the enormity of it all. I can see two towering glass buildings soaring above us and turn to see another pair on the opposite side. All of us, including Rush, are pressed against the windows in awe, trying to take in what is around us.

Middle England is a crossroads where our four Realms meet. Each Realm has a tower which serves as a trading and political hub. The people working there are in charge of bartering with each other and allocating our rations, not that I have ever known anyone visit Martindale. Sometimes, if something serious is happening, the screens will show us pictures from Middle England but the images are nothing compared to the sheer majesty of the place. As well as the four towers, there are other smaller but equally impressive buildings. People hurry between them, looking identical in dark suits.

As we edge slowly through the junction, I try to predict the exact point which means I am at the cross section of the Realms; where I am either in all four at the same time, or none at all, depending on which way you look at it.

When we accelerate away, I realise I have left the North for the first time ever. I exchange a look with Wray as we sense this is actually happening. I assume we are now in the South but there are no announcements. As the train continues, the scenery is much the same as it is in the North, although there do seem to be more places that have been rebuilt.

It doesn't feel like long before the carriage doors slide open and one of the Kingsmen enters, telling us we should arrive at Windsor Castle within half an hour. As he turns to leave, he glances at the marks on Rush's face. Although I didn't hit him there, he must have landed awkwardly because one of his eyes has already blackened.

'Is everything all right here?' he asks, peering around the cabin, but Rush nods and doesn't elaborate.

The man's eyes are narrow and he looks at us all, wondering if there is something he has missed, but doesn't add anything before leaving the room.

After a while, the train slows again and we drop into a tunnel that continues for a few miles until we stop completely. Our carriage is well lit but it is difficult to see anything outside. I press my face against the glass again and think I can make out another train next to us. The atmosphere is more apprehensive and I can feel the nervous energy humming between us.

There are voices nearby but we all stay sitting as the noise of the train dies. The lights flicker and then go out completely. I feel Wray fidgeting next to me and a shuffling of movement in the carriage. I wonder if Rush will use this moment to get his revenge and grasp around for Wray. I take his hand more for my own comfort than his, before the lights sputter back to life. I glance around the room but Rush is still in the same seat he was before, meeting my eyes for a moment and then looking away.

The door swishes open and someone, who I first assume

to be a Kingsman, strides in. It is only when I take a second glance that I realise the man in front of me is the Minister Prime. Everything I have seen of him on screen is nothing compared to the way he looks in real life. He towers over everyone and even if Opie was here, he would barely reach the man's shoulders. From where I am sitting, my eyes are level with his thighs, which seem broader than my waist. He is wearing thick dark gloves, his hands as big as the plates we eat from at home and, although his uniform is nearly the same as a regular Kingsman's, it seems lighter and sleeker, almost absorbing the overhead light, instead of reflecting it. His eyes skim quickly around the cabin, taking us all in briefly before he rocks back onto his heels.

'You will all now be shown to your quarters,' he says. His voice is deep and brimming with authority as he points to the side I am sitting on, and then indicates the other side. 'Girls with her, boys over there. This evening there will be a banquet where you will be formally introduced to the King as his Offerings.'

After another glimpse around, he turns and thunders back out of the carriage, his boots echoing loudly. As he leaves, the other girls hover around me, as Wray nervously crosses to the other side. He catches my eye and I give him a gentle nod to let him know I will see him later. Two Kingsmen enter and, without speaking, one of them flashes a hand in our direction, telling us to follow him. I am at the front as the two Elite girls fall in line behind me. I make one final glance towards Wray, who is at the back of the five boys, as we exit the carriage and step onto a stone platform.

The Kingsman's pace is quick and I feel slightly restricted in the dress, although not as much as the female Elite whose sparkling silver gown is even tighter and more elaborate than mine. Jela is almost running to keep pace. Pietra doesn't speak but I can hear her footsteps behind me.

The train must have stopped under the castle as we are led up a winding set of stone steps and I feel the temperature rising. The stairs open onto a corridor lit by rows of what I first think are candles, before I realise they have small flame-shaped light bulbs on top of white stems. The Kingsman doesn't stop, turning left out of the passage, but I pause to look in both directions. The walls are grey and made of solid-looking thick stone and there is a deep red carpet on the floor. The candle lights stretch as far into the distance, leaving me to wonder how much power they have here compared to Martindale. I catch up with the Kingsman before he can turn to look for us. I try to remember the route back to the top of the stairway, but quickly lose track of the tight twists and turns. In the top corners of many of the corridors and stairways are small cameras attached to the ceiling with blinking lights underneath. Some of them swivel to follow our route, adding to my unease.

Eventually, the Kingsman pushes through a heavy wooden

door and leads us into a large room where the luxury is unlike anything I have ever encountered. The carpet is thick and bouncy and there are beds twice the width of mine at home placed around the edge. We step inside as the door bangs loudly closed behind us. Four girls are already in the room and one of them tells us they are from the South. I stand in the centre, wondering if any of the beds have been assigned. Pietra and Jela are already sitting on beds next to each other, close to the others. Something about the way the door closed didn't sound right, so I try the handle but it is instantly clear we are locked in. The room is lit by a row of windows, but these are also locked, the glass rippled in a way that makes it impossible to see through.

I choose the bed furthest away, lying on it and staring at the ceiling as I enjoy the way it supports my body. At home, I know every inch of my bed, the uncomfortable ridges and the springs that have long since broken. I wonder if I will be able to sleep with this new-found comfort. Next to each bed is a tall, thin wardrobe. Inside are a handful of dresses as well as white jumpsuits and boots, none of which I would choose to wear at home.

I listen to the girls talking and realise I have never really spent much time with other females through my life. Aside from my mother, I have been surrounded by boys. Even on the train, I felt drawn to Wray as opposed to the females.

The other six girls are chatting excitedly about their journeys and how they felt about being chosen.

I am already the outsider.

I check my thinkwatch but, as I guessed would happen, the communication function isn't working. Usually, I would be able to send messages to my mother, Colt, Opie, or anyone else if I knew their ID. Here, the signal is dead.

Throughout the afternoon, girls from the other Realms arrive until there are fifteen of us dotted around. The female Trog from the south, who seems to be called Faith, has taken the bed in the opposite corner to me, although no one seems to be picking on her in the way Rush tried to target Wray. For the most part, I keep to myself, not knowing how to make the small-talk which seems to come so easily to others. I feel as if my mind is already a step ahead of where the others are. For them, this is exciting; the extravagance of our room is something to be enjoyed. I think of the cameras, the locked door and the windows we can't see out of and cannot open.

The voices are silenced as a woman opens our door and tells us it is time to go to the banquet. She is wearing a flowing green gown that stretches to the floor. I don't recognise her and she doesn't introduce herself. I choose to stay in the dress I already had on, although some of the girls have changed into something fancier from the wardrobes.

We file out behind the woman in green but I deliberately

make sure I am at the back. The maze-like corridors across a selection of floors make it impossible to track our route. As I find myself wondering if the layout is deliberate, I also worry that I have already become paranoid. It is hard to feel differently as cameras continue to turn as we do.

Despite all this, I feel awestruck as we are led through wide, thick wooden doors into a hall. The first thing I notice is the massive high ceiling, which is unlike anything I have ever seen. It is painted with images of various animals, of which I recognise only a few, but the bright colours are exquisite and the detail amazing. Banked rows of seats flank the room and we are directed to a rectangular area in the centre. I look up to see various people in the chairs staring down upon us and it is hard not to be intimidated. I am not used to being the centre of attention. A line of boys enter from a door on the other side and I spy Wray at the back, staring up high towards the people above us. In the middle of the area is a long wooden table, with benches running alongside it. One by one we sit, girls on one side, boys on the other, with Wray opposite me. I catch his eye and wink, which he returns with a smile.

Above us, the Minister Prime is sitting in a box, with more cameras above him pointing towards us. He looks at us unmoving as other voices chatter on. I watch him closely as he slowly stands, then holds his arm out to the side, demanding silence with an authority nobody dares challenge. Instantly the room is quiet before he raises his arms. Everyone stands in the seats above us and we follow the unspoken command. Underneath the box, trumpeters wearing red and white uniforms raise their instruments to their mouths and launch into the national anthem.

I have never been that patriotic but still feel a tingle shoot down my spine as the doors next to the Minister Prime are opened by two Kingsmen, revealing the King standing at the back of the box in a flowing cherry gown. To see him on screen and on the various posters that are put up around Martindale is one thing, but there is something about witnessing him in person which is hard to describe. His hair is as bright as on screen, his frame just as imposing, but in person there is something more. He has an aura around him, making you feel drawn to his presence. I've always thought Opie had something similar, although much of that was because of his height. This is something different and, perhaps for the first time in my life, I can see why he was able to end a war that we have always been told could have destroyed us all.

He walks towards a huge throne next to the Minister Prime and offers a small wave before trying to sit. As I watch, something doesn't seem quite right. The King falls the last few centimetres onto his seat, hitting his head on a curved part near the top of the throne. If it hurt, then he doesn't react, instead leaning against the head rest and blinking quickly as if trying to stop himself falling asleep. I feel a sense of confusion around the room, the hush of his entrance being replaced by murmurs of bewilderment. Angrily, the Minister Prime extends his arm, demanding a silence which is instantly granted.

On the other side of the King is the woman in green who led us into the hall. She stands and surveys us before introducing herself as Deputy Minister Prime Ignacia. She has dark black hair, styled high in a way I have never seen before. Her voice is deep but full of authority, although she has a way of making it sound as if she isn't talking down to us.

She welcomes us as this year's Offerings and then asks for those from the South to stay standing while everyone else sits. There is a ripple of applause from the seats above but I continue to watch the King, who appears to be struggling to stay awake. His eyes are closing for seconds at a time before opening again. The way I felt intimidated by his charisma a few moments ago now seems misplaced.

After the South, the West's Offerings stand and are clapped, before it is our turn. It feels slightly silly to be praised simply for being who you are but I go with it and enjoy seeing Wray's reaction. He turns a full circle, taking in the reception, before we sit again.

After we have all been introduced, Ignacia says it is time for the official welcoming banquet, at which a large set of double doors open and people dressed in white trousers and smocks appear carrying plates of food. Suddenly there is noise again, whispered approval passing around the table and the sound of metal knives and forks being raised.

The meal is unlike anything I have ever known. Huge platters of meats are placed in front of us: pork, chicken, beef, lamb along with potatoes, vegetables, breads, gravies, and many other things I don't even know the names for. Wray's eyes are bulging as an entire turkey is placed in front of him. At first there is a politeness, with us all looking at each other, before it quickly becomes a free-for-all. All around the table are Offerings grabbing at the food, tearing chunks of meat as we eat with our hands. Before the food arrived, I did not feel hungry but now I am famished, breaking all the manners my mother ever taught me as I join in the frenzy. It isn't just the amount of food which I find astonishing, it is the taste. The meats are juicy and rich, the bread warm and soft. I barely know where to reach next, our various arms and cutlery crossing as we stretch across each other.

Wray is eating a large drumstick from the turkey with his hands. He grins at me between mouthfuls and I can tell he, like me, has never seen anything like it. In my mind I make a note of everything I want to try but I am barely a quarter of the way through when I feel my stomach begin to seize. I fill a goblet with water and wash it down but, if anything,

I feel fuller. Around me, I can see the other Offerings reaching a similar point but I look to the box to see the King still eating. In one hand, he has a bread roll while he is grasping a bottle of wine in the other. I wonder where his appetite comes from considering he must see this type of spread whenever he wants.

His head is bouncing from side to side and I suddenly realise who he reminds me of. In Martindale, there is a man named Mayall who always seems to have a bottle of wine near him. He disappears whenever the Kingsmen are around but frequently sleeps on the streets, even on the coldest evenings. As the King's eyes roll back in his head, I understand that he is drunk. The images of our leader flashed to us on screen always show him as strong and noble; nothing like the man I see above me who cannot feed himself fast enough and looks as if he may topple over. I feel embarrassed about my own behaviour, eating with my hands and shovelling food as if it is normal, when my mother and Colt will be in our cold house this evening with next to nothing.

Across the table a few seats away from Wray, one of the other Offerings is watching me. As I catch his eye, he looks away quickly but then glances up again to see if I am still peering at him. He is one of the Elites from the West and has black hair and dark, olive skin. Somehow I can tell he is thinking something similar to me about the food. He offers a half-smile, widening his eyes as if to say 'What can we do?'

and I like him instantly. He reaches for a piece of squishy yellow fruit I have never tried before. He hasn't said a word but he is right, of course. We are unable to do anything about the wider situation around our Realms but that doesn't mean we should deprive ourselves – especially as there is more food in front of us than we might usually eat all week. My stomach feels full but satisfied as I also chew slowly on a piece of the yellow fruit and give my new friend a knowing nod.

As the sound of eating begins to wane, the people in the white uniforms emerge from the doors again, clearing the remaining food and our plates. I start to wonder what will happen to what is left but the doors quickly open again and before I know what is happening, there are plates of extravagant desserts in front of us. I have tried chocolate a couple of times but have never seen anything like the cakes in front of us which are dripping in it. That is barely the start, though, as other creations covered in cream, fruits and many other things I can't even describe are placed in front of us. My belly is bulging against the fabric of the dress but I almost feel obliged to keep eating if only to try the amazing new foods. None of us know exactly what is in store and this could be the only time a feast such as this is put on for us.

The chocolate cake is soft in the centre with a thick covering that is so rich I feel myself gagging. I eat a thin slice though, before cutting another piece, this time from a cake with strawberries on the top. Wray is still eating with his hands, while the Elite boy from the West is licking his fingers, having admitted defeat. I point at a spot on my chin before he realises what I am trying to say and wipes away a smear of cream.

Eventually the tables are cleared and the sounds in the room change to that of glasses and goblets being slurped from and placed on the table. Then, I turn to see the Minister Prime standing with his arm outstretched and the room falls into complete silence. His facial expression has not changed since we arrived and it is only now that I realise he didn't seem to be eating when everyone else was. On his right-hand side, the King has finished but there are pieces of food stuck in his beard and he is still holding a wine bottle.

'Welcome to Windsor,' the Minister says, somehow making it sound threatening. 'I thank you all for coming and hope you will be up to the highest of standards.'

I shiver but not because of the cold; it is because his words feel as if they are flowing through me. It is strange that he thanked us for coming seeing as none of us had a choice.

'I know you will all be wondering what is in store for you but those questions will be answered tomorrow, for now . . .'

He doesn't get to finish his sentence as there is a large clattering noise. Across the table, Wray has knocked his goblet onto the floor and dives under the table to grab it. He emerges looking nervous and embarrassed, holding the metal cup aloft and placing it on the table, bowing his head towards the Minister and saying sorry.

The Minister Prime exchanges a look with the King, who rises to his feet. At first I think he is going to speak but instead he walks towards the row of steps which lead down towards us. He holds the rail but I can see him wobbling slightly and it seems as if everyone is holding their breath. The Minister Prime is still standing but even he has narrowed his eyes as he watches the King, curious as to what is happening.

The King stumbles towards a Kingsman at the bottom of the stairs and pulls a sword out of the officer's belt. It appears heavy and unwieldy as he unsteadily waves it around, before seeming to figure out its weight and straightening himself. As he peers towards our table, the atmosphere changes. Wray looks at the King and then glances towards me. He is licking his lips, his eyes darting between the two of us. Above us, there is a hush but, whereas the earlier ones felt respectful, this seems full of fear.

As he bounces the sword up and down in his grip, the King continues to approach, passing me and walking around the edge of the table until he is standing next to Wray. The next few seconds slow almost to a stop as Wray stares up at the man standing over him and then turns to me, his eyes wide as he knows what is going to happen. Nobody speaks or moves as the King pulls the sword back before thrusting forward with a loud heave of effort.

In an instant, a droplet of what I know is blood lands on my cheek as the whites of Wray's eyes stare into me, asking why he had to die.

10

I see the next few minutes in flashes. Wray slumps to the side as people start screaming. The King is laughing, throwing the sword to the floor in disdain and then strolling back towards the stairs. I hear movement as a handful of Kingsmen swarm and then the Minister Prime is saying something. There are words such as 'calm' and 'move' but I'm not even sure they are complete sentences. Instead, I just see Wray's dead, frightened eyes asking for an answer I can't give him.

I am vaguely aware of being in a line of people trooping through the corridors at speed before I find myself back in the dormitory. I sit on my bed as no one dares speak. Instead, we stare at each other, using each other's shock as a reminder that what we have just seen actually happened. Some of the girls take off their dresses, trying unsuccessfully to wipe away the spatters of blood as I look down to notice reddened darker spots on the material of mine. I remember the feeling of something hitting my face and lick my fingers, scrubbing at my skin in an effort to wipe away what I think is there.

It is hard to know what is the more shocking: that poor Wray is dead, or that our King – the person we have grown up idolising – could have stabbed him so callously.

In a blink, I understand what the word 'Offering' means: we are exactly that, free for the King to do what he wants with. Whether he puts us to work, or skewers us through a chair, we are his.

In the bathroom, I hear somebody being sick and wonder if it is the physical shock of what we have seen, or if she has come to the same realisation I have.

As my senses return and the room drifts into focus I stand and walk around, trying the door once more and examining the windows. As before, we are locked in and I know this will be the way I have to get used to living.

I can't help but think of Colt and my mother and feel relieved they are not a part of this. Then I remember the way Wray told me that being chosen as an Offering was the proudest moment of his mother's life. There is a lump in my throat but I force myself to swallow it, desperate not to show any emotion in front of the strangers around me.

People are beginning to find their voices but we still seem to be split along our selection lines. The eight Elites are at the far end of the room from me, while I have managed to take the bed with the most space around it. The Trog, Faith, is by herself on the bed in the corner closest to me, so I walk across and ask if she is okay. She seems grateful that someone has acknowledged her. Wray was also a Trog and so she must be wondering if that was why he was killed. I try to reassure her, although I have no idea.

Faith explains that she has been ill recently, seemingly desperate to convince me there is a good reason why she is a Trog. I tell her I understand. The truth is it really doesn't matter what you are if the King you have grown up being told to worship can do such a thing.

Faith is short with untidy blonde hair and an ill-fitting dress which clings to her unflatteringly. She is desperate to understand something that to me is senseless, insisting the King must have been confused or ill, or any number of other arguments which don't stand up to what we all saw.

The chattering stops instantly as the door unlocks with a heavy clunk. Some of the girls are only partially dressed and, as they reach for towels or clothes to cover themselves, it feels as if we are all holding our breath. None of us knows what to expect as Ignacia sweeps in, still wearing the green gown. She stands in the doorway, looking around the room, before drawing herself up as straight as she can to address us.

'Hello, ladies,' she says, glancing from side to side, trying to engage us all. 'I just wanted to apologise for the . . . *accident* earlier on. Hopefully you can all stay calm about things.' She pauses and rocks back on her heels as if expecting somebody to reply. As if her calling Wray's death an 'accident' makes it one. I'm not sure she even believes what she's saying. She certainly doesn't hold the authority the Minister Prime has, her eyes darting back and forth looking for a confirmation that doesn't come.

'I do have another reason for being here,' she adds. 'Which one of you was wearing a silvery dress earlier? It was quite long, apparently.'

She peers from side to side, waiting for someone to own up but nobody does. Given the fact we are still in shock from what we witnessed in the hall, it is unsurprising.

Ignacia frowns as she is forced to start looking around the room a second time. She discounts me as I still have on my purple dress, while Faith probably isn't the shape she is looking for. As she turns towards the Elite end of the room, the girls move stealthily to one side, revealing Jela, who is sitting on her bed in her underwear and a towel. Her long blonde hair is wet and the way she is wrapped in the material makes her appear tiny and vulnerable.

'Was it you?' Ignacia asks, stepping towards Jela, who nods but seems confused.

'Where is the dress?'

Jela nods towards the wardrobe next to the bed. 'It's got blood on it,' she adds quickly.

'The King has requested your presence this evening,' Ignacia says firmly, indicating towards the wardrobe. 'He requested you wear that dress specifically.'

Jela looks sideways at Pietra on the adjacent bed but the other Elite says nothing, instead pulling the bed covers around herself.

'What does he want with her?' I find myself saying. My voice echoes around the room as everyone turns to look at me. Ignacia studies me too, her head cocked at an angle, before she purses her lips and finally speaks.

'He has requested that she visit his quarters.'

'Will she be coming back?' I ask, although it sounds like someone else's voice.

Ignacia doesn't reply instantly and it feels as if she doesn't know the answer.

'Probably not tonight,' is all she can eventually add but the three words make it clear to us all that we are in the middle of a dangerous game. If we don't play, we end up like Wray; if we do then Jela's fate may well be ours too.

Either way, as Jela's soft sobs reverberate around the room, no one is in any doubt that there is a very good reason why nobody ever sees the Offerings again.

11

Ignacia is right about Jela not returning, although I sense it isn't just me who lies awake hoping the door will open at some point during the night. My stomach is full and uncomfortable but I think the sickening sensation I have is more to do with what I have seen in the past few hours than what I have eaten. I sleep in fits and starts, sometimes jolting awake when I feel as if someone is nearby, even when the rest of the room is unmoving. Eventually, as the darkness outside the windows slowly turns into the dim dredges of morning, I allow my eyes to stay open, lying still until someone else dares to move first.

Aside from the light, we have no concept of time as there are no clocks and our thinkwatches have been useless since we arrived. Some of the girls seem more traumatised by this than anything else, which is perhaps no surprise considering thinkwatches are part of our daily lives. They provide us with reminders and alerts and allow us to interact with our neighbours. It isn't quite the same for me as I have seen the inner workings of mine and spent years trying to find ways to subtly manipulate it.

As we hear the sounds of the door unbolting, we all look as one, hoping to see Jela returning, but instead it is Ignacia again. Her hair is flatter and she is now wearing an impressive dark brown robe. She doesn't mention Jela and tells us that she is there to take us to our morning welcome and then we will be told what roles we are to perform while in service to the King. In the short period of time she gives us to change into our jumpsuits, I feel a sense of us all becoming resigned to our fates. Faith doesn't look up from her bed and nobody wants to catch another's eyes.

Ignacia leads us through the bewildering warren of corridors and up more stone steps. At first I think we are returning to the main hall but quickly lose my bearings. Eventually, we reach a room with rows of tables. The male Offerings are already there but their unease mirrors ours as they struggle to make eye contact. The space reminds me of our classroom – there is a huge screen at the front, although it is larger and cleaner. After we have all sat, Ignacia presses a button on the wall and the display comes to life.

Old-fashioned vehicles are skimming across the screen as a voice informs us that, in the not too distant past, we were overrun with cars. The film goes on to tell us the story we have all been brought up with. Twenty-five years ago, the oil ran out. It had been a gradual process with nations around the world panicking and then countries declaring war on each other. For most, it was quick and brutal with nuclear weapons destroying much of the Middle East. For us, there was civil war with the starving lower classes – the rebels – fighting against the ruling upper classes – the nationalists.

My mother has always been reluctant to talk about these events, but what she did say was how bad it was in the lead-up to the outbreak of fighting. With little food to eat, people did what they could to survive but it wasn't enough and everything spiralled from there.

Millions died as armies loyal to the ruling nationalists battled the lower classes over eight long years. The screen shows us images of men, women and children lying dead, some through violence, some through hunger. We might have heard these things passed down through our parents but this is the first time I have ever had to see anything like this. The nauseating feeling in my stomach is only growing as we're shown huge pits of burned, blackened bodies. Someone at the back starts to sob at the sight of a dead child who is lying in the dirt clutching a soft brown teddy bear.

I can feel my emotions being played with as the screen pales to white before an image of King Victor fades into view. A hardened woman's voice tells us that he stood up to both sides, uniting the country behind him by providing another way that didn't involve fighting. She doesn't say anything else but my mother has told me in the past that people were tired of the battle and that he came along at the right time for people to support him. I always asked what was different – people were hungry before the war, hungry during it and, aside from the feast of last night, I can barely remember a day where I haven't been hungry myself.

Her words were always the same: 'You don't understand.'

Although she is not as patriotic as someone like Opie's father, Mum has always assured me life is better with the King than it was before.

I continue to watch the pictures of him in a hospital talking to an injured soldier and another of him helping to rebuild a damaged house, heaving bricks and smoothing cement. He is younger and thinner, a far cry from the man we saw last night. As delicate music plays gently in the background, I am forced to remind myself what he did to Wray because it would be too easy to think of him as the kind, uniting person being shown on the screen.

After becoming our leader, the King divided the nation into four Realms, where we were expected to work together for the well-being of us all. The East and the West farm their lands, providing food for us. In the East they also fish, while the West is also responsible for defence. The images tell us this is where our nuclear weapons are stored deep underground if we are forced to defend ourselves. It feels as much of a threat as an assurance.

The South deals with finance, international trade and future research. In the North we produce textiles and electronics. The film misses off the part where we act as a giant dump for everyone else too. Despite that, I feel a longing for home as the screen shows us vast greenery, small untouched villages and enormous lakes. I don't know exactly where they are but the thought they are in my Realm makes me feel proud.

The broadcast tells us about the King's innovations: the thinkwatches which help us live our daily lives and the cross-country trains which are the main way of transporting people and goods.

Finally, it moves on to the Reckoning. I am hoping there may be some explanation but instead it tells us that the King devised a test for all his subjects; something which would figure out how everyone was best suited to serving the country. It shows us rows of soldiers, laboratories full of people in white coats and a group of workers helping to build a bridge. Given everything I have seen in the past day, I want to feel hostile but it all seems so sensible. Is it really such a bad thing to utilise everyone in the best way in order to enhance all of our lives? I want to say no, to think that the way people such as Wray and Faith are discarded is wrong but then I remember all the dead people I have just seen on screen.

The screen fades to an image of Offerings being led onto a train, telling us that this is the way the four Realms repay the King for the sacrifices he made. That each year, he takes thirty young people to assist him in making the country better by doing whatever he deems necessary. None of that fits with keeping us locked inside and murdering Wray, but then I suppose that wouldn't be the best thing to put into a film which is telling us how lucky we are.

It finishes with a mother and son being given a basket of food, 'to show the King's gratitude for your service', and it's hard not to see Mum and Colt in their places. I try to console myself that, despite what could happen to me, they will at least be looked after.

As the footage ends, the lights switch back on and a ripple of applause spreads around the room. At first, it is just one or two people but quickly everybody starts to clap. Not wanting to be singled out, I join in too, hammering my hands together loudly as the noise turns into cheers. Ignacia is standing at the front, a curious half-smile on her face as if she knew what was going to happen. Quickly it has become a competition to see who can make the most noise. People are banging the tables; others are making hooting noises that sound more like the ones I am used to from the woods.

After a while, Ignacia raises her hand to quieten us and says the King would be grateful to hear of our appreciation.

It is as if last night did not happen.

'All of our Offerings are given roles to perform to serve the King,' Ignacia says. 'These will be judged based upon your performance in the Reckoning.' She presses something on her thinkwatch and ours burst into life. I feel mine buzzing at first before the screen lights up, displaying the word 'technology'.

'You should all now see where we have judged you to best aid your country,' she adds. Around me, everyone is checking their wrists and I feel a hum of satisfaction. I assume most people, like me, have been given jobs within areas they have an interest in.

Ignacia seems cheerier than the previous night as she tells us it is time for a tour – but her demeanour makes things all the more confusing. Is being an Offering a blessing or a curse? It is hard to reconcile the differences with everything we have seen.

More identical corridors, more echoing footsteps and then we are outside. As we exit into a courtyard through wide wooden doors, I realise it is the first time I have been anywhere but inside since stepping onto the train. The air is cool but refreshing as I gulp it desperately, enjoying the feeling as it fills my lungs. I look at the deep, endless blue of the sky and the fluffy clouds before Ignacia's voice brings me back to the present.

She asks who has been assigned to the barracks and nods approvingly as a few boys and one girl raise their hands. It seems strange that there is a need for an army of this type when we all know there are bombs that could destroy us all so easily, but then there are many things I don't understand about the mix between the old and new. Ignacia leads us towards a door at the far end and then invites those assigned to the barracks to go inside and meet their Head Kingsman.

She explains that each of us will have a Head Kingsman to answer to and then leads us towards another door at the far end of the courtyard. I stay towards the back, taking my time to enjoy the last remnants of what feels like freedom before we are back inside again.

More corridors, more stone, more footsteps. The dark-skinned Elite boy who was looking at me last night catches my eye again but he is harder to read this time. We are all nervous, not knowing how to deal with the situation we find ourselves in. I realise I have spoken fewer words since arriving at the castle than I have at any point in my life.

Intoxicating smells drift around us as we enter a giant kitchen. There are piles of vegetables and racks of meat which makes me hungry again. I have become so used to eating once a day that the longing in my stomach at this time of the morning feels unnatural and fills me with guilt. Faith, the Elite boy and a couple more Offerings are left in the kitchen as we move further into the castle.

A few more of the Offerings are left in an area where they make clothes and I realise the castle is divided much like our Realms are but on a smaller scale.

We make more stops in various areas, some with an introduction, some without. As our numbers have thinned, a strange thing has happened; with a growing excitement our little group seems to be latching onto the hope that being an Offering isn't as bad as people feared last night. I remember the way Faith tried to explain the King's behaviour and, even though none of us left on the tour have said it out loud, the fact we are talking to each other again is a sign that we are becoming more optimistic. One girl from the South tells another that she can't wait to get to work and it is as if we have all blanked Wray and Jela from our minds. I sense it too, the combination of the footage, the tour and Ignacia making me feel as if everything will be all right.

As we move, I have been looking for potential ways out; unguarded doors, corridors where there are no cameras, walls which could be low enough to climb and windows which might be worth trying to see if they open. But the further we travel, the more I feel resigned. I can't explain my own feelings but suddenly I'm wondering if Wray did something wrong after all. Perhaps he was incredibly disrespectful to the King? Maybe Jela is a fair price considering all he has done for us?

Soon we arrive at an area where Ignacia tells us she does her daily work. At the far end of the corridor I can see a couple of Kingsmen but she doesn't take us that far, instead leading us through a doorway into another passageway with openings on either side. She asks which of us have been marked as clerical and three people put their hands up. She points to a door on the left and says it is the Minister Prime's office, then the one opposite, which is hers. I peer through the open door to see banks of electrical items, including thinkpads, thinkwatches and other things I don't recognise. The clutter of items reminds me of my objects from home and suddenly I realise the one thing I have missed. Despite the more positive thoughts of what it means to be an Offering, I wonder what happened to last year's – and every year's before that. We didn't see anyone around the barracks and there were only one or two people in the kitchen and textiles area. If Wray was a one-off and we are so valued, then where are last year's thirty? Plus those from all the years before?

I hear footsteps echoing away from me and find I have fallen behind Ignacia and our remaining numbers, lost in my own thoughts. As I turn, I bump into someone's solid chest and step backwards, muttering an apology and hoping

RECKONING

I'm not in trouble for being on my own in this area. The person apologises too and, as I look into his face, it is as if I have gone back in time. Staring down at me, almost as confused as I am, is Hart – Martindale's last Offering.

12

I struggle to know what to say. When he left our village, Hart had a distinctive smile with large, well-built arms that came from years of helping out with various things around the place. He would unload supplies from the trains and deliver them. Now his face is thin, the bones jutting into his cheeks, and there is a hollowness around his eyes. His brown hair has grown out slightly, but it is still short and slightly patchy, with a tuft sticking out at the back. He squints, trying to place where he knows me from before I whisper 'Silver Blackthorn'. At first his eyes widen in recognition but then, before I can speak any further, he gives a slight shake of his head, brushing past me and entering one of the offices without a word.

I am in shock at seeing such a familiar face but have no choice other than to follow the sound of the footsteps rapidly retreating into the distance. I have barely caught up when the few of us who are left are whisked through to the electronics laboratories where Ignacia tells me I will be working. She introduces me to 'Head Kingsman Porter' and then takes everyone else out of the room, leaving me as the only Offering to work here.

The lab has rows of screens and thinkpad-like objects placed on benches and tables, as well as a desk in the back corner of the room which is piled high with various salvaged electrical pieces. I can see an old-fashioned phone similar to those that litter the gully outside Martindale, plus various broken thinkpads, thinkwatches and screens. My vision feels hazy as all I can really think of is Hart's skeletal appearance and the way he dashed away quickly to stop us being seen together.

Porter is supposed to be looking after me, or bossing me around depending on which way you look at it, but he is hunched over a desk in the corner and the brief look he gives me shows irritation more than anything else. He is barely taller than I am but somewhere around his forties, with brown hair scraped across his head. Most people that age fought in the war, so I am not surprised to see a scar that loops around his mouth. He is wearing the same uniform that a Kingsman would, but has no weapons holster.

As I hover uncomfortably in the middle of the room, Porter looks over his glasses at me a second time, seemingly unhappy that I am still there, and then gives a loud tut. No one else is around, so I can only assume it is for my benefit.

'What did you say your name was?' he asks, even though I haven't spoken since arriving.

'Silver Blackthorn,' I say, trying to be polite.

He doesn't move from the desk, tutting again and continuing to eye me across the room.

'Are you any good with this stuff?' He points to the pile of electrical items in the corner. His tone doesn't sound too interested so I mutter something vague. I try not to speak too much about what I can intuitively do with technology at the best of times, let alone to someone I don't know.

I wonder how much the Reckoning knew when it decided to make me a Member.

Porter nods acceptingly, although I'm not sure he has really listened to my answer.

'I suppose I'd better introduce you,' he says, beckoning me over and opening a door on the far wall.

The second room is smaller but there are three people sitting on high stools facing away from me. None of them turns until Porter tells them to. The only girl is holding a soldering iron, while the other two each have half-assembled thinkpads in their hands. Porter introduces us but the only name which sticks is 'Lumin', who has dark skin and is even more uninterested in me than Porter is. Perhaps because of this, Porter tells him to talk me through what we're doing and then leaves without looking at me.

Again I wait, feeling self-conscious in the middle of the room. On each side of me, there are metal benches with a strange mix of parts dumped on top. There are electronics

I have never seen before mixed in with scrap metal and dis-
assembled broken objects that look older than I am.

I realise Lumin is watching me, his lips clamped together
in apparent disapproval. He is a strange-looking person, not
unattractive but he seems to have a sense of aggravation
about him, his features tight in a permanent frown.

'So, you're the only one this year?' he says.

I shrug, not knowing how to reply.

'There were two last time,' he continues. 'None of them
are still here, of course.'

I think about Wray last night and assume that is the type
of outcome he is referring to.

'Are you an Offering?' I ask, trying to gain some control
over the interrogation.

'What do you think?' he shoots back.

The girl with the soldering iron spins around in her chair
and rolls her eyes at me. 'Don't mind him,' she says. 'I'm
Hari. We're all Offerings . . . well, what's left. Lumin's from
two years ago, I'm four and he's five.' She nudges the
person next to her, introducing him as Mira, and I feel guilty
about not remembering their names the first time around. It
means Lumin is only eighteen, quite a frightening thought
considering how much older he looks. I wonder what he
must have seen in the past two years to make him age so
much. 'Are you North?' she adds, continuing after I have

nodded. 'I remember you from last night. You were wearing purple, yes?'

'It was my mother's,' I say, instantly wishing I could take it back. It feels as if I have already given too much of myself away by admitting it.

She nods as if remembering when she was in my position and I realise at least some of the older Offerings must have been in the crowd who were above us looking down. I want to ask more questions but Lumin takes charge, as Porter asked him to.

'Enough chatting,' he says. 'Come here.'

There are four thinkpads in front of him, each with something different on the screen. One is filled with fire but Lumin presses a button to turn it off before I can take too close an interest. He points from one thinkpad to the next. 'Notice anything?' he asks.

My eyes flick through the screens. 'Are those images from cameras from around the castle?'

'At least you're not completely useless,' he says without a hint of it being a joke. 'All of the cameras are attracted automatically to movement. We're trying to work on a system that will stop them being attracted to Kingsmen, instead just focusing on anybody else.'

I think about what he's saying for a moment. 'So you have access to the security system?'

'Why, are you trying to escape?' Lumin's tone is sneering but I feel more worried by the way I blurted out the question. 'Do you think they're that stupid? If you're thinking like that already, you're not going to last long.'

'I didn't mean that,' I protest, even though I did.

Lumin shakes his head dismissively. 'Try it if you want and see what happens. Anyway, the Kingsmen's thinkwatches work on a different frequency to ours, so it should be a simple case of reprogramming the system that operates the cameras, right?'

'I guess . . .'

'Except the system was built before the war and has been patched up through the years, when it needed to be created from scratch. That leaves us trying to mix old and new to make something work.' He points to the bench of clutter behind me, then back to the thinkpads. 'Those are from one of the cameras we have taken apart, while these give us access to the monitoring system.'

'Limited access,' Mira interrupts without looking up. 'I wouldn't go digging if I were you.'

Lumin smiles gently for the first time and I wonder if he was going to let me find that out for myself. The implication is pretty clear that everything we do is being monitored somewhere along the line.

'Is this what you're all working on?' I ask.

'Don't be stupid,' Lumin replies. 'There are much

bigger priorities but there's no way your thinkwatch will have the privileges.'

I check my thinkwatch momentarily and it is still working, although the button for communicate is unresponsive.

Lumin slides out of the way, allowing me to sit, before huffing his way out of the lab and entering the main area where Porter is. At first I don't do anything, instead taking in the dim surroundings. There are no windows and only the one door, with a long thin light across the ceiling providing the only illumination. It feels strange being in a room lit by anything other than the sun or a candle.

'Don't mind him,' Hari says, not looking up.

I want to ask about the fates of last year's Offerings but am not sure I want to know the answer.

'Just keep your head down, do the work, don't be stupid, and you'll be fine,' she adds.

'Thanks.'

'Are you an Elite?' she asks.

I show her the orange face of my thinkwatch. 'Member.'

'Fair enough.' She twists her wrist around to show me the grey-black face of hers. I can just about make out the shape of the crown imprinted into it. 'We're Elites from the South, Lumin's a Member from the East. What's the North like?'

'It's greener than down here.'

She smiles and returns to her work as I turn to one of

the thinkpads, pressing my palm and thinkwatch into it until I feel it responding.

'What are you working on?' I ask, trying to sound conversational but Hari simply laughs.

'If you want to last around here, the first rule is don't ask questions.'

I don't reply but it's clear I have already been careless. I turn back to the thinkpads and start trying to figure out how everything works. At first, I consider asking but then wonder if throwing me in at the deep end is Porter's way of discovering if I am any use. Given everything that has happened in the past day, it is hard to judge what people's motivations may be. For Lumin, perhaps it is as simple as staying alive. Porter could be the crotchety man he seems to be, or he could be the person deciding who stays and who goes. He is a Kingsman after all.

It is barely a few minutes before I find myself being able to flick between various cameras around the castle. For the most part, there doesn't seem to be much going on as they show a host of empty corridors but it is hard to resist the urge to keep searching for unguarded doors and unbarred windows. From what I can tell, there is nothing monitoring our dormitories, although there are a few cameras that I don't have access to. As Lumin indicated, the system is a clumsy mess of mismatched technology but, luckily for me, it is the type of thing I have been messing around with my whole life. I try to slow myself, not wanting to make things look too easy, instead trying to watch what the others are doing from the corner of my eye.

Hari's thinkpad is showing moving images of something I assume is a bomb falling to the ground and then a large explosion. It doesn't seem real, more like some sort of simulation, but she is making small tweaks to whatever she is working on before running it again. She glances sideways towards me and, although I don't make any sudden movements to incriminate myself, she angles her screen away.

A couple of hours drag by as I go through the motions of working on the security system before Lumin and Porter enter the room. Porter checks my progress as I talk him through a few possible solutions I have. He continues to show a lack of interest but does stop at one point to tap something into his thinkwatch.

'Good, good,' he mutters, watching the other screens, instead of mine. I already have a pretty good idea of how to fix things but, instead of doing it, I have offered a few things that probably won't work but sound possible. I know I sound naive but that's what I want. Competent and useful – not a threat.

'You may as well head back to your dorm,' he says, addressing me. 'You lot can head off too.'

I follow Lumin towards the door, confused that we are being allowed to move around without an escort. As he hurries away from me, I stand in the corridor, unsure of what I should be doing. The other two exit and say good-bye to each other, although there doesn't seem to be any warmth to it.

'You're wondering why we can come and go as we please, aren't you?' Hari asks.

She sounds friendly but I'm not ready to trust anyone. 'Am I that obvious?' I reply, trying to sound as adolescent as I did to Porter.

If she sees through me, then she doesn't show it. 'Think about it,' she says. 'Where are you going to go? Try the doors and the windows and see how many open. Even if they did, where would it get you? Another courtyard with more high walls?' She nods at a camera mounted above the door of the lab. 'Not to mention the army of red lights keeping an eye out. We can all go where we want because there's nowhere to go.'

'I don't know where the dorm is,' I say, realising she is right but not wanting to believe it.

She points along the corridor and gives me a series of directions, which I surprise myself by being able to recite back. I want to ask where she stays but don't get a chance as she edges past me and disappears into the distance, her footsteps echoing along the hard stone floor.

I glance up to the blinking light under the camera and then set off the way I was told.

As I trudge through the corridors, I am trying to make a mental note of where everything is. I am so lost in my thoughts that I can only gasp in shock as someone puts a hand across my mouth and yanks me roughly through a doorway.

13

My instinct is to shout for help – or simply bite and kick –
but, as I am spun around, I find myself face to face with
Hart. His stare tells me to stay quiet as he slowly releases his
fingers from around my face and whispers an apology. My
eyes dart around the room, which is some sort of storage
area stocked with uniforms and cleaning utensils. It is as
low-tech as something we might have in Martindale but I
can't see any blinking camera lights.

Hart notices my movement and nods approvingly.
'You'll get used to where they are soon enough.'

There is so much I want to ask him but I don't get a
chance before he closes the door quietly. 'How are my
parents?'

'They're fine . . .'

'Are they both still alive?'

'Yes.'

Hart nods slowly and then repeats the question, unsure
he can trust me. His eyes are flickering all over the place,
making me feel nervous.

'Honestly, they're both fine,' I say, resting a hand on his

upper arm. He is wearing a white uniform much like mine but shudders at my touch. Even through the material, I am astounded by how thin he feels, especially considering I had the biggest meal of my life last night. I had been assuming that was the norm.

I let him go but he is still nodding. 'That's good,' he says, repeating it over and over.

'Are you all right?'

He doesn't seem to notice I've spoken. 'Is Martindale still there?'

'Of course . . .'

'Good, good . . .' He sounds flat and distant and there is no joy in his response.

On his wrist I see the dark-faced thinkwatch we were all so keen to spy when we found out Martindale had an Elite. 'What happened to you?' I ask softly.

His pupils focus on me but I can't read him. 'I saw you last night from a distance,' he says. 'I was at the top looking down and couldn't figure out if you were the girl I knew from home. It was only when you told me your name this morning that it all fell into place. You took a risk wearing that dress; I'm surprised you're still here.'

I think of Jela the night before and know he is telling me that if she wasn't so effortlessly pretty, then it could have been me Ignacia came calling for.

'They took another girl. What's going to happen to her?'

Hart shrugs. 'She belongs to the King now. You might see her at the weekly feast. It depends how quickly he gets bored with her.'

'What happens to us all?'

At first I don't think Hart is going to respond but then I realise he is listening for the sound of somebody passing. Footsteps reverberate around the corridor outside and then fade into the distance. If Hart is trying to make me nervous, then he's going the right way about it.

'One way or the other, we all end up going the same way,' he says. 'There are only two people left from my year.'

'You and Lumin?'

Hart seems confused at my knowledge for a moment but then nods. 'If you reach the end of the year, you get a small room of your own on one of the top floors. We're all on borrowed time though.'

'How many of you live up there?'

Hart shakes his head. 'Maybe twenty? I don't know.'

I try to do the adding up in my head. The war ended seventeen years ago but, before this year, there had been fourteen Reckonings, with thirty Offerings each year. That means there are only twenty people left out of over four hundred Offerings. Lumin's attitude and Hart's nervousness suddenly makes a lot more sense because simply staying alive is an achievement in itself.

'What happens to everyone?' I say, repeating my question that he never really answered.

'Didn't you see what happened to that kid last night?'

I stumble over my words. As if I could have forgotten. 'Of course, he was opposite me . . .'

'Then you know it is whatever the King wants to happen to us all. A few are sent overseas as gifts but you never hear from them. Most are dead.'

'But how has this been happening for so long with no one finding out?'

Hart looks at me as if I am stupid. The areas around his eyes are dark, although the rest of his face is pale and I feel a shudder go through me that I wish I could control. He doesn't answer but there's no need because it is obvious. Everything we are told comes either through our screens, thinkpads or thinkwatches. If none of those reveals what happens to the Offerings, then how are we supposed to know? Instead, stories are spread about marrying exotic leaders abroad or leading armies, so being an Offering doesn't sound too bad.

'Have my parents been getting their extra rations?' Hart asks, as if abruptly remembering.

'Yes, sometimes they share them with the smaller children around the village.' I smile at the thought. 'Your mum gave my friend Opie some bread because he helped her fix a door that wasn't closing. It had swollen in the damp and was sticking.'

Hart smiles and for the first time it feels as if I'm actually talking to him and not an impersonator. 'So she and Dad are really okay?'

'Yes, they just miss you; the whole village does.'

'Really?'

'Really. When I was chosen, people kept telling me to look out for you. Your dad told me to tell you your mother is fine. That was when we all thought being an Offering was . . . different.'

Hart peers over his shoulder and then leans against the door before sitting on the floor. Unsure of what to do, I follow his lead, resting on the ground next to him.

'Did they send you off?' he asks.

'Yes, it was like yours but there were more people and the cameras were there. Don't you get to see the Offering here?'

Hart shakes his head. 'We don't see anything from outside.'

That was the impression I was beginning to get. 'How have you survived so long?'

'Don't get noticed. It will be hard for you.'

'How do you mean?'

'You're pretty.'

'Oh.'

I feel embarrassed and don't know how to reply. It's nice of him to say but I've never thought of myself in that way.

'You shouldn't wear that dress again,' he adds. 'Be plain and blend in. It's the only way.'

From what he is saying, keeping my head down while I'm working for Porter now seems a necessity rather than just an aspiration. If you're too bad then you're expendable, too good then you're a threat.

'Tell me about the past two years,' I say.

Hart coughs quietly and I'm not sure he's going to respond as an eerie silence fills the room. I can hear shuffling movements in the distance but nothing nearby; the only light is coming from a small window high in the brickwork on the wall opposite. At the back of the room are rows of folded-down chairs but, considering we have both been brought up with so little, it isn't surprising we are sitting on the floor.

'It's not locked,' Hart says, nodding towards the window. 'But there's a big drop on the other side, plus it would only get you into the courtyard where the barracks are.' He pauses for a moment and then answers the question, although he speaks so quietly that I have to re-run his words in my head as if to confirm he has said what I think. 'Every week you get through the feasts is an achievement,' he tells me.

'How come you're so thin if we feast every week?' I ask, knowing it's not the point he's making.

'Sometimes it's hard to be hungry when you know what's coming. Neither of us are a stranger to hunger, are we?'

He's right, of course – I'm not sure how other areas might live but Martindale isn't a place awash with food.

'What's coming?' I ask.

Hart makes a noise which is a half-laugh, half-sigh. 'That depends on what mood the King is in. A few weeks ago, there were maybe half-a-dozen Offerings left from last year. Gradually that table where you sit gets smaller and smaller. For whatever reason, he was angry and threw a full bottle of wine onto the floor – then he ordered the two lads closest to him to fight each other. They were confused but, by then, everyone knows he's serious. Kingsmen gave them their swords and that was that. He was roaring away while these two kids sliced each other to pieces for his amusement.'

'That's horrible . . .'

For the first time, Hart seems to be thinking clearly and his words come out uninterrupted. 'By the time it was over, they had killed each other. The King was so furious at not having a winner he stormed down to the central area, grabbed the sword out of one of their hands, and then stabbed one of the other Offerings just because he could. That was three of them gone in a matter of minutes.'

My lack of surprise is more worrying to me than anything else. 'Is that normal?'

'Sort of. That's the worst I've seen, usually it's more like your lad last night. He does whatever he wants.'

'Doesn't anyone do anything to stop him?'

Hart snorts. 'Like who?'

'I don't know . . .'

I'm struggling to find the right words, as the full extent of what it is to be an Offering is beginning to dawn on me. 'I don't understand how all of this can have been going on for so long with nobody saying or doing anything.'

'What would you do? You know what it's like outside – everyone loves the King. He's the man who stopped us all fighting. You've seen the footage.'

I have but none of it shows this version of him. It's hard to reconcile the two sides of the same man and to separate everything we have grown up being told with what I have actually witnessed in the castle.

'So is this it, then?' I say. 'We're stuck here waiting for our eventual fate until next year's lot come along?'

'What do you suggest?'

'Hasn't anyone escaped, or at least tried?'

Hart laughs mockingly and I feel myself tensing. Out of

everyone, he should understand the most what I'm talking about. We come from the same place and have seen the same things.

'Of course people have tried,' he says condescendingly.

'So what happened?'

'Let's just say they weren't successful.'

'Did they die?'

'The lucky ones did.'

'I don't understand what you mean.'

Hart sniggers again and I can feel my anger boiling. 'If it is so easy to escape, why do you think people haven't done it? The only doors and windows you'll ever find open don't lead anywhere important. Some have tried running, others jumping, but no one has got away. When they're caught, they disappear for days and then you might see them again at a banquet where they are made an example of – to warn everyone what happens if you try to get away.'

Hart takes a moment to breathe. 'You can't even kill yourself,' he adds, although that wasn't what I was thinking. 'In my year, someone tried but the doctors kept them alive so the King could think of his own way to do it.'

He doesn't elaborate but I don't want him to anyway. He's probably right that the lucky ones are killed before they get caught.

Hart pushes himself up until he is standing and holds

out a hand to pull me up. 'We've probably been in here too long,' he says. 'Never forget the cameras and don't be seen in pairs. They are always on the lookout for people who seem too close to each other.'

I think of the way Lumin and Mira hurried off on their own, while Hari was uneasy standing next to me underneath the camera. I try to catch his stare but Hart is facing the door, holding the handle and listening for movement.

'Do you work in the Minister Prime's office?' I ask.

'Yes, it's just office stuff. Easy to go unnoticed if you don't do anything stupid.'

'What types of thing do you have access to?'

'. . . *If* you don't do anything stupid . . .'

His point is clear and I realise he has given up. If he had similar thoughts of escaping or somehow letting other people know what our King is actually like, then they are long gone.

'Can I come see you?'

Hart shakes his head. 'Haven't you been listening? Don't make friends and don't give them a reason to notice you.'

'Who do you mean by "them"?'

'Everyone – the Ministers, the Kingsmen, the King, whoever you are working with, or for. They want us all to work against each other.'

Hart sounds paranoid but I nod an acceptance as he

opens the door, checks both ways, and leaves without another word. I step into the corridor and, as he heads away from me, I wonder if that is to be my fate: a broken person living without hope.

14

Even though Hart spoke about not being hungry, the rest of the week gives me an idea of why he is so thin. The only food we receive each evening is a basket of bread and fruit in our room. Everyone seems happy to share and Faith tells me that she has learned from working in the kitchens that the feasts for Offerings will only happen once a week. I am eating less than I did when I lived in Martindale but quickly fall into the routine of accepting the pains in my stomach. Faith says there is no easy way to smuggle food out of the kitchens, not that I would have asked.

Hart told me how he sees things and, over the course of the week, everyone seems to have discovered for themselves what our lives are to be like. The fact that none of us have seen or heard from Jela since she was taken only adds to our unease.

Each day is much the same as the last. We get up and go to our respective jobs, then return and spend the evening in our dorms in near silence. I feel closest to Faith but she is as savvy as me and we both realise it is dangerous to be too friendly. I don't see Hart again but I do begin to get to know the corridors a lot better, memorising where the cameras are and checking the various doors and windows in case Hart is mistaken. I am determined not to end up lost and broken like him but struggle to find anything that could give me hope. Instead, I feel alone. My mind constantly drifts back to my mother, Colt, Opie and Imp and I can only trust they are being treated to the same extra provisions that Hart's parents were.

On the morning of the next banquet, Ignacia visits the dorm to tell us we should dress our best in the evening. New outfits are delivered to our wardrobes and many of the others spend hours showering, clipping and shaving before choosing their best dresses. I take Hart's advice and do enough to be passable without being too obvious. A few of the others seem to have put two and two together about Jela and I know I should tell the rest what Hart has told me but already I am thinking of myself.

I choose a long dress but it doesn't hug me like my mother's does and it is plain and black. Among the sparkly, short creations many of the others have gone for, it is entirely unnoticeable. My only consideration of clothes in the past was what would keep me the warmest. Having to give such serious thought to something like this seems completely silly.

As I sit on my bed, I catch Faith's eye and she clearly has the same ideas I do. She is wearing a light yellow dress and, although it would be short on some of the girls, her height means it reaches her knees. She grins and then holds up a high-heeled shoe as if asking if that's what she should choose. I shrug and point to my own, which are flat and comfortable. My dress covers them anyway but I stand and push myself up onto my toes to see what it would feel like to be those few inches taller. As I try to spin, I stumble clumsily, automatically reaching ahead to stop myself falling. At first I think I have misjudged where the wall is but then my hand presses against the wood panelling that runs around the lower half of the room. I just about manage to hold myself up and no one except Faith has noticed. She laughs quietly to herself and turns away.

For some reason I am now drawn to the wood. The top halves of the walls are painted a greyish colour but below that, roughly at the height of my chest, are dark varnished wood panels which run diagonally. The section my hands fell against feels particularly thin, so, after a check over my shoulder to make sure no one is paying me any attention, I run my hands along the grain until I reach an area a metre or so away which is distinctly thicker. I crouch on the floor using my bed as a shield and trace the palm of my hand across this segment, trying to figure out where it begins and ends. The only person who might be able to see me would be Faith but she is still facing away. It doesn't take long for me to discover there is a section roughly a metre square that is thinner than the rest. I can feel my heart beating in a mixture of excitement and apprehension as I sit on the floor with my back against it and press backwards. I am sure it is some sort of hidden door but it doesn't give way, no matter how hard I push.

Before I can examine it any further, the main door opens and Ignacia glides into the room in a purple dress that looks a lot like the one I wore at the last feast. Her hair is higher than last week, although she seems slightly rushed as she tells us it is time to go.

Through the week we have been left to find our own way around the castle, or at least the parts of it where there don't seem to be any Kingsmen. We have only visited the main hall once and I'm not sure I would be able to find it again but Ignacia leads the way, moving quickly and not checking behind her as some of us struggle to keep up.

We enter the hall opposite the male Offerings again and there is a ripple of something that feels like constrained excitement from our side. I look up to the royal box to see Jela sitting there, wearing an elaborate red dress. I wonder if she will acknowledge us or give any indication that she is all right, but she simply stares into the distance, blank and empty.

I try to look up towards the higher seats to see if I can spot Hart, Lumin, Porter or any of the others, but the lights are bright and focused directly on us, meaning I can't see anything.

Things begin much as last week, with the Minister Prime demanding silence before the anthem and the King's entrance. The King seems more in control of himself this week but less interested in us. As the food is placed on the table, I force myself to eat slower, knowing everything that Hart told me is coming true. Rather than enjoy the meal, I am instead worrying about what the King might have in store for us later. Across the table, the Elite boy from the West makes eye contact but I quickly look away with a delicate shake of my head, trying to tell him that any sort of acknowledgment is dangerous, especially here.

The food is as delicious as before but this time I try to concentrate on eating certain things, rather than trying a bit of everything. After only a week, my body feels weaker than it did in Martindale, so I stick mainly to the meat. I consider concealing some but my dress wouldn't make that easy and I suspect the potential punishment would not be worth it.

As we are all still eating, I hear a heaving, guttural noise coming from the royal box and look up to see the King bent over double being sick on the floor. The sight is so surreal that everyone around the table has stopped eating to watch. It is only as the Minister Prime starts to rise to his feet that we collectively realise we should not be staring.

I turn back to my plate as the Minister Prime sits again but out of the corner of my eye I see the King wiping his mouth with the back of his sleeve and then calling for more food. At first I think he is ill and it is only when I feel my stomach beginning to strain that I understand the truth; he has made himself vomit simply so he can keep eating. I risk another look upwards, watching as he swigs heartily from a bottle of wine while holding some sort of meat in the other hand. All of a sudden, it feels wrong to eat. While everyone in Martindale spends weeks and months trading and bartering over petty amounts, he is here forcing himself to be ill simply so he can eat more.

Because Wray is no longer there, the boys' benches have been shunted along and they have a little more space. I look directly across to where there is more of a gap than there should be and think of poor, frightened Wray's eyes, then risk another glance at the King. He has more food stuck in his beard than I would usually eat in a day at home. I have never truly hated anyone in the past but I now despise him. It is hard to imagine how he has somehow become so respected outside the walls and I know the easy thing to do is follow Hart's example by not standing out. Although it might get me through this year, perhaps another, I know I am only going to end up the same as Wray in the end.

Somehow, I need to find a way to fight back.

Across the table, the Elite boy is staring at me. I refuse

to meet his eyes and hope no one else has noticed. I wonder if he even knows how reckless he is being, putting both of us in danger. I can't begin to imagine what he might want; we've never even spoken.

As I continue to will him to stop looking at me, the gentle chatter of noise halts instantly and I don't need to look around to know the Minister Prime is standing with his arm out. He starts speaking, every syllable rolling from his tongue in a way that makes me shudder. He thanks us for our efforts through the week and emphasises he has been getting some good reports back about us from the various Head Kingsmen. I hadn't thought that Porter might be feeding back information but I guess it is no surprise. It's not as if I have done anything out of the ordinary in any case.

There are a few mutterings around the table but nobody risks anything too disruptive.

He tells us that it is a learning process for everybody as we get to grips with our new surroundings and, for a moment, it genuinely sounds as if he is trying to be helpful. Then his true intention becomes clear.

'None of you should forget, of course, that being here is a privilege. You are all our King's subjects and there are rules we all must abide by. If any of you were to come forward to reveal any untoward behaviour among your fellow Offerings, it would be looked upon most favourably.

I should warn you that the opposite is also true, however. If any unpatriotic behaviour is found and it is later discovered that others of you were aware, then you will be treated as harshly as those directly involved.'

I can remember Hart's words exactly – 'They want us all to work against each other' – and it is clear that, over the course of the week, pretty much everything he told me is true. The Minister Prime will know that people within the group are beginning to bond, which is something he will not abide. I know I will have to be more careful, even around someone like Faith. The Minister Prime wants us to look at everyone as a potential enemy and it is now hard not to.

After the meal and the speech, there are no further incidents, as the King seems too busy eating and drinking to pay any attention to us.

Later, the dorm is quieter than usual, with even the pockets of people who had become friendly now worried about inadvertently saying something out of place that could be fed back to someone in authority. Wearing us down has taken barely a week, so perhaps it is understand-able why Lumin and Hart behave as they do after two years.

As the lights go out and everyone settles down to sleep, I lie awake listening to everyone's stirrings. On a few occasions I am ready to slide out of bed and return to examining the wall, only to stop myself as another girl rolls over or mutters in her sleep. To someone who had her own room at home, even if it was small, it is amazing how noisy a group of people can be while they are supposed to be sleeping.

A hint of moonlight shines through the windows and I allow my eyes to adjust to the dark as much as possible. Eventually I sit and squint into the gloominess of the far end of the room. I watch for a few minutes but, despite the odd murmur and rustling, nobody appears to be awake. Gradually, I slip between the sheets of my bed until my bare feet feel the carpet beneath me. It is only a few steps from my bed to the wall but I hold my breath over each one until I am again pressed up against the wood panelling. If anything, the discrepancy between the thinner and thicker parts now feels more apparent in the dark and it is easier to find the minuscule gap between the hidden door and the rest of the wood.

So many thoughts rush through my head; have any previous Offerings ever found this? Does Ignacia or anyone else know about it? Is it just a cupboard or a passageway? Where could it lead? Is it monitored? Is it a trap? A test?

I have to calm myself and focus on the first thing before any of that: can I actually open it? Slowly I trace my fingers around the gap, using my nails to find the corners and trying to squeeze the tips of my fingers into the opening.

All I discover is that the gap narrows on one side, which is where I guess the hinges are.

Faith is shuffling in the bed closest to me, so I stop and rest the back of my head against the wall, holding my breath and listening in case she has disturbed anyone else. As I lean into the wall, I hear a gentle clicking noise before I find myself falling backwards. It is too late to stop myself as my head bounces off a cold stone floor, leaving me confused both because of what has happened and because of the unexpected bump. For a few moments, I don't move, but lie there listening. When I am certain nobody has heard, I slowly roll over and then move myself into a kneeling position.

The thinner section of wood has swung away from the bedroom, to reveal something which is too dark to see properly. In the dark I try to figure out how the door opened and realise there is a push-panel in the top right which my head was pressing against. It looks and feels exactly the same as the rest of the panelling and the only way you would know it was there was if you were already aware of it – or by accident.

I take one last look into the bedroom, trying to see if anyone is moving, and then retreat into the space behind the door, pushing it almost fully closed and finding myself in complete darkness. Using my hands to guide me, I trace the stone and creep forward, unable to stop shivering as the cold seeps through my body. A voice in my head is telling me to be sensible and return to the room but the thought of ending up like Hart keeps driving me forward until I reach another wood panel. It has taken me under a minute to creep along the passage in the same direction, so it isn't long, and I try to think my way around the outer corridors to work out where I might be, but I have no idea. My fingers quickly find a clasp on the second wood panel and I wait, holding onto it and trying to build up the courage to find out what is on the other side. Eventually I tell myself that if I have got this far, then I have already made my decision. I slowly pull the door inwards before poking my head out and risking a glance in both directions.

On the other side I find a corridor that looks similar to most of the others in the castle – except that there is a large window at one end. The single pane is so large it seems almost like some sort of lookout point. In the fraction of a second I allow myself to look around before retreating, I can't see anything other than the dim moonlight that fills the corridor. More importantly, I can't see anyone else in the area and no sign of any cameras. I run through the images in my head, over and over, trying to remember anything that could mean danger, but then I act impulsively, reopening the panel and taking a longer amount of time to take in the surroundings, before crawling into the larger new corridor and pulling the panel shut.

The area is quieter than the dorm. Slowly I creep towards the window, expecting to have someone jump out at any moment but there are no obvious doors along the panelled walls and the window is a dead end. Trying to stop myself shivering, I look through the glass at the remnants of a town that still hasn't recovered from the war. There are piles of bricks and rubble dotted as far as I can see, the only buildings apparently on the brink of collapse, shored up with various makeshift pieces of wood and stone. Despite the destruction, the bright white of the moon provides an astonishing view outside the castle. I press against the glass and try to stare around an impossible angle towards the central section of the castle, but it is hard to see anything other than the fact I am in an area furthest away from the middle. It is a long way down but, if I could somehow survive the steep drop, I would be outside the grounds and a short distance away from the cover and shelter the rubble would provide. In my head, I know it is impossible but that doesn't stop me thinking through the scenarios.

I am so lost in my imagination that the first time I realise someone has crept up on me is when I feel a hand gripping my shoulder, making me shriek with surprise.

15

In the fraction of a second it takes me to turn, the faces of the Minister Prime, Ignacia, a Kingsman and even the King himself flash before my eyes. I wonder what my punishment will be; will it happen in front of everyone and will it affect Colt and my mother? Instead it is a face that in many ways is even more shocking: the Elite from the West who spent the evening staring at me across the banquet table.

'Shh,' he whispers before telling me his name is Imrin.

I am unsure how to respond but he seems as surprised as I feel. 'Is there a passage out of your room too?' he asks.

I feel a slight panic, remembering the Minister Prime's order that we should report anything suspicious. It seems too obvious that Imrin is here at the same time as me. Has he been following me somehow? Or was it a trap all along?

The moonlight is reflecting from Imrin's smooth dark skin and when it becomes clear I'm not going to answer, he tries again. 'I'm sorry for scaring you. I was just . . . excited. I sleep in the corner of the boy's dorm and I found this by accident a few days ago. I followed it and it brought me out by this window. I've been coming back each night just to stare at the outside world. You're the first person I've seen here.'

I think over his words as his black eyes stare at me. If it wasn't for what Hart had told me, and the Minister Prime's order, I would believe him.

'Show me,' I say.

He takes my hand and I feel an instant spark of exhilaration. It's hard to describe but it is like the feeling I have when I am with Opie, a sense of excitement. I let him lead me towards the wall directly opposite where I had emerged. His skin is warm and somehow reassuring. He lets my hand go and presses a spot on the wood until the panel clicks inwards, exactly as mine did.

'Our dorm is through there,' he whispers, taking a step inside. He motions for me to follow but I shake my head and he re-emerges. 'Did you find something similar?' It is clear he already knows the answer but if he is some sort of spy, then I suppose I'm in trouble anyway.

'Ours is here,' I say, showing him the latch on our door, directly opposite his.

If he already knew the location of ours, then he hides the fact very well, his face a picture of intrigue. I return to the window and feel Imrin's presence behind me.

'What's it like in the girl's dorm?' he asks.

I am trying to be suspicious but there is something so likeable about him that it is hard not to feel engaged. He has an intensity to his eyes that makes it seem like there is no one else in the world but you. 'What's it like in yours?' I counter, turning to face him.

'Everyone's terrified after what happened to that Wray kid on the first night. One of the others didn't come back from his job either, so we're two down already. Everybody thinks they're going to be next.'

He doesn't sound scared but that could be his way; Opie is the same. 'Ours is just quiet,' I say. 'Hardly anyone speaks to each other, especially after tonight with the Minister Prime's speech.'

'Ours is like that too. I was worried about coming out tonight . . .'

'Why did you, then?'

Imrin's brow ripples in what I first think is displeasure but then I realise that he doesn't know. His shrug confirms his silent answer and I understand he could ask me the same thing.

'Where do you work?' he asks instead.

'In the tech department – there are only a few of us.'

'I work in the kitchens.'

He is only telling me what I already know because I saw him being dropped off but it is nice to have someone to talk to.

'I guess it's less fun at the feast each week when you have to help put it together?'

He returns my thin smile. 'We have to put together something like that every day of the week. Just because we are not feasting, it doesn't mean the King isn't.'

'Do the older Offerings talk to you?'

'Not really. There aren't many of them . . .'

Hearing it from someone else somehow makes it more real and I find myself trusting Imrin all too easily.

'What's at the other end of the corridor?' I ask, nodding towards the fork in the opposite direction from the window.

'I don't really know. I poked my head around a few days ago and it is another corridor – but I saw a camera around that corner. It was facing the other way and I haven't tried again since.'

I'm not surprised as there are cameras everywhere but it still feels nice to have this window area as my own – our own – to get away from everyone else. I figure the next time I am in the security camera system without Porter, Lumin or anyone else watching me too closely, I will try to figure out where we are. Imrin and I talk about the positions of our dorms in relation to the hall and where we work, which gives me something of a start.

Goosebumps rise on my arm and my back arches backwards as a gentle breeze ripples through the air – from where I do not know. Imrin reaches out, perhaps instinctively, to touch my hand and ask if I'm okay and I don't shy away; instead I pull him towards me and let him put his arms around me. Somehow, despite the temperature, his body is wonderfully comforting.

I guide him back to the passage that leads to my dorm and open the door, then we sit inside the tunnel, him still resting a hand around my shoulder while the other one rubs my skin to warm me up. It is nice to feel actual contact with somebody after over a week of isolating myself. I have been so used to playing around with Opie, Imp and Colt that it is only now that I realise how much I have missed the touch of another person. Something about Imrin feels natural, as if I don't have to try to be someone else in his presence. I find him fascinating.

'What do you think these tunnels are?' he asks.

Between us, we cannot come up with a better answer other than that the castle has been here for a long time and that it may hold many other secrets. Whether anyone else knows about them is something we can't know. I would guess they would probably have been blocked if they were widely known about.

Imrin tells me his family came to the country four generations ago from India and that he has three older sisters and three younger sisters. He is the only son and his mother has spent years doting on him, while his father has an injury from the war that hasn't healed. They have been supported by his older sisters for as long as he can remember. I try to stop myself revealing too much but he is witty and seems so honest – plus he has a quality about him that is hard to describe. It might be the way he speaks, purring the words in a way that makes you want to get comfortable and listen.

In truth, I probably see a lot of me in him. He has rebelled in the same small way that I have, which is why we are here. There is also an obvious parallel in the way he is surrounded by girls compared to the way I have so many boys in my life. I tell him about Colt but not Opie or his family as we start talking about where we come from.

At first he tells me how he has distant family members who live in India but, because of the way things are, it is impossible for them to have any contact. Where we are now feels completely foreign to me, so to hear about other countries is incredibly strange. I recognise the names but little else. The last his family knew was that India was in the middle of a war that had been going on for the whole of his lifetime. We have always been told that all of the other countries are dangerous but I have been doubting everything since my arrival.

'Are you an Elite?' he asks and I realise we have been talking for all this time without either of us asking the most obvious question, or checking each other's wrists. For most people, it would come up first.

'I'm a Member. You?'

'Elite,' he says, although he's not showing off. He almost

sounds embarrassed admitting it. 'The first in my family. My sisters are Members or Inters.'

'What do they do?'

'We run a farm and all work together. When my result came out, everyone thought I would be sent somewhere else.'

'Not here though?'

Imrin laughs gently. 'No, I guess not.'

As he tells me about his sisters, who are, apparently, all bigger and stronger than him, I almost forget where I am. Suddenly I am transported back to Martindale, sitting around a fire in the woods with Opie laughing about the trouble his brothers have got themselves into.

I tell him a little about my village and a few of the people there, although I'm not ready to open up completely yet.

The fact we know so little about each other's areas only reinforces Hart's point that we are completely divided. He was talking about being here as Offerings but it is true of the outside too. The results of the Reckoning each year decide which Realms get the most provisions. It is supposed to be an aspiration to be an Elite, not just to give yourself a better life but to help everyone you live with too. None of us wants to be part of a Reckoning where the North finishes fourth, giving us less than the previous year. Despite that, we barely know anything about those we are trying to beat.

As I begin to say we should be going back to bed, Imrin

asks about the girl sitting next to the King and I
how Jela was taken from the dorm and that the
we have seen her since is beside the King at the la

I stand, hunched under the low ceiling and
return to bed, when I think of one final thing. 'W
you staring at me over dinner?'

Even in the swirling darkness, I can tell he is
rassed. 'I just thought you had nice eyes,' he says.

It's not what I expected, or wanted, and I don't
how to reply, other than a limp-sounding 'thanks'.

'Are you going to come back tomorrow?' he asks,
hand on the hidden door to return to the corridor.

'Maybe, if everyone is asleep and I can stay awake.'

'Me too.'

I already know I will be sneaking out every night if I
think I can get away with it but I tell myself I should keep
my intentions private.

'We need to be careful,' I say. 'If we're going to do thi
. . . do anything . . . we can't be friends anywhere othe
than here. We can't talk to each other or be seen togethe
We have to be complete strangers.'

I'm not sure he understands quite what I mean but
says 'okay' and then he is gone with a gentle click of
wooden panel.

As I make my way back to the bedroom, I have
remind myself that little has changed; we are still priso

erhaps it is just because I now have someone to talk to, but something feels different – as if I now have a compulsion to believe that everything will be all right in the end.

Before I re-enter the bedroom, I press my ear against the panel and listen until I am sure everything inside is silent. I gently pull the door open and creep back into the room, each of my footsteps punctuated by a small intake of breath until I feel the scrambled bed sheets around me once more. I can hear the faint rattle of the windows as the breeze hums its chorus outside and, as someone at the other end of the room turns over noisily, I slide down to the bottom of the bed and close my eyes, dreaming of Martindale.

*   *   *

Although I have become used to sleeping while the elements scratch at the outside of our house in Martindale, I have never been a deep sleeper. Sometimes the howl of the wind or the tip-tapping of rain invades my dreams and I lie half-awake, half-asleep, knowing exactly where I am but still being able to rest. I have even fallen asleep by the gully once or twice, huddled close to a fire built by either Opie or myself, or snuggled underneath one of the thick woollen blankets we sometimes take with us.

As I jolt awake at the sound of Ignacia's voice, I am utterly confused. My eyelids are heavy and, as they open slightly, I see people already dressed, while somehow I have

still continued sleeping. I hear the words 'hurry' and 'now' and realise she is talking to me. The accusing eyes of the other girls are watching as I stumble out of bed and grab my work clothes from the wardrobe. Everything seems to have a thin grey haze about it as I try to remember if last night was a dream. I recall the passage, the window and Imrin; but then I also remember the woods, a fire, and Opie. Or was it Imrin in the woods and Opie in the passage?

'Come on, we have to go,' a voice says, and I turn to see Faith standing in the doorway. Half of the girls have already left with Ignacia and I can hear their footsteps echoing.

'I'm coming,' I say, hopping towards the door, battling with a shoe.

Together, Faith and I catch up to the rest of the group. She tells me that Ignacia came to the room and told us we were all needed in the main hall, although she doesn't know why.

'You were talking in your sleep,' she adds ominously.

'What did I say?'

'I don't know, you were mumbling.'

For a moment, I was worried that I had given something away and, as last night's memories swirl into something that seems vaguely coherent, I wonder if talking in my sleep is something I have always done.

The hall is not decked out in its usual regal way. The lights are off and there is no spread awaiting us at the banqueting table. Instead, the Minister Prime is standing with his hands behind his back, eyeing each of us as we are led across the floor until we are standing in a semi-circle around him. Ignacia goes to his side and then I hear a clunk as the doors are closed. As I turn to see Kingsmen standing rigidly in front of the exits, my heart sinks.

Nothing good is going to happen this morning.

The Minister Prime speaks sharply without moving. 'Which one of you is Pietra?'

Everyone's eyes shoot sideways at Pietra, who takes a nervous step forward. Her long brown hair is plaited behind her and she is trying to stand tall but doesn't seem too confident. I remember her on the train, next to Rush, sneering and laughing, and I wonder what she has done wrong. Regardless of what I thought of her then, I'm not sure I want to see what could happen to her here.

'Did I not tell you all yesterday that unpatriotic behaviour would result in harsh treatment?' the Minister Prime demands.

For a moment, Pietra doesn't reply. She rocks nervously from one foot to the other and is trembling as she replies. 'Yes, Sir.'

'And did I not inform everyone here that revealing untoward behaviour would be looked upon most favourably?'

'Yes, Sir.'

The Minister Prime leans back gently onto his heels and

looks along the line. 'You should all know,' he says, pausing for effect, 'that Pietra here took my words as literally as I meant you all to and reported something very grave to us this morning.'

He pauses again, licking his lips as his piercing holes of eyes flicker across each of us. 'Now, who would like to step forward and confess?'

16

It is almost as if his words have punched me in the stomach. I remember the rustling from last night when I returned to the room. Pietra must have heard me and reported it this morning while I was sleeping.

The Minister Prime's eyes continue to skim between us, determined for someone to say something. 'I will punish you all if nobody steps forward.' The way he speaks reminds me of the sensation you get when you are ripping something in half. The tones ripple through you in a way that feels exhilarating, yet a little scary at the same time. Everything he says reeks of power.

I try to step forward but my legs feel heavy and refuse to listen to my command. I open my mouth to say something but can only let out a vague croak. My body is wracked with guilt and fear. What will happen to Colt and my mother? Inwardly, I scream at myself but then, one pace at a time, I see another girl stepping into the circle, her head bowed, her gentle sobbing filling the room.

The Minister Prime glances sideways to Ignacia who nods briefly and then looks away.

'What is your name?' he booms.

'Bryony.'

'Bryony what?'

'Bryony Gaitlin, Sir.'

The Minister Prime smiles, although his thin lips don't separate until he speaks. 'Are you from the East, Ms Gaitlin?'

'Yes.'

'And you are an Intermediate?'

'Yes.'

'What would you like to confess?'

There is a silence as Bryony raises her head slightly. Although we have shared the dorm, I haven't spoken to her since we arrived. She has reddish hair, cut short, and is glancing quickly from side to side. Bryony is now level with Pietra, who is the only person not watching the girl with the trembling voice.

'I took food from the kitchen.'

'You did what?'

Bryony's voice is louder the second time. 'I took food from the kitchen, Sir.'

'Were the rules explained to you about stealing?'

'Yes, Sir.'

'Do you not respect our King?'

'Yes, Sir.'

By now, the Minister's voice has built to a climax. 'Then *why* have you disrespected his good grace?'

We all know there is no answer Bryony can give that will get her out of trouble and I cannot believe how close I came to confessing to something they didn't know about.

Bryony's voice has dropped again. 'I was hungry.'

With a flick of his eyes, the Minister Prime has Kingsmen descending on Bryony. She doesn't resist but they grab her roughly anyway, hauling her out of the main doors.

Everyone stands in silence and Pietra is still in the centre of us. I stare at the back of her head, telling her without words that I hate her.

'We have removed the food she took,' the Minister says strictly, before turning his attention back to Pietra. 'You will, of course, be rewarded for your loyalty. There will be extra rations for you waiting in your room tonight.' He turns his attention back to the rest of us. 'I hope you have all learned a lesson this morning.'

I have learned two lessons: firstly that Pietra cannot be trusted and secondly that if I am going to sneak out and explore, I need to be more careful about it.

'Ms Gaitlin has been taken to the dungeons and when our King decides she has learned enough of a lesson, she will be given other more appropriate work.' The Minister Prime does not expand but, regardless of what that work may entail, none of us thinks it is going to be pleasant for her.

I spend the rest of the day quietly seething as I work in the laboratories. There are so many things I would like to say to Pietra in the evening but none of them would be sensible. It is clear that we are all utterly divided after barely a week and the only person I think I can trust is someone I have spoken to only once.

Perhaps the only silver lining is that my work isn't that bad. I made sure it took me the entire week but I solved the issue with the cameras – only to be scoffed at by Lumin who told me it was never an issue anyway. Instead it was a test to see how well I could do. They had all gone through it, with Lumin boasting that he had completed the task in three days. Not wanting to point out I could have done it in less than one hour, I let him have his moment and succeed in both keeping my head down and gaining a little sympathy from Hari. Mira doesn't say much to anyone.

Inside the lab, when neither Lumin nor Porter are around, Hari is perfectly friendly – but she barely acknowledges me if anyone else is present and it is that approach I know I should copy. In a quiet moment, I ask her about the dungeons as I had never heard of anything like this until the Minister Prime mentioned it. Hari says they are under the hall and it is where they lock up and punish anyone who has broken the rules. The fact we are all locked up anyway doesn't escape me but it is useful knowledge in the wider picture of understanding the castle's layout. I wonder if there might be an extra exit down there, although I'm not overly keen on finding out.

Porter is gradually growing on me. He doesn't say much and delegates everything but the most important jobs to us but he doesn't come across like some of the other people who wear the Kingsman uniform. He seems more apathetic to the cause, as opposed to driven by it, but I cannot convince myself he is someone I should trust.

He does seem to have an inkling of what I am capable of, however, and has kept me in the main lab with him since I completed the initial task. He is working on a wider project that should help our electronic items use electricity more efficiently and, for the first time, I begin to see some of the good work that goes on around the castle. Every now and then, Porter will ask my opinion on something. A lot of his questions surpass any previous knowledge I have but I tell him the first thing that drops into my head and he looks back down at his machine with a 'hmm', without letting me know if I have been useful or not.

Most of my time is spent fixing things, mainly thinkpads but the occasional thinkwatch too. Tinkering with the spare parts makes me think of home, although it feels odd and almost too easy to have genuine extras to be using, instead of having to hunt through piles of scrap to try to find something I can work with. He gives me some burned-out thinkpads that he says belong to the Home Affairs department and I easily manage to transfer wires from what he tells me is an old tower computer to fix them. I didn't know what they were called in the past but there are stacks of them in the gully outside Martindale, piles of plastic, silicon and metal winding into each other. If he seems impressed then he hides it well and I ask enough questions I already know the answers to, making the work seem harder than it is.

There is an access device which Porter keeps in his top drawer to reprogram things officially. Each time I need it, I have to ask permission and, though I am tempted to find out what else it could do with my thinkwatch, I resist the urge, at least for now. I spend the day submerged in work.

There is a very different atmosphere in the dorm when I return. Pietra is sitting on her bed with a bowl of bread and fruit but instead of the other Elites being around her – or the silence of recent days – there is a poisonous feel to the air.

'Would you like something *extra* to eat?' Pietra asks sweetly as I walk past. It is the first time she has spoken to me since the train.

I make certain to reply equally sweetly as I make my way back to my bed – there is no point in deliberately antagonising someone the Minister Prime is happy with. 'I'm fine, thank you.'

All but a couple of the other girls are also on their beds, including Faith, who offers me a half-smile, which I return. Nobody is speaking but it feels as if I am in a tin can where the lid is about to blow off.

'You do know I did this for all of us?' Pietra says loudly, addressing everyone. She sounds aggrieved but close to tears as well. We all turn to look towards her as she stands and points to the food. 'You could at least be grateful.'

I want to reply but know I shouldn't. Anything said in front of the other girls could find its way back to Ignacia or the Minister Prime. Faith puts me to shame, though, spitting a fury I can only feel. 'You did it for yourself.'

Everyone's eyes shift from Pietra to Faith and then back again, although it is one of the other Elites who replies, 'Who cares what you think, Trog?'

Faith laughs, showing a maturity I wish I had. I'm angrier on her behalf than she is. 'Jela was an Elite and it didn't do her much good.'

She is right, of course, but it is still shocking to hear Jela's name used in such a way.

'Go on,' Faith adds, 'report me. See if I care.'

One of the other girls starts talking about sticking together, which sounds nice in theory but would take a lot more trust than any of us have for each other. She is shot down anyway as the name-calling intensifies between Faith, Pietra and a few of the other girls. I feel nothing but guilt as I sit on my bed, watching instead of defending as I realise, again, that we are divided in every way – from our Realms, to our ranks, to thirteen girls who simply cannot get on with one another. The argument rages until one of the Kingsmen storms in and tells everyone to stop shouting. We all look nervously at each other as he asks if there is a problem he should be aware of but everyone stays silent. I realise with a small amount of relief that the dispute will not go any further.

After that, aside from a few mutterings in various corners of the room, there is near enough silence again. Through saying nothing, I have managed to isolate myself even further as I can't bring myself to meet Faith's eyes during the rest of the evening until the lights turn themselves off.

I lie awake waiting for everyone's shuffling to stop and then head back towards the panel next to my bed. Within a couple of minutes, I am standing at the large window peering out over wisps of fog slowly descending on the battered remains of the town. The moon isn't as bright as it was the previous evening but there is something wonderfully ethereal as Imrin whispers in my ear, 'Beautiful, isn't it?'

It's slightly unnerving how he has crept up on me again but I have to agree.

'I didn't know if you'd come,' I say, not turning.

'What else have I got to look forward to?'

'Did you hear about this morning?'

Imrin says that the head chef Kingsman gave the boys a massive telling-off that morning, reminding them of the penalty for stealing food. Then he pulls a bread roll out from a pocket and grins at me. 'We all do it,' he says. 'But I suppose some of us don't have anyone to trust or share with.'

He splits it and gives me half. At first I take small pinches but then end up gorging the final bit. The hunger here is far worse than at home because the food is tantalisingly close. In Martindale, you get used to not eating on certain days and doing everything you can to bump your rations up. Here, we feast once a week, but because there is next to nothing in the days in between, it is almost painful to eat after the first plateful.

As we finish, we stand together looking out over the town. There is something comforting and peaceful about the scene and when Imrin reaches out to hold my hand again, I let him.

'What are we going to do?' he asks after what seems like an age.

'What would you like to do?'

Imrin takes a deep breath as the silvery swirling mist continues to gather over the tops of the trees in the distance. 'I don't want to die here,' he says simply, putting into words something that has been in the back of my mind since Wray was killed in front of me.

It sounds obvious but it is almost as if his words crystallise the vague thoughts that have been swimming in my mind. I grip his hand tighter to let him know I agree and then say the words I have been trying to convince myself of.

'Let's escape, then.'

17

Saying you want to escape is the easy part; actually figuring out how to do it is not quite so simple. Over the next couple of weeks, Imrin becomes my constant reminder that I am getting nowhere. I know I would probably be better on my own; but our regular evenings staring out towards the real world are what help me through the days. Sometimes we say nothing, other times we talk about what we want to do when we get out; how we're going to find a remote town and hide away with our families. It is complete fantasy and yet it is something to hold on to. I still don't tell him about Opie. Now and then we talk about a potential way out but we always go in circles, bogged down by talk of cameras, Kingsmen, huge walls and locked doors. The depressing truth is that neither of us knows what we are doing and so we revert back to finding ways of comforting each other through smuggled morsels of food and talking about scenarios we both know will never happen.

One evening we talk about our Reckonings. It feels so intimate, as if giving away a part of myself, and yet Imrin is

the perfect person to talk to because he has no precon-
ceptions of who I should be. I tell him things I could never
tell Opie because of the way we grew up together. Imrin's
Reckoning was very different to mine. I felt as if I was in
a conversation with the machine, fighting back and forth,
protecting the memories it wanted and then trying to
question it. Imrin was overwhelmed by it. When it showed
him images of his sisters burning, he fell to pieces,
screaming and shouting at it to stop. But it continued,
torturing him by finding out how far it could go. After-
wards he was disorientated and emotional and didn't speak
to anyone until his thinkwatch told him he was an Elite. He
says he doesn't understand how a grading like that could
happen but I cannot offer any help either. He is fascinated
to hear how different mine was, although I feel a rawness
talking about it that I didn't have at the time. Somehow the
memory has intensified to the point where I'm not sure
what I felt then and how I feel about it now. Neither of us
really understands what happened during our Reckonings
but perhaps some of it comes down to how badly you want
something. I was never too bothered about being an Elite,
I was simply inquisitive about what the process was. Imrin
tells me he always wanted to be an Elite and even gave
reasons why it should grant his wish. If it had asked me that
question, I would have laughed. If it asked Opie, he would
have crumbled, stumbling over a reply that wouldn't have

convinced himself, let alone anyone or anything else. I wonder if we'll ever know exactly what the process is.

Imrin is so easy to talk to but, while we continue to meet when it is safe to do so, I feel an impending sense that my time is running out as two more boys and another girl disappear. She simply did not return to the dorm after work. No one told us anything, and none of us dared to ask. A day later and a bed and wardrobe are removed from our room. We whisper to each other about her being sent abroad and married off, or imprisoned and punished, but none of us knows. Perhaps she is just a reminder that we should never feel too comfortable.

As time passes, my clothes begin to feel looser, even though Imrin is bringing food for me almost every evening. I tell him not to but I can tell from the way he looks at me that he has noticed how thin I am becoming.

Eventually, after hours of talking through improbable, if not impossible, circumstances that could lead to our escape, between us we come to the conclusion that the only way we know that definitely provides a way out is the way we came in – on a shuttle train. Imrin says there is a delivery of food once a week on a regular time and day, but neither of us knows how we can get to it unseen.

Each day I walk a slightly different route from the dorm to the stairwell where we entered, before moving on to the laboratories. Most areas are covered by cameras but, in the short moments that Porter leaves me alone, I check the security system I had access to on my first day and note the angles and coverage of each device. It takes a few days but I am able to plot a route which can get me from the lab to the stairwell while only being caught on camera three times – in places which wouldn't be unusual.

It takes me longer to figure out something similar for Imrin as I am unfamiliar with the parts of the castle in which he works – and being spotted around there without a good reason is not a good idea. It takes a while, but eventually we have a way to get to the stairwell without raising suspicion.

On a morning on which the delivery isn't due, we do a test run. I tell Porter I have forgotten something in the dorm and then hurry along the route I have memorised, reaching the corridor by the stairwell a few moments after Imrin does. We pass each other with nothing more than a nod before returning to work but that night we talk excitedly about what we are going to do when we get out. It is still a fantasy, of course, but the feeling that we have achieved something worthwhile is enough to keep us planning.

The biggest problem is getting through the door that seals the passage to the train from the rest of the castle. On the wall next to the entrance stairwell is a scanner of some sort. It is a silver, square-shaped box fixed to the wall at waist height that has a white reflective panel on the front and looks a little like the surface of a thinkpad. Neither of us has seen one before, and there don't appear to be any others in obvious places around the castle. I find myself going out of my way to walk past it when I can, hoping there will be a careless Kingsman showing off its secrets but there never is. One time, I take a risk, brushing my think-watch against it but it doesn't even have the good grace to beep a warning at me. Instead it does nothing.

The nights have been getting colder, so when Imrin and I meet we sit a little inside the passage that leads to the girls' dorm. Our forays out after dark are now so frequent that we have amassed a small selection of blankets pilfered from our rooms and we huddle underneath them whispering to each other, our spot dimly illuminated by the faint trickle of white moonlight through the gap around the hidden door.

'Talk me through your delivery day,' I suggest as we try to figure out a way around the problem.

'It always happens at the same time,' Imrin starts. 'We spend an hour and a half rearranging all the supplies we still have to make sure we have room for the new produce. There's loads of it from all around the country: frozen meat joints and fish, plus fruits, vegetables, nuts, herbs and so on. Everything is divided up into the areas they came from.'

'Why?'

'I don't know. Perhaps it is to measure each area's usefulness? It's odd but I always get a little buzz when I see the crates from the West.'

I understand what he means. It is probably down to the years of growing up in one place, isolated from anyone who comes from a different Realm.

He sounds embarrassed, so I try to reassure him. 'Last week, Porter received a crate of new parts which he said came from the North. When I saw the markings on the side, I felt that same spark.'

He shuffles closer so our shoulders are touching as he pulls the blanket up higher until just our faces are poking out. The passage is chilly and I can see small streams of breath escaping into the gloom as we talk.

'What happens with the delivery?' I ask.

'There are four Kingsmen – the same people each week.'

'Are they from the castle?'

'I don't think so. Their uniforms are slightly different colours and they don't have the King's seal that the ones around here do.'

'So they probably come from the train?'

'I suppose. They bring each Realm's produce one at a time because it takes the four of them to carry it all. It is a mixture of foods, most of it we use, some we don't. I'm not even sure I know what it all is.'

'We know it takes roughly five minutes to walk from the passageway to the kitchen, so that's forty minutes or so for return journeys that take in all four Realms' food supplies. What do you do during that time?'

'We all unpack and stack.'

'Would you be able to sneak away?'

Imrin sighs. 'I'd never be allowed to go for a toilet break, or anything official, but I suppose among all the madness, if I was careful, I could get out without being noticed. It would be risky.'

'Okay, so let's say the third delivery has arrived and everyone in the kitchen is running around frantically. The Kingsmen leave and you manage to sneak out, following our route to the exit. Because you have to go the longer way around, you would be getting there more or less as the Kingsmen would be coming back out with the final amount of food.'

'Right, so if you arrive at around that time, it gives us ten minutes or so to get down the steps and find our way onto the train.'

A faint breeze skims through the air. We are largely sheltered by the hidden doors at either end but the temperature still drops slightly. I start massaging my hands together but Imrin takes them in his and rubs them, instantly making me feel warmer. Despite the cold and the fact we are sitting, I feel far more comfortable here than I do in bed.

'What haven't we figured out?' he asks.

'Assuming the Kingsmen close it behind them, we are going to have to get through the door at the top of the steps – but we also don't know if there will be any other Kingsmen waiting at the bottom.'

'What are we going to do if there are?'

I don't reply for a moment because there is no simple answer. 'If we want to get out, we are going to have to take a risk at some point.'

It is Imrin's turn to stay silent as I watch his breath spiralling into oblivion. The light catches the browner parts of his eyes as they stare into the darkness across from us. I can almost hear his mind ticking over as he thinks the same thoughts as me.

'Will there be anything in your system about that door?' Imrin asks.

'Not on the machines I have access to but Porter has far more on his. I've seen things over his shoulder before and occasionally he has set things up for me to use. It might be on there.'

'Will you be able to get access to it?'

'Not easily.'

'You don't have to, we can find another way.'

Imrin sounds sincere but I know he is simply trying to give me a get-out; we both know what I am going to have to do.

'I'll make you a deal,' I say. 'On this week's delivery day, you try to disappear for five minutes and see if you're missed. Meanwhile, I'll do what I can to find out how to get through the door.'

'Are you sure you'll be okay?'

'No . . . are you?'

'No.'

We turn to face each other and have to stifle our giggles as somehow the prospect of being caught seems hilarious.

I spend the rest of the week trying to watch Porter as much as I think I can get away with. On one occasion, he allows me to use his computer to complete a task but he spends the whole time hovering around the office, although I don't think he is suspicious. Imrin and I have agreed not to meet until after that week's delivery as it isn't worth pushing our luck until we have the information we need. As I spend the lonely evenings surrounded by people who either won't talk to me, or who I am too embarrassed to talk to, I start to miss him but my dreams are a cluttered mish-mash of memories. Some nights I am with Opie, laughing and joking in the secret passageway, while others I am fighting and playing with Imrin in the woods outside Martindale. The two are interchangeable in my thoughts and I don't know how to separate them.

The morning before the next food delivery, I arrive in the labs to find Lumin sitting at Porter's desk, tapping away at a thinkpad. I try to act casually, scanning my thinkwatch to get onto my machine before continuing with my work in the silence I am so used to before I finally ask the obvious. 'Where's Porter?'

'Kingsman Porter,' Lumin snaps back.

'Where's Kingsman Porter?' I correct myself, trying to sound calm.

'Not here.'

His tone is dismissive but I don't want to push him too much by trying to undermine whatever authority he thinks he has over me.

'Do you know how long he's going to be?'

'Yes.'

'How long?'

'Until he gets back.'

Lumin is still tapping away and hasn't looked up. It is pretty clear he is unwilling to tell me anything, so I try a different track. 'I'm working on a project for him and need a bit of help.'

'What project?' Lumin still doesn't look up but his fingers have stopped fizzing around the thinkpad. I know I've got him.

'I'm not supposed to say.'

'Why not?'

'He told me not to.'

It is a complete fabrication but Lumin reacts as I hoped

he would, spinning around to face me and glaring in annoyance.

'Why would he trust you with something and not me?'

'I don't know. If it's any consolation, he didn't mention you personally – he just told me not to tell anyone about it.'

The lie flows easily and I know Lumin won't follow it up with Porter. He will be too annoyed at the prospect of Hari finding out.

'He probably feels it is something beneath me.' Lumin's eyes flare across the room, daring me to dispute it and tell him it is because I'm better than he is. I know how easy it would be to push his buttons but let it go with a shrug.

'So do you know when he is going to be back?'

Lumin looks at his thinkwatch. 'Around an hour.'

That means I have an hour to get onto his machine. I could tell Lumin I need to use it for the project but that seems too obvious, plus it wouldn't get him out of the room.

I walk across to a workbench where the crate from the North I mentioned to Imrin is placed and start to rummage through it. There are replacement thinkpad screens, touch sensors, springs, and anything else I would need to rebuild our thinkpads and thinkwatches from scratch. Towards the bottom, I find what I'm looking for and carry it across to where Lumin is sitting.

'Can you help me with this?' I ask.

He looks at the object and then at me, his eyebrows arched in annoyance. 'What do you need?'

'I'm working on a repair job and need this sticky silicon to put it back together but I can't get the lid off.'

The can has a long thin nozzle with a plastic cap, a looped handle at the other end and a trigger that squeezes the gel out. Lumin huffs but takes it from me and tries to pull the lid free. What he doesn't know is that I have already squirted a small amount of the liquid into it and then pushed the lid down hard. It works like a springy glue, holding the cap in place. Lumin struggles as he holds the can and tries to yank it off one-handed. Annoyed at looking weak in front of me, he asks me to hold it and then uses two hands to tug.

I crouch, which allows me angle the nozzle towards his face as he pulls and then, as the cap slips free, I squeeze the trigger hard, shooting a jet of the liquid into his face. To make it seem like more of an accident, I rock backwards, falling until I am on the floor ending up against the wall. My exaggeration is unnecessary as Lumin is shrieking.

It is hard not to feel sorry for him as he tries to claw the liquid out of his eye. As I reach towards him apologising, he brushes me away. 'Get off,' he yells, pushing me roughly.

'You should go to medical,' I reply and don't have to fake my concern. I know it won't cause any lasting damage but, having had an accident with an old piece of kit I fished from the scrap outside Martindale, I know it hurts. At first I don't think he is going to listen but then he storms towards the door without a word, slamming it as he leaves.

I check my thinkwatch and know I should have at least fifty minutes before Porter returns. The door to the second part of the lab is firmly closed from this side, so Hari and Mira cannot emerge without knocking, which means there is only one door I have to focus on – the one Lumin just left through.

I sit in front of Porter's machine and work as quickly as I can, scanning through the documents and files and looking for any blueprint or list of specifications that may relate to the scanner by the stairwell. A clatter in the adjacent laboratory makes me pause but there is no knock at the door, so I ignore it. Around half of Porter's files are protected by passwords which I don't try to get through. I do stumble across a floor plan for the boys' dormitory and notice there is no hidden passage on it. I would like to take longer to try to figure out the exact route of the passage to the girls' dormitory but force myself to close the file and keep searching for what I am looking for. I see blueprints for various pieces of technology, some I know, some I don't, before I finally notice a folder marked 'access' that was hidden away within a list of others.

I skim through a long list of filenames that seem unrelated to anything and have to resort to opening them all one at a time. I check my thinkwatch every few minutes, watching time tick away, having not found what I need. I try to work quicker but my hand is shaking with the realisation that this could be my only chance. Jargon continues to fill the screen as I scan through the words looking for anything useful until, just as I am about to close a file, I notice a few lines at the bottom that mention an order number. I quickly jump back into the inventory and am so engrossed at hunting through the numbers that, as I find the right one, I almost don't hear the click of the door opening behind me.

18

'Silver?'

Porter's voice is inquisitive, not angry, as I hear him moving around the room. Lumin's assessment that he would be 'around an hour' was at least double what it actually was.

I emerge from under his desk, where I dived when I heard the door opening, and deliberately lift my head too quickly, bashing it into the hard wood of the table. I cry out in pain and although Porter doesn't show too much sympathy, he does at least ask how I am before querying why I was under his desk.

Rubbing my head as I look for empathy that doesn't come, I speak slowly, faking pain I don't really feel. 'There was this fizzing sound and the lights flickered. It sounded like it was coming from here,' I say.

It sounds vaguely plausible. At least once every other day or so, there is some sort of issue with the power around the castle. Sometimes everything turns off and then sizzles back to life almost instantly, on other occasions we are without electricity for a few minutes at a time.

Porter's eyes narrow. 'That happens all the time.'

'I know but this sounded different – I thought I would check.'

He looks at me closely but I wince in false pain and continue to rub my head as I stand. 'That hurt,' I add.

'Did you find anything?'

'One of the connectors was a bit loose so I shoved it back in and the noise stopped. Then I heard you calling my name and whacked my head.'

Porter nods but I'm not sure if it is because he believes me. His eyes shoot around the room. 'Where's Lumin?'

'He got some silicon in his eye and went to medical.'

Another nod.

As I return to my side of the room, I can feel him watching but he says nothing, even when he sits down at the screen I hastily swiped out of.

*   *   *

'So you got it?'

Imrin's voice sounds excited and I realise he can see straight through my attempts at trying to play it cool. The night is colder than the last time we were in the passageway together. We sit wrapped under two blankets watching our breath.

I have to force my teeth from chattering as I reply. 'It responds to the borodron used in Kingsmen uniforms.'

'Oh, so there's no way through?'

'What makes you think that?'

Imrin blows into his hands. 'We don't have access to anything like that.'

'No, but I've seen the order sheets. There are small amounts of it in the textiles department. They have it there to help out with minor armour repairs.'

He sounds unsure. 'Do the scanners need anything other than borodron?'

'I don't think so.'

'Do you know anyone who works in textiles?'

I shake my head, although it's too dim for him to see. 'One of the girls in our dorm works there but Pietra is the last person I could ask.'

'There's a lad on our side who is in there.'

'Do you get on?'

Imrin lifts the blanket slightly. 'He got me this. Don't ask me how he smuggled it out but I swapped half-a-dozen fruit buns for it.'

'You never get me fruit buns.'

Imrin knows I am teasing. 'That's because I had to give them to him. If you want to place an order, I'll see what I can do.'

'How about an entire pig on a spit?'

Imrin squeezes me just above the waist, his fingers

tickling until I squeal and put a hand in front of my mouth to stop myself.

'You're going to get us caught,' I say.

'You're the one being noisy.'

I elbow him playfully. He recoils before tickling me again, until I am lying on top of him, one knee hovering dangerously close to an area he wouldn't want me to slam it into. 'Do you give up?' I whisper.

'Yes.'

'Are you going to get me my pig on a spit?'

'When we're outside, I'll catch you a pig and you can roast it yourself.'

'Promise?'

'Promise.'

I release him and we huddle together under the blanket. I have completely forgotten what we were arguing about until Imrin asks me what the name of the material was. I tell him and he repeats it to himself a couple of times.

'I'll ask him if there's any chance,' Imrin says. 'But it will probably cost me. I might not be able to get you anything extra for a week or so.'

'I'm fine.'

'Are you sure? You're so thin.'

Imrin's voice is full of concern but I shrug it off, even though I know he is right. I have had to ask Ignacia for smaller work clothes and trace my ribs through my clothing almost subconsciously until I feel Imrin's hand holding mine.

'I'll try to get you something anyway,' he says. I turn to look at him just as the narrow stream of moonlight intensifies. Presumably it is now shining through the clouds but it catches him at such an angle that I can see the pores of his soft caramel-coloured skin.

'What?' he asks, but it is not his words that have me entranced, it is the way he is looking at me, like Opie used to, as if we have known each other our whole lives.

I feel his hand on my side and want to respond but, as I draw towards him, we hear a clatter in the corridor outside. Instantly we pull apart and my heart races as the moment is lost. We see the shadow of someone passing the door and heading towards the window, their boots echoing loudly.

For a moment or two, neither of us can bring ourselves to even breathe until the shadow passes back the other way.

'I should go,' Imrin says and I don't disagree as he peeks out of the door and then scampers across the hallway before disappearing. I return silently to the room trying to focus on our plan but instead finding my thoughts clouded by what might have happened between us if it wasn't for the interruption.

* * *

At the banquet the following evening, Imrin gives a gentle shake of his head across the table to let me know he hasn't been successful yet. But he does flick his head towards one of the boys sitting a few seats down from him, letting me know someone is on the case. Aside from that moment, I don't look anywhere other than my plate, forcing myself to eat, even when my stomach feels full. I know it will likely be the only thing of substance I get all week and just hope that I can keep it all down, focusing on the meats and fruits instead of bread.

As I am finishing, everyone goes silent and I turn, expecting to see the Minister Prime standing. Instead, it is the King. Next to him, Jela is staring towards us, her eyes empty of feeling or recognition, but one is rimmed by a heavy purple and black mark that even from a distance looks painful.

The King clears his throat noisily and then wipes something away from his beard. He is wearing the same robes as always but tonight he does appear to be coherent. His voice sounds like the one I have heard many times before on screen and as with the Minister Prime, it holds an authority. The Minister Prime's voice instils fear but the King has a turn of phrase that is so charming, it makes you feel as if he is an old family friend.

'My subjects,' he says, not needing a microphone to make his voice boom around the room. He then stares towards us. 'My Offerings . . . I would like to offer my sincere thanks for your cooperation this year. It is wonderful to see so many new faces.'

He appears oblivious to the fact that the 'new' faces are diminishing rapidly but seems to have an almost childlike sense of playfulness as he grins at us.

'Now we have become a little more acquainted with each other over these past few weeks, I figure it is time to have a little fun.' He clicks his fingers and Kingsmen rush to the table and start removing the leftover food, then they take away the table and benches until we are left standing around, looking at each other in confusion.

The King sounds polite as he continues, although none of us is fooled into thinking we have a choice about his next request. 'If you would, I'd now like you to separate into your Realms and then choose someone to represent you – girl or boy.'

Everyone looks at each other before we drift off towards our corners. With Jela next to the King, Pietra is the only other girl left from my Realm. Wray is dead, leaving Rush, the other Elite male I first sat with on the train, plus our male Inter and Member. I instinctively think it is going to be a battle to not volunteer but, before anyone can speak, Rush says he will do it. He stares at me as he speaks, knowing that everyone around us saw what I did to him on the train, silently challenging me to say I'm better than he is.

The truth is, I'm happy with anyone who isn't me stepping forward.

'Good luck,' I say, meaning it, as he steps towards the centre of what is now an amphitheatre, steep banks of seats stretching up towards the ceiling filled with people I can only see the outlines of in the bright overhead lights. I look nervously towards the group of people from the West and am glad to see it isn't Imrin moving forward. Faith is not representing the South either.

All of the volunteers are boys, with Rush just about the biggest of the group. The rest of us are crowded around the edge of the arena, leaving a large space in the centre where the four volunteers stand nervously.

'Excellent, excellent,' the King says with a lick of his lips. 'First things first, bring her up.'

Everyone's eyes turn as the main doors open with a clang and two Kingsmen bring in Bryony, who Pietra told on for stealing food. She can barely stand by herself. She is thinner than I am, her hair a straggle of knots, her eyes bruised and beaten. They drag her to the group from the East and drop her on the floor before turning without a second glance and heading back to the door. Pietra shuffles awkwardly next to me, staring at the floor. The King allows Bryony's gentle whimpers to filter around the room for a few moments before continuing as if nothing untoward has happened.

'Four strapping young men . . . there's only one thing for it.' He glances towards the Minister Prime, who offers a smile and a nod before the King turns back towards us.

'Gentlemen, it is time for a little tradition which we have had around here for a few years now, where I look to find my champion. You are to be the first four competitors this year. For the winner, you and your Realm's Offerings will be invited back for a private breakfast with me tomorrow. For the losers, well . . .'

He gives a nod towards the Kingsmen by the door, who approach the volunteers, hands gripping their sword handles. I see the boys tense, as Rush bends his knees in a fighting stance. Instead of violence, the Kingsmen offer each of the boys a sword before returning to their spots.

The four of them eye each other anxiously as what is going to happen begins to dawn on them. I see Rush taking a few steps away from the rest of the group.

The King laughs at the sight in front of him. 'Of the four of you, I only want to see one left standing. I do not care how you do it as long as you are entertaining. You will start the next time I click my fingers.'

He edges back to his seat to get comfortable while the boys separate, eyeing each other. The boy from the East is almost as tall as Rush but probably a little bulkier. He is twirling the sword in his hand, clearly relishing what is about to happen. The Offering from the South is the smallest by quite a long way and reminds me of Wray in stature. The sword seems too big for him and, although he is trying to grasp it confidently, everyone can tell he doesn't want to be there. The boy from the West is somewhere in the middle but is hopping from one foot to the other as if to signal that he has speed on his side. Rush, meanwhile, is still standing with his knees slightly bent, looking between the other three and ready for action.

Although we knew it was coming, it is a shock when the snap of the King's fingers echoes around the room. The hush that surrounded us from above is transformed into an audible 'ooh' as everyone gets ready for the action.

Straight away, the Offering from the East tears across the space until he is bearing down upon the one from the South, who seems fixed to the spot in fear. With an exaggerated swish of the sword, the smaller boy is on the ground in a pool of blood in seconds. The King brays and takes a swig from his bottle of wine.

It is hard to judge the atmosphere. There is a sense of excitement from the people above us but it is hard to know whether this is for the King's gratification or because they are genuinely enjoying what is playing out. I look across to the Offerings from the South and one of the girls is in tears. Meanwhile, the three remaining boys are still circling each other.

Rush is slowly moving backwards while keeping an eye

on the other two, but I'm not entirely sure he knows where he is going as he is heading straight towards the Kingsmen by the door. As one of them steps forward, I start to shout to Rush but it is too late as the guard clubs him to the floor from behind and then shoves him back towards the centre. I hold my breath, suddenly concerned about the fortunes of someone I had knocked to the ground myself a few weeks ago. The Offering from the West holds back but the one from the East, still splashed with blood from his first kill, tears forward, sword in the air.

Everything seems to slow as his momentum carries the sword forward, swinging it towards Rush, who rolls out of the way and scrambles to his feet. The boy from the East overbalances from the weight of the sword and, as he tries to steady himself, the one from the West launches forward and spears him through the back.

There is a gasp of shock and possibly approval around the room as the second Offering falls. The triumphant boy from the West takes the sword from the dead boy, and turns to face Rush, who is rubbing the back of his head and trying to get his balance.

The King is clapping and stamping his feet in approval, the Minister Prime is patting the fingers of his right hand into his left palm with little enthusiasm.

The boy from the West seems shaken and I realise that if this isn't the type of thing you revel in, then it is as hard for the winner as anyone else. He is trying to maintain a distance from Rush, but keeps glancing towards the fallen body. I can tell he is almost willing the dead boy to stand, just so it wasn't him that struck the killing blow.

Rush's head seems to have cleared as he advances, sword raised. The swagger has returned to his stance as he steps over the first body. The boy from the West stops and allows Rush to get nearer and then, as our Offering lunges forward, the other boy reels back, his sword swishing through the air towards Rush. There is a gasp but, from the angle I am at, I can see he has overbalanced, missing Rush and stumbling to the floor, the sword still in his hand.

There is no emotion in his face as Rush turns, raises his sword, and plunges it deep into the side of the boy from the West, before kicking him away and collapsing to his knees, drenched with sweat and blood.

The King roars with delight and his applause echoes around the room until, slowly, perhaps reluctantly, everyone else begins to join in. The Minister Prime rises after a while and calls for silence, before indicating for the Kingsmen to take Rush to the medical area and then sending everyone else back to their dormitories.

The shuffling of chairs above us is drowned out by the chortles of the King. I refuse to look at the wreckage behind me as we all file out. Instead, I hover towards the back and wait until the Offerings from the West are near us.

I catch Imrin's gaze for a fraction of a second but that is all it takes. His eyes tell me what his lips don't have to – if we're going to go, it has to be before the next feast.

19

I'm not in the mood to sneak out that night, although I can't sleep either. Bryony is back in the dorm and spends a lot of the evening moaning with pain and we are all too afraid to comfort her in case it somehow gets us in trouble.

In the morning, Ignacia arrives to take Pietra and myself to breakfast. Refusing isn't an option but it is hardly something I feel proud about. We are led towards the main hall but carry on past it to an area of the castle I have never been in before. My eyes flick around, trying to remember the details but all I really see are cameras – lots of them. Wherever we are must be somewhere important, but Ignacia is walking too quickly for me to memorise it all.

Soon, she takes us through a large heavy-looking set of wooden doors that leads into a room decked in the same shade of red that the King wears. There are flags and drapes around the walls, plus a large coloured glass window illuminates the room like a kaleidoscope. Ignacia offers us seats and it is only when I hear the King's voice that I realise I am staring at the window.

'Stunning, isn't it?'

The King is sitting at the head of the table with Jela at his side but he is looking straight at me. I sit quickly, desperate not to have to engage with him but it is too late.

'I commissioned it especially,' he adds, still watching me. 'What do you think?'

I stare at the window again, which shows him, sword in hand, standing triumphantly over the leaders of the rebel and nationalist armies. From the few things we have been told about the end of the war, I assume this must be only symbolic, not an actual event, but the fact the King has had this scene created in stained glass shows that perception is more important than reality.

'It's beautiful,' I say, knowing there was no other response I could give. In many ways, I'm not even lying – the craftsmanship is incredible.

The King smiles and nods. 'It was done by one of you, an Offering, a few years ago. I forget his name . . .' He looks around the room but the only people there are Jela, myself, Pietra, Rush, the other three boys and two Kingsmen, one by the door, the other on the King's shoulder. He looks at Jela, somehow expecting her to know the name of someone from before her time, before shaking his head in annoyance.

'Anyway, it doesn't matter,' the King adds. 'I had his hands cut off when he had finished. There was no way I was going to risk him creating anything with somebody else's image in it.'

He claps his hand on the table, making everyone jump before telling us to eat.

Given everything I have already seen, I didn't think I could be shocked by anything else but the callousness of the King while talking about someone who has created such a startling tribute for him is beyond comprehension.

Opposite Jela is Rush, who the King is now focusing all of his attention on, asking questions about his upbringing and enthusing about his performance the previous evening, even though, as I remember it, he didn't do very much. As he turns to face the King, I can see a deep gash through the still-matted hair on the back of his head.

With each question, he answers with a gentle bow of the head and a respectful 'Your Majesty' until the King tells him that it isn't necessary.

Again, I concentrate on the meats, devouring the wafer-thin slices of ham, turkey and chicken, along with dollops of chutney and pickle. I try to put out of my mind that three people had to die for me to eat like this. Each mouthful feels as if I am revelling in their blood. I try to focus on Imrin telling me how thin I was looking and as I gently finger the jagged edges of my ribs through my work clothes, I switch off and eat as much as I can without drawing attention to myself.

With the King's attention on Rush, I try to catch Jela's eye but it doesn't take long to realise that she is gone. She is sitting up straight in her chair, delicately cutting her food into small pieces, but her eyes are vacant as they stare impassively at the plate, then the wall and then back again. Up close, her eye looks a lot worse than it did last night. The lid is halfway closed, decorated by a rainbow of colours that almost mask the jagged scratch which zigzags above her eyebrow. When she finishes, she puts her cutlery down neatly on either side of the plate and then sits unmoving as the King scoffs pastries and continues to make sure Rush's plate is full.

I can only wonder if Rush knows how dangerous a game he has fallen into. Being popular might be good while it lasts, but how long before the King wants to see him perform again to ensure his first performance wasn't a fluke? How long before he is traded to some other country as currency? Or sent out onto a far-flung battlefield somewhere? Perhaps that's what he wants but I'm happier keeping my head down.

After we are dismissed, I spend the rest of the day going through the motions in the labs, unhappy I chose to eat the food that had only been given because people died. Lumin has no after-effects from the accident with his eye, although he hasn't spoken to me since. Porter, meanwhile, seems to have forgotten the incident with me under his desk.

That night I sneak out, sitting at the far end of the passage on my own, shivering under the blankets. I sit in the shadow, close my eyes and think of home, only realising I have fallen asleep as I hear a gentle click when the door swings inwards, catching on my legs.

'Silver?' Imrin whispers.

'Who else?'

I shuffle along until he is next to me and cover him with the blankets.

'You're freezing,' he says.

'I've been waiting for you.'

'People were awake, I couldn't get out.'

'Did you get it?'

Imrin reaches into his gown and takes out a thin, square object, handing it to me. It is difficult to describe as it weighs next to nothing, but the borodron feels sleek, like it should be a heavy piece of metal. I hold two of the corners and flex it back and forth in a way that feels as if it shouldn't be possible.

'It's so . . . strange,' I say, struggling for a better word. I have never felt anything like it before. 'Did you have to do much to get it?'

'Not really, there's a proper black market going on in our dorm. The good thing is that everyone is in debt to everyone else for something. No one is going to end up telling on anyone else, because they'll end up taking themselves down too.'

'It's the exact opposite in our dorm; nobody even talks

about stuff like that since Pietra did her thing. I guess boys are more corruptible than girls.' I give him a gentle nudge but he points out that perhaps that means girls are more likely to turn on each other than boys. From my experience, I can't argue.

We agree not to meet the next night as the day after is when the delivery will happen. We run through our plan one final time and, if anything, it sounds too easy. Imrin says that he managed to get out of the kitchen and back in unnoticed last time. The last time I told Porter I needed to go to the bathroom, he told me to 'call it a bog' and stop annoying him. Every day he says or does something that makes me wonder how he reached the position he is in.

After we have run through everything over and over until I am bored, I take Imrin's arm and drape it around me, resting my head on his shoulder. He starts to say something but I shush him and we sit in silence until I feel my eyelids drooping and my mind slipping away until I am in Martindale again. The thought of home is always my safety blanket.

Imrin jolts me awake and says I should return to bed. We run through the schedule one final time before I yawn a goodnight and head back to the dorm.

*   *   *

The next day and a bit drags more than any period of time I have ever known. In my head, I keep trying to talk myself out of our plan, thinking of all the things that could go wrong: Porter stopping me from leaving, Imrin being caught on his way out, alarms sounding if the door opens, Kingsmen that might be waiting at the bottom of the steps, as well as any number of other things.

When I wake up on the morning of the delivery I have to steady myself because my hands are shaking. I have used the sponges in our bathroom to clean Wray's blood from my mother's dress, and now I wrap the fabric around my waist. It is easily hidden by the bagginess of the work clothes I have. Aside from Imrin, it is the one thing I have no intention of leaving behind.

When I arrive in the main lab, Porter is already there, tinkering away on his thinkpad. He grunts something without looking, which I assume is a 'good morning'.

'Am I in here today?' I ask, even though his answer is always the same.

'Yes, but you're my Lumin today, he's at the medical bay.'

'What's wrong with him?'

'No idea but he's holding our work up, so it better be something good.'

I wonder why he's there – he has never missed a day of work before and the only experience I've known of people visiting the medical bay has been when they've been harmed. Could something have happened to him?

Either way, I'm not sure if it is going to make it more difficult for me to slip away myself, so I sit at my bench and reply in the same casual fashion. 'I've got to see Ignacia later.'

The question fires straight back: 'Why?'

'I'm not sure. It's at her request.'

I am prising open a damaged thinkpad, waiting to see if Porter is going to object, but instead he mumbles something about it 'always being him' as we carry on working.

It almost seems as if time is going backwards. I wonder if Imrin's day is going as he expects. I know his schedule as well as he does, so as I check the time again, I know those working in the kitchen will now be bundling last week's food together and getting rid of anything that can't be used.

I think of the old battered metal clock that sits above the sink in my house in Martindale. It is a dim cream colour, round with hands that point to numerals around the edges, rather than the numbers we are all so used to. It is the only one of its type I have ever seen as everyone relies on their thinkwatches to know what they should be doing. Mum taught me how to use it, saying that although I didn't need to know, it was her way of showing me what life used to be like. I think she kept it from before the war. When she was showing me how it worked, I didn't understand but now it is nice to remember.

I close my eyes and think of the noise it made before the battery ran out.

Tick-tock.

As I stare at the digital numbers on my thinkwatch, I can almost hear the ticking from one second to the next until, finally, it is the moment for me to go. I know timing is everything, so I tell Porter I have to go a full minute early, just in case he argues. As it is, he mumbles something that ends in the word 'off', and then I am out of the door.

It is almost as if crossing into the corridor starts my heart beating faster – suddenly it is thudding in my chest as I hurry along the route I would now know even if my eyes were shut. Around each bend I expect to see a Kingsman who will stop me and ask where I'm going, but, as with my practice runs, there is nobody. I move past the few cameras on my route without looking at them until I reach the final bend. I peer around the corner and observe as two Kingsmen struggle past, carrying a crate of food each, exactly as Imrin said they would. As soon as they are out of sight, I dash for the door, knowing we have just ten minutes. I check my thinkwatch again and then set off along the corridor in the direction I know Imrin should be coming from.

I reach into my pocket and nervously finger the square of borodron, flexing it back and forth, whispering Imrin's name under my breath and checking my thinkwatch again.

Nine minutes.

I walk back to the door and look both ways along the corridor. I cannot even pace because of the proximity of the cameras.

Eight minutes.

'Come on, Imrin,' I whisper, before taking the borodron out of my pocket and pressing it against the scanner as planned. I expect there to be a problem but instead the door hisses upwards, allowing a draft of air to fizz through the space and chill my arms. All I can see ahead are the spiralling steps.

Seven and a half minutes.

I move forward and go down the first few steps, enjoying the feel of the cool air, my skin tingling in a way I haven't felt since I left Martindale. I edge slowly down the stairs, constantly expecting someone to stop me, but there is no one.

Seven minutes.

I know the time is coming where I am going to have to make a decision: wait for Imrin or go it alone. After another half-a-dozen steps, I stop and wait. The air is cooler here but the temperature is reassuring instead of disturbing. I close my eyes and listen to a faint dripping noise before making my decision, hurrying up the stairs again until I am back in the corridor. As I turn, I collide with something solid.

'I couldn't get away,' Imrin mutters, out of breath, but his explanation is irrelevant.

Six minutes.

'Come on,' I say, leading the way through the open door as quickly as I can. I swipe the scanner on the inside with the borodron, making the door fizz back into place, and then we scamper down the stone steps, trying not to make too much noise.

As we get to the bottom I stop by the opening and quickly glance around, fully expecting to see a mass of Kingsmen milling about.

Instead, the area is empty except for a dozen or so discarded crates scattered on the ground. What's more, there is a train waiting on the platform. Aside from there being fewer carriages, it is very similar to the one which brought us to the castle.

There are still five minutes to spare as Imrin and I walk onto the platform hand-in-hand.

'Is this really it?' Imrin says, his voice full of the disbelief I feel.

There is a faint pencil-thin shaft of light stretching from the far end of the tunnel but it is the air I cannot stop enjoying, taking deep full breaths through my nose and reluctantly letting it back out through my mouth.

'Let's go,' I say, gripping Imrin's hand harder and scampering towards the carriage with the open door.

Inside there are stacks of crates and I clamber over the first set, heading towards the back corner of the carriage by climbing over and around the remaining objects. We are not in the clear yet and there is every chance we could still be discovered at some point, so our best hope is to stow away as far from the door as possible. Once we are away from the castle and out in the open, we might be able to jump when we reach a grassy area, giving us a better chance than simply staying on board until we are discovered. After that, neither of us knows where we might go, but it is surely preferable to waiting for our fates here.

I think of my mother and Colt and wonder if I am being selfish. Am I getting myself out of trouble, only to land them in it? I tell myself no, but the truth is that I don't really know. I am hoping that the communicator on my thinkwatch will work when we get outside the castle walls, meaning I should be able to contact them and give them warning that they might be in danger.

It is that thought that is running through my mind as I reach the back of the carriage. There is a pile of thick plastic sheets and blankets that will be perfect to hide under. I check my thinkwatch one final time before I reach out and pull the covers clear, knowing we have a little over four minutes to spare.

Since leaving the labs, I have expected to run into somebody the whole time, but as the person hiding under the covers stares up at me, eyes wide in shock, I can do nothing but gasp in absolute horror.

20

Lumin looks frantically from me to Imrin and back again. 'Silver?'

I stumble over what to say but, above anything, I can hear the tick-tocking of my mum's clock in my head.

'We've got to go,' I say, addressing Imrin as I pick the sheets back up from the ground. He doesn't argue as I turn to Lumin.

'You're not going to tell, are you?' Lumin asks, panic in his voice.

I shake my head. 'Good luck with getting away. If I knew how you felt about everything, then perhaps we could have worked together?'

Lumin motions as if to say something but I don't give him the opportunity, dropping the covers over his head and rushing back the way I came. I risk a glance at my thinkwatch.

Under two minutes.

'Come on,' I say to Imrin, too loudly, tearing up the stairs two at a time until we reach the top, where I swipe the borodron against the scanner, scramble through, and then swipe it once more to make the door hum into place. I hurry across the hallway with Imrin just behind me and we throw ourselves around a corner just as the heavy stamp of Kingsmen boots echo in the corridor we have just been standing in. There is the murmur of low voices and the noise of the door as it slides back into place. We are alone but the silence is deafening and already I am missing the chilling breeze on my skin.

'I'm sorry,' I say. 'We could have gone too but it didn't feel right. There's so much more chance of three of us being caught, rather than one or two. It wouldn't have been fair to him.'

Imrin's face is hard to read. His lips are tight and his eyes don't seem to have the same intensity as when we are together in the evenings. Perhaps it is because I have hardly ever seen him in the daylight but I suspect it is because he knows our biggest chance of getting away has gone.

'Who was he?'

'Lumin, he works in the labs.'

'Is he the one who gave you lots of grief?'

'Yes, I didn't know he was looking for a way out too. I guess he had the same idea we did.' My eyes flicker down to my thinkwatch. 'We have to go or we'll be noticed. We've been away too long anyway.'

Imrin nods an acceptance and turns to leave.

'Am I going to see you tonight?' I ask.

Imrin doesn't answer, instead hurrying into the distance.

I dash back the way I came until I arrive at the labs and then stop before I reach the camera directly over the door. I smooth my hair down and straighten my clothes before opening the door and walking back to my workbench without a word.

I spend the rest of the afternoon waiting for someone to storm in, demanding to know where Lumin is but, as we reach the end of the day, I convince myself he has really got away. I wonder if there's any chance he won't be found and hope that Imrin and I will have an opportunity ourselves to try again next week.

Back at the dormitory in the evening, it is clear something isn't right as there is a frantic scramble with people getting changed.

'What's going on?' I ask one of the girls near the door who is actually speaking to me.

'Ignacia was here five minutes ago and told us we have to be in the dining hall tonight. She told us we have to look our best.'

'Just the girls, or the boys too?'

'No idea, she didn't say.'

'Is it another banquet?'

'I've no idea – *she didn't say.*' The girl speaks slowly as if I am stupid, so I apologise and return to my bed. Things feel off and I wonder if it is something to do with Lumin. If it is, it doesn't explain why they need us dressed up.

While people hurry back and forth, I do what I always do: make myself presentable without going over the top. Even though it doesn't cling to me the way it used to, I don't want to risk wearing my mother's dress, instead choosing a blue outfit from the wardrobe that is shorter and less flattering. I tie my hair back into a ponytail and make the token effort of visiting the bathroom – where I spend minutes staring into my own eyes in the mirror. I'm not even sure I recognise myself. My face is thinner than I ever remember and the area around my eyes is dark, much like Hart's. I run my fingers along the material of my dress, feeling my ribs poking through, my thin fingers sliding into the gaps between the bones.

'That's horrible,' I hear from behind me and look into the mirror to see Pietra standing there, eyeing me.

I straighten myself up and spin to face her, spitting a furious reply – 'Don't even talk to me' – before stomping past her back into the bedroom.

In truth, it isn't even her words that hurt, it is the way I feel about my own body. I think of myself as a shadow of the person who could hold my own with Opie. All of the exercise I used to get in the woods: the running, lifting, chasing, play-fighting and climbing. Now, I do nothing but hide in the mediocrity I will be showing off tonight.

I am doing enough to survive but it isn't the same as living.

Before long, we are trooping along the corridors towards the main hall. I have gone for flat, comfortable shoes again but most of the girls are wearing heels as we clip-clop our way along the paths that now seem so familiar. There is so little to occupy ourselves with away from work that I assume most of them see dressing up as just about the only form of entertainment. As we are led into the hall, it is immediately obvious that something is different. The King is already there, standing in his box and looking down upon us as we parade in one at a time with Ignacia at the front.

The usual banqueting tables are nowhere to be seen and the male Offerings are already sitting on benches at the back of the room. Ignacia leads us along an S-shaped route around the floor until we reach an adjacent bench where we each sit. The lighting also seems different and for the first time since our opening entrance, the bright overhead spotlights aren't making us squint as we look up towards the banked rows of seats. I look to see if I can spot Hart, Porter, Mira or Hari but, if they are seated there, they are lost among the other faces peering down towards us.

From the far end of the arena I cannot see Jela in her usual place; instead the seat is empty. The King is still standing, staring towards us until he sits with a nod towards the Minister Prime, who rises to his feet and holds out an arm, demanding a hush he already has. He speaks slowly, wrapping his tongue around each word. 'You are all, no doubt, wondering why you have been called here this evening.' He pauses, as if inviting one of us to confirm that's true but the silence continues to hang in the air. 'It is not, as you might have thought, for a feast, nor is it because our beloved monarch is continuing to look for another champion.'

Another pause as I feel a few of us on the bench shuffling uneasily.

'It is, however, because we have an escapee in our midst . . .'

I feel my heart leap and struggle to keep my mouth closed as the main doors clang open and three Kingsmen drag the unmistakeable shape of Lumin into the arena. Even in the dimmer light, I can see the bruises on his face as his battered, broken body is held up by the men. As they reach the centre of the area, they sling him to the floor where he lies unmoving.

'This man's name is Lumin Barrow,' the Minister Prime says, addressing us. 'He was in the position you are now two years ago. By the good grace of our King, he has been granted all the hospitality and support anyone could have hoped for but today he tried to repay that by leaving this place.'

Lumin rolls over on the floor, crawling towards us.

Blood and dirt are smeared across his head as his eyes stare crookedly across the room towards me. I shake my head the merest amount to tell him it wasn't me who told but I cannot tell if he sees it.

The Minister Prime's voice booms ferociously. 'Lumin Barrow, do you confess to your crimes?'

As he rolls over, I see that Lumin's clothes are ripped, blood seeping through the holes and oozing down his leg. He groans in pain, collapsing onto his back.

Annoyed by the lack of reply, the Minister Prime signals towards the Kingsmen. As they approach, Lumin coughs and splutters something I do not hear properly but that I can only assume is an admission of guilt as the guards stop mid-stride.

The King stands and looks disdainfully down upon Lumin. I'm not sure he is even that bothered about the escape attempt; he seems more annoyed at whatever he had planned for the evening being disrupted. He squints towards our benches and then clears his throat. 'Where is my champion?'

Everyone's eyes shoot sideways towards Rush, who slowly rises to his feet and walks forward at the King's request. One of the Kingsmen marches over and hands Rush a coil of something black, but it is too far away for me to know exactly what it is until the King speaks again: 'Have you ever used a whip, boy?'

'No.'

'Well, now is your chance to learn.'

Four Kingsmen step forward and pin Lumin to the ground, turning him over and standing on his wrists and ankles so he cannot move. The King tells Rush to tug Lumin's shirt up over his head until the bare flesh of his back is exposed. At first, I think I am going to be spared witnessing the worst because we are a fair distance away but then, horribly, there is a steady buzzing as large screens descend in the four corners of the room, clicking into place. Someone I don't recognise comes forward holding a camera but the King mutters 'not yet', and then orders the Kingsmen to pull Lumin up so that he can see one of the screens.

At first it is blank but then it pops and sizzles into life until a grey-coloured building appears. Whoever is filming there appears to be moving as the images are shaky. They approach a property which seems very similar to the type of house my mother and Colt live in. The roof juts at a disjointed angle, but there are two front windows and a mucky once-white door.

Everyone's attention is suddenly thrown back to Lumin as he howls in agony. At first I think someone must have struck him but he is being held up by two of the Kingsmen. The truth sinks in moments before the King speaks.

'This is where Mr Barrow grew up. If he has no respect for my house, then I have no respect for his.'

Within seconds there is a whooshing sound from the screens and the building is on fire. Bright orange flames lick the roof as a thick blackness fills the screen, smoke billowing towards us until it is almost impossible to see anything at all. All the while, there are screams of terror and the sound of running footsteps. Eventually, there is a 'plip' sound and the screens switch to a close-up of Lumin. He looks far worse in detail, cuts and scrapes along most of his face and dried flakes of dark blood mixing with fresh gouges. He is whimpering and opening his mouth as if trying to speak, although nothing is coming out.

'Your parents and your sister have been arrested and will stay secured until I decide otherwise.'

As he sits, the Kingsmen take their cue and tear Lumin's shirt from his body before pinning him to the ground again. The screens focus on his back as Rush wraps the whip around his hand. His eyes flicker sideways and I think he is shaking a little but, under the gaze of the King and with four Kingsmen close by, we all know he has no choice.

His arm arches forward and the whip fizzes through the air before landing across Lumin's back with a fleshy crack. There is a gasp around the arena as the image on the screen zooms in on the thin, deep wound. It is a mangled mess of pink as the King yells 'again'. Once more the whip flashes through the air and lands with a snap which echoes so viciously, it feels as if it is tearing through our ears. The girl two seats away from me is trying to stifle tears but no one seems to notice as a third and fourth slap of the whip collides with flesh. Lumin screamed in pain at the first two strikes but he is silent now; the four marks on his skin have criss-crossed each other, leaving a section that is such a mixture of pink, purple, red and black that it is almost as if I am seeing a new colour.

Rush steps back and drops the whip to the floor and I can see he is definitely trembling now as he stumbles back towards us. The King says nothing but has a satisfied smirk on his face as the Minister Prime stands and raises his arm for silence.

'You should, of course, now all be aware that we check all transport in and out of the castle,' he says. 'Now get out of my sight.'

21

In the dorm that evening, there is a new kind of silence. Before we've not spoken to each other through fear, jealousy, anger, or simply because we don't like each other. This evening, it is because there is nothing we can say. For me personally, it is a mixture of revulsion and relief at how close Imrin and I came to suffering the same fate. I remember hoping my thinkwatch would work outside the walls to contact my mother and Colt, but I would not have even got that far and the imprisonment and humiliation which will no doubt await Lumin's family could have been set for mine instead.

As we are getting ready to go to sleep, an alarm sounds so loudly that I cannot hear the gasps of surprise around the room. People's lips are moving, querying what is going on, but all I can hear is the ringing sound. In the gap around the door, a red light is flashing. We hear voices and foot-steps for an hour or so until it is quiet again.

Because the noise has lasted for so long, it takes a few moments for my ears to recognise when the alarm has ended. I can feel the ringing long after I lie on my bed and close my eyes. I really want to sneak out to see if Imrin is waiting for me but I was already nervous after seeing what happened to Lumin. Now, following the alarm, I stay where I am, staring into my closed eyelids and wondering exactly what has happened.

The next morning, no one knows what to expect. The dorm door unlocks and, with the lack of any other instruction, everyone flocks to their various jobs. Porter is already in the laboratory but doesn't greet us as Hari, Mira and I enter. The other two go into the back lab as I settle on my bench and continue working my way through the list of repairs that need to be done.

I am so used to working in silence that I jump a little when I hear the word 'Silver'. I turn to see Porter holding his glasses in one hand, examining me. I have never seen him without his glasses before but it accentuates his wrinkles and he looks older. I'm confused by his gentle tone as he has never addressed me like that before.

'It's all right,' he adds. 'I know I'm just a grumpy old man.'

I want to tell him he's not but, as a smile spreads across his face, it's clear that he knows what I'm thinking.

'You don't have to pretend,' he says. 'I know you and Lumin didn't really get on but last night was difficult for me . . .'

His voice cracks as he tails off.

'I know he was good around here . . .' I stumble over my words before I realise how uncaring that sounds.

Porter smiles weakly. 'Now you know why I don't allow myself to get too close to any of you. Many, many Offerings have come through here and one by one, you all go back out the door again.'

He sounds close to tears and I'm not sure how to react. I have come to know him as a crotchety, slightly eccentric old man who orders me around – but now he suddenly seems like a real person.

'How did you end up with that?' I ask, nodding towards his Kingsman's uniform that seems more out of place than ever.

I know I am taking a risk but he glances down at himself and shakes his head. 'Depending on your viewpoint, I was either in the right place at the right time, or the wrong place at the wrong time. After the war ended, it was chaos. Victor . . . the King . . . had come along and everyone was desperate for the fighting to end. That didn't mean there was any structure in place, though. The whole country had been brought to its knees, so Victor chose people from both sides to come and work with him. I was in my early twenties and my father was one of the members of the nationalist government that was dissolved. Somehow I was one of the people who ended up as part of Victor's team to help put everything back together. I was always good with the tech side of things, so I ended up doing this.'

'Working with Offerings?'

Porter shakes his head and then wearily rubs the bridge of his nose. 'Not at first. We had various people left over from the war – but Victor soon tired of them and demanded new, fresh young people be brought in. That's where the idea of the Reckoning and Offerings came in. We would test everyone at the age of sixteen to find a selection of boys and girls across the country, then bring them here to help put everything together again. The core thinking wasn't so bad, I suppose, a cross section of abilities, genders and backgrounds, but it didn't really work out like that.'

'Why?'

'Have you ever heard of the saying "Power corrupts"?'

I shake my head.

'I guess you wouldn't have. We used to say it in the old days but it's nonsense anyway. Power only corrupts if you're corruptible in the first place. Victor always had a vicious, nasty streak about him but no one other than those of us who worked close to him ever saw it. To everyone outside, he was the conquering, uniting hero. As I, and others, got to know him, we realised that he only became that hero through chance. He just arrived at a time where everyone was ready to stop fighting and then, because of his bloodline, people thought he was something he's not. Anyway, he gets bored. Once a year, thirty of you will be brought in and theoretically you are here to help us make life easier for everyone. In reality, hardly any of you get through twelve months before the next lot comes along.'

I have never heard anyone talk with such knowledge, although it is hard to detect whether Porter is angry; he simply sounds tired.

'Was it always like this?'

Porter shrugs. 'More or less. Any of us who said anything in the early days simply disappeared until it got to the point where no one spoke out.'

At this point, I sense a shame in his voice but it is no more than mine; he has been trying to keep his head down in much the same way that I have – except that he has been doing it for seventeen years.

'What's the Reckoning?' I ask.

The question seems to take Porter by surprise as he blinks rapidly. 'I, um . . .'

I half-turn back to my bench. 'Sorry, I shouldn't have asked . . .'

'No, it's fine.' I spin back as Porter takes a sip of something from a cup on his desk and sighs deeply. 'I'm not sure I can even answer that question. It was some sort of technology that was being worked on before the war started. I've always presumed it was being developed during it as well. There used to be a different Minister Prime . . .'

'Really?' I interrupt. I have only ever known the current one.

Porter nods. 'Admittedly, this was right at the very start. This current Minister Prime's actual name is Bathix but the first one was Xyalis.'

'I've never heard of him.'

'You wouldn't have done. I think most of the people who were around then have largely forgotten. He was only in place for a few months but the Reckoning was based on his invention. Like I said, the Offering initially wasn't necessarily a bad idea – it was never meant to turn into this. When Victor's temper began getting out of hand, that was when Xyalis spoke up.'

The induction footage told us the King invented the Reckoning, which is what we have always assumed is true. I believe Porter when he says that isn't what occurred.

'What happened?' I ask.

'He was the first who went missing. One evening, he told us something had to be done, the next moment Bathix was in place and Victor carried on as if nothing had happened. Slowly but surely, the rest of us did as well.'

'Was he killed?'

Porter glances towards the door and takes another drink. 'I have no idea. With pretty much everyone else, their bodies were paraded to warn us of the consequences of going against the King. With Xyalis, he just disappeared.

Nobody knows but I suspect he was killed in his sleep and it was only when that caused more passive dissent that Victor decided he would start making examples of people.'

'I didn't get on as badly with Lumin as you might think.'

My mention of the name brings Porter back to the present but he shakes his head gently as if it doesn't matter anyway. 'You're doing the right thing, young Silver. Keep your head down, don't be noticed, and don't do anything stupid. I've been doing it for seventeen years.'

I'm almost embarrassed that he has noticed my nothingness. 'What was the alarm for last night?'

'Lockdown. We get them now and then, probably less often than we used to. There are still pockets of people not loyal to the King out there. We all know it but no one says anything. Sometimes, when it seems like there might be an eruption of violence close to the castle, the sirens sound and we're all locked into wherever we are. It might last an hour or two, but anything up to a day or so. It always passes.'

'There's still fighting?'

Porter nods but it is still hard to take in. I have never heard of anything other than adulation for the King.

'How long has it been going on?'

With a shrug of his shoulders and a puff through his lips, Porter seems dismissive. 'I suppose it never stopped. I guess some people always knew we were replacing one system that didn't work with another.'

He looks at me closely, before putting his glasses back on, and spinning back around to his work. 'Don't go thinking silly thoughts, Ms Blackthorn. You're doing just fine.'

It is another hour before he speaks to me again, beckoning me over to Lumin's old machine and bringing up the screen with the security cameras on that I worked on during my first day.

'Seem familiar?' he asks.

'Yes.'

'I knew you would be able to solve that test easily. I could see it in you as soon as you walked into the room and started looking at the spare parts.'

'You noticed?'

'More than you might think. Before he . . . before last night, Lumin was working on something for me far more advanced than that initial project. It's easy to get the cameras to respond to your thinkwatches instead of the Kingsmen's. What we can't do, or what I've not had time to do, is to get them to switch off completely when there is nothing to see and then switch back on when there is.'

'Why would you need them to do that?' Porter squints at me over the top of his glasses, wanting me to answer my own question. 'Because of the power issue?' I add.

'Exactly. You can't have helped but notice how many

cameras there are around here. They all use energy that could be better funnelled elsewhere. We've been trying to find a way that makes them go into a standby mode until it recognises one of your thinkwatches nearby. Then it will switch back on and continue to work as normal.'

'Who monitors them?'

Porter looks at me more intently. 'Dangerous questions,' is all he says before returning to where he was working. I realise I am pushing it.

I'm not entirely sure where to begin but, as I begin to familiarise myself with the system, I notice I have far more access than I did the first time. And that's when I have an idea . . .

* * *

As I enter the dorm that evening, there is a shock waiting as Jela sits on a bed directly opposite the door. She doesn't look up as I say her name and one of the other girls gives me a shrug as if to say they have all tried that already. I cross to Jela's bed and sit next to her, asking if she is all right. She doesn't respond, instead reaching for a brush and running it through her hair while staring towards the windows.

'It's good to see you, Jela,' I say, although she doesn't seem to hear me.

She is wearing the same silvery dress as on the train when we first arrived, although it has lost a lot of the sparkle it once had and has a few grubby, grimy patches on it. Her blonde hair is longer than it was before but I can see a patch behind her ear that is bald where a large clump has been pulled out. The flecked colours around her eye have now faded into one large purple bruise and, as I rest a hand on her shoulder, she pulls away sharply and instinctively.

'Sorry,' I add, unsure of what else I can tell her.

To my surprise, she pushes the brush into my hand and I slowly and gently run it through her hair until it is knot-less. She makes no sound as I place the brush on the bed next to her and say I am on the far side of the room if she ever wants someone to talk to.

Shortly after everyone has returned and we have shared out the thin helpings of bread and fruit, the door is heaved open and Ignacia enters. She looks angry and at first I think someone has been caught doing something wrong again. Instead, what she says is much, much worse.

'Which one of you was wearing the long green dress last night?'

Suddenly it dawns on us all not only why we had to dress up the previous evening – but also why Jela has returned. In Porter's words, the King 'gets bored'.

No one speaks up, but the look on the face of one of the girls close to the door gives her away as Ignacia snaps: 'Come on then, take the dress, it's time to go.'

The girl murmurs an anguished 'no' but Ignacia is firm.

'You can either come with me now, or I'll call the Kingsmen in. Either way, it's time to go.'

Her tone is harsh but I realise she is doing the girl a favour in some ways. Perhaps she approves of the King's requests, perhaps not. Either way, she is doing what the rest of us who want to stay alive are doing – exactly what it takes.

The girl reaches into her cupboard and takes out a wondrous cyan silky dress, folding it over in her arms, before taking one final look at Jela and leaving the room.

As the door locks back into place, we look at each other and there is a bond we haven't had before. Faith meets my eyes for the first time in a while in a knowing exchange of simultaneous sorrow and relief that it wasn't us.

It takes far longer for everyone to finish shuffling around in their beds after the lights have gone out, which perhaps isn't surprising; no one is having happy dreams tonight.

As it finally becomes late enough to sneak out, I sit at the end of the passage huddled under the blankets waiting for Imrin, knowing that somehow I not only have to find a way out – but that I have to warn my mother and Colt to find somewhere safe before I manage it.

22

I am jolted awake by someone shaking my arm. 'Silver,' Imrin's voice hisses as my eyes shoot open and flash from side to side. We are in the tunnel and I have fallen asleep.

'What time is it?' I mumble.

'Late. Come on, I have something to show you.'

I struggle to come to my senses as Imrin leads me out of the passage from the girl's dorm into the tunnel on the boy's side. As he closes the door, I realise I have never been in here before, though it is much the same as the other one.

On the floor are rolls of paper. I have become so used to doing everything on screens that I had almost forgotten the pencils, pens and paper from when I was young. They seem somewhat alien. Imrin flattens out one of the rolls and tells me to look. My eyes feel heavy as I struggle to focus.

'What is it?' I ask.

'I started mapping out as much of the castle as we know about.' He points to a spot. 'This is where we are. I've guessed some of it, like the position of your dorm, but you can help with that, obviously.'

There is excitement and pride in his whispers. I rub my

eyes and yawn, then take a proper look. Slowly the lines and shapes swarm into focus and I can see what he has created.

'The floor below us is over here,' he says, scrambling for something in the darkness as I continue to look at what's in front of me. The lines are slightly wobbly but it is easy to see where everything goes.

'We should mark the cameras on,' I say.

'Good idea.'

Together we draw the cameras we can remember and, on paper, there seems far fewer than it feels there should be.

'It could have been us . . .' Imrin says, not mentioning Lumin's name.

'I know.'

'It got me thinking about how, if we are really going to do this, we have to plan so much better. Last time, we could have run into anyone on those stairs, or the platform, but we were reckless because we wanted to get away.' Imrin points to the map. 'This can help us plan where everything is. We can mark the doors, windows, cameras, places where the Kingsmen congregate and everything else. We might end up with little more than we already have but it's better than nothing.'

He is right on both counts; we probably will end up with nothing extra but as long as we're careful, it can't do any harm to properly plan. It also allows me to finally get a bearing on where our corridor with the window might actually be.

As we fill in as much as we know, there are still huge gaps in our knowledge. We have no idea what the medical bay is like, or the dungeons. Areas around the Minister Prime's offices, the section behind the main hall, where we assume the King lives, and plenty of other corridors are unknown too. Despite that, it does feel as if we are actually doing something worthwhile.

Imrin has an excitement to his voice that I find hard to share.

'Before we do anything, we are going to have to find a way to contact our families,' I say. 'Remember what happened to Lumin. I don't want that happening to Colt, my mum or . . . anyone else.' I nearly mention Opie's name but stop myself in time.

Imrin nods. 'Perhaps through doing all of this, we'll find something we didn't know about before? Besides, would your mother really want to know this is how you're living? If we can find a completely safe way of getting out, we can figure the rest out as we go along.'

I'm not as sure as Imrin, but it doesn't seem the right time to shoot him down.

'There is something else I've been thinking about too,' he adds. 'It occurred to me when we were in the hall with . . .'

'. . . Lumin. You can say his name.'

'With Lumin. I thought about the Kingsmen. There were only four of them that whole time. How many have you ever seen together?'

I think about what he's saying and it dawns on me too. 'Maybe seven or eight?'

'Exactly. There are the people who run our areas; your Porter guy, the one from the kitchens and presumably others in charge of key areas – but they're not fully trained and armed like the ones who guard the doors. So let's say it's not eight, let's double it, triple it – that's still only twenty-four or twenty-five. Plus the Minister Prime. Not many, is it? And that's a maximum.'

'There could be lots more.'

'Maybe, but where are they? Think about our first night when there were thirty of us. How many guards were there? Six? Wouldn't that have been the night to give us a big show of force?'

'I guess . . .'

'Or the night where the King was looking for his champion? There were only four guards and they all gave their swords away.'

I try to think if there were any others waiting in the wings but, apart from one standing behind the King in the box, there wasn't anyone. 'But if there are so few of them, why would they give their weapons away? Any of the boys could have turned on the guards and overpowered them with the swords.'

Imrin is already ahead of me. 'Only if you had an idea that you had a chance. Besides, it was new and frightening. None of us knew what to expect – we are all so used to people disappearing and others like Wray being killed that we've fallen in line.'

I stare at the map thinking over what Imrin is saying. It almost ties into what Porter told me earlier in the day. Could it really be true?

'There must be more Kingsmen . . .' I'm trying to convince myself more than Imrin but he sounds confident.

'There probably are – they are out and about in the main cities. This place is pretty secure, isn't it? Think how many exits we've come up with – the train tunnel in and out and the obvious main doors at the front. All you have to do is man those. Think how easily we made our way through all the corridors. We went the long way around to avoid the cameras but there were no Kingsmen. Perhaps there are other exits through the King's quarters or the dungeons – we don't know – but that's how you could make something look far more secure than it actually is. Meanwhile, the bulk of his men are off in the cities and towns. How many have you ever seen around Martindale?'

I don't even have to think. 'There were loads on Reckoning day, but only one or two apart from that – and not all the time. Sometimes, we would go weeks or months without seeing any.'

'Exactly, which is the same as where I come from. But think of what we see on screen – armies of Kingsmen. They probably do exist, just not here. Everyone assumes there are huge numbers of people ready to fight for the King because that's what we're always shown. But we're always shown what a brave, bold person he is too and we know the truth of that.'

I tell Imrin what Porter told me about people still fighting, but that only supports his point that the King may have an army that are off fighting elsewhere.

'I suppose that could be why there are so many cameras,' I add. 'If you had enough men, you wouldn't need them. It's easier to have one person, somewhere, watching them and then direct Kingsmen to where they're needed, rather than have guards on every corner.'

'Or maybe you don't even need the one person – there might be an electronic control. Have you ever heard of anything?'

I tell him that Porter told me I was asking something dangerous when I came up with that exact question.

Imrin sounds suspicious. 'Why did he tell you all of that?'

'I don't know. I think he was upset over Lumin.'

I tell Imrin the rest of what Porter told me but it only

makes him more sure that he is right. I am not as convinced as he seems but it is somewhat comforting to think it could be true.

'How do you think Lumin is doing?' I ask after Imrin has rolled his maps back up.

His enthusiasm seeps away and I hear him gulp. 'Not well . . .' His words slip away before he adds something, softer than before. 'Can I show you something?'

'That depends on what it is.'

Imrin laughs gently with no real feeling, then he pulls his top over his head. His torso isn't as skeletal as mine but it is covered in horizontal red marks and slim slices through his skin.

'What happened?'

'Working in the kitchen is a dangerous place when you have knives, hot pans, cutlery and an angry Kingsman.'

He starts to expand but I shush him, not wanting to know the details. I trace the outline of the marks with my fingers as he winces at first but then relaxes slightly, holding his stomach taut.

'Does it hurt?'

'Not as much as it did.'

'Why didn't you show me before?'

Imrin jumps slightly as my cool fingers slide across the warmth of his belly button. 'I don't know. I guess I wanted to keep something to myself.'

'You can tell me anything you want.'

My words sound hollow, as I know I haven't told him about Opie, but he apologises for something he doesn't have to, compounding my guilt.

As my fingers rest on him, our eyes meet and I realise he is still in pain. Before I know what I am doing, my lips are on his, my hands sliding around to his back as I pull him towards me. He flinches as our stomachs bump together but it instantly becomes a giggle as I feel his fingers clasping my back. The way he touches me, holds me, feels so natural that I almost forget where I am before I hear him whispering delicately in my ear that we need to be quiet.

After that, the rest of the night is a blur until I wake up in my bed the next morning realising that, for the first time since I arrived at the castle, Opie hasn't been in my dreams once.

* * *

Spurred on by Imrin's ideas the night before, I throw myself into work the next day, at the same time trying to take advantage of any moments Porter is not around to watch over me. Despite the way he opened up to me, I'm not ready to trust anyone more than I have to.

When Porter disappears into the back lab for a few minutes, I raid the supply crate, pocketing a couple of tiny parts and a screwdriver which I don't think will be missed.

After he leaves completely for the afternoon, I spend ten minutes removing the back panel from my thinkwatch – the first time I have done so since leaving Martindale – switching one of the parts for a newer one from the crate, and then putting it back together. Even though my fingers don't seem to want to work as quickly as I try to force them to, I finish in plenty of time.

That evening, I spend a short while sitting with a still-mute Jela, brushing her hair. She doesn't let anyone else near her and, as far as I can tell, hasn't spoken a word since returning. She hasn't been assigned to work anywhere and spends each day in the dormitory, I assume doing nothing.

I softly whisper in her ear the things that are most vivid to me from the outside. 'In Martindale, there is this huge field just past Mrs Cusack's house,' I say. 'In the winter it is frozen over but, as it gets warmer, it is completely taken over by wildflowers that stretch as far as you can see. Most of them are this purple colour but there are reds and blues too. There is a period of maybe a week or two just after they flower where the smell drifts across the whole village. You'll see all the younger girls with flowers in their hair and loads of people will decorate their windows with the petals.'

Jela angles back towards me as I gently brush through a knot. 'Do you have anything like that?' I ask, not expecting, or getting, a response.

'On the other side, there is this huge wooded area,' I

add. 'There used to be a lake in the centre but it is empty now. There is this area of trees and bushes that links the village to the lake where I reckon I know every twig and branch. I call it the gully. If I closed my eyes now, I could talk you through it. I have seen some of the trees grow – they're younger than me. The bigger ones will drop seeds and then the next spring, you will see these little saplings that get covered in leaves and mulch the next time it is autumn. Do you have anywhere like that which makes you so happy you don't even have words for it?'

Another knot, more silence.

My memories are more reassuring for me than anyone else as I continue speaking gently into her ear. 'It's strange because everyone loves the summer when it's warmer, but my favourite time is at the end when autumn comes. You have these wonderful rain storms when it is dry one moment and then, in what seems like no time, the clouds roll in and empty themselves all over you. My friend runs for it most of the time; he doesn't like it – but I love those first few drops that hit you on the head, and the noise as they start to fall slowly and then build into a giant crescendo of sound, bouncing off the trees and the ground. Then your hair becomes plastered to your head and you have to pull it away from your face to see what's going on. My mum is always messaging my thinkwatch, asking where I am, but she already knows the answer. And then, when I turn up a bit late, she always says the same thing: "You look like a drowned rat, Silver Blackthorn". She's been telling me that since I was four years old.'

The memory makes me giggle and it is only then that I realise my nose is blocked and there are tears running down my face. The hairbrush is on the bed but I don't remember putting it down and one of my hands is resting on Jela's hips. She hasn't shaken me away.

'I like rain too,' she says, almost too quietly for me to hear.

I place my other hand on hers and whisper in her ear that one day, somehow, I'll take her to Martindale so she can feel my rain and visit my woods. As I stand to return to my bed, I realise at least three or four of the other girls have been listening. None of them says anything as I walk past, but the way one of them is dabbing her eyes tells me that I'm not the only one who is missing home.

23

Despite my breakthrough of sorts with Jela, she says nothing for the rest of the evening and the way she screams, fidgets and throws off her covers after the lights have gone out means I have to take extra care before sneaking out. She is on the bed next to Pietra and it is hard to tell from the other side of the room whether it is just Jela who is making the noise. After a while, I gamble that it is only her and head into the hidden tunnel. Imrin has transferred the maps into my side of the passageway, so we sit under the blankets adding a few extra corridors and cameras that we have gone looking for through the day.

Neither of us mentions the previous night, which, at least for now, is fine by me.

'Come with me,' I say, taking Imrin's hand and leading him through the door out into the main corridor.

We stop to look through the window, where the thin clouds are failing to block the bright white moonlight from flooding the area. Part of me wants to stay and watch but it is late already, so I tug Imrin away towards the far end of the passageway. I release his hand and touch the screen of my thinkwatch, then step away from the safety of our dead end onto the wider corridor and begin walking away from him.

Imrin's eyes are wide and scared as he hisses my name.

'It's all right,' I assure him as I stop moving and check my thinkwatch's screen before meeting his eyes.

'There are cameras at either end.'

'I know. One of them is too far away to see me.'

'What about the other one? What are you doing?' Imrin hasn't stepped towards me and is still hidden from view.

'Do you trust me?'

'I don't . . . yes.'

I hold out my hand. 'Then come here.'

At first I don't think he is going to but, after a moment, he stares into my eyes and steps forward, looking uncertainly at the fixed red camera light.

'What are you doing?' he asks, eyes on the camera.

I check my thinkwatch again, the light overhead catching the gentle orange colour of the face. 'Twenty-nine, twenty-eight . . .'

Imrin clutches me but is clearly confused. 'You're going to get us caught.'

'Twenty-four . . . I'm not. Tell me what you see.'

He is pressed up against me and I can feel his heart beating quickly. It makes me feel excited. 'A camera, I see a camera . . .' He is stumbling over his words.

'Nineteen . . . what else?'

'I don't know, a red light.'

'Sixteen . . . exactly, what about it?'

'That it's on and pointing at us.'

'Thirteen . . . look again.'

Imrin's voice is shaking now, his heart thumping through his clothes but I want him to see it. 'Silver . . .'

'Eleven. Tell me what you see, Imrin.'

'The camera is pointing at us and the red light is on.'

'Eight . . . Exactly, but what about it specifically?'

Imrin's breathing has increased and then I feel it in his body as his fingers tighten around me. 'The light isn't blinking!'

I snatch his hand and yank him back into our corridor. 'Four, three, two, one. That's right, blinking light means it is recording, steady red light means it is on but not sending images.'

'But . . . how?'

I lead Imrin back to our spot and we wrap ourselves in the blankets, even though he isn't cold. 'After what happened with Lumin,' I whisper, 'Porter put me on a new project working with the cameras. I haven't figured the whole thing out yet – but what I have done is reconfigure my thinkwatch so that I can stand in front of the cameras and they aren't able to recognise me.'

Imrin raises his arm. 'Isn't mine going to give us away?'

'As long as you are close to me, mine overrides it because it works on a stronger frequency. I found the information on the system.'

'So what does that mean?'

I point to the blank areas of the map we haven't figured out yet. 'The thinkwatch gives me ninety seconds before the camera resets itself.'

'Can you use the ninety seconds over and over?'

'Not quite, I tried it with the camera directly outside the lab. I get the ninety seconds, then the light starts blinking. I tried it a second time and got around a minute before it reset itself again. I've been going through the camera logs over the last couple of days and it looks like they're on twelve-hour cycles.'

'So you can get a ninety-second window and then something like another sixty seconds, then you can't do anything for twelve hours?'

'Exactly, after that anything I've managed to reconfigure is overridden by the original system. It's not amazing but it's better than the position we were in yesterday.'

'Well . . . not quite . . .'

I can see Imrin's cheeky grin in the faint light through the door and pinch him on the arm.

'Do you want to go exploring?' I ask, feeling my own heart beating. It feels rebellious and exciting. Exactly what I shouldn't be doing but perhaps that is why I'm so thrilled.

'Where?'

'If we turn right out of the corridor, I've used up one of my goes on that first camera. We could go that way but we wouldn't be able to get back – so let's go left. If we're careful not to pass any camera twice, we will be able to trace our route back.'

'There could be anyone out walking around . . .'

'I thought you said last night there were no guards?'

I'm teasing but Imrin squirms. 'I know, but . . .'

'We've got ninety seconds a camera, so we can go slowly and listen out for anything. We don't have to go far; I just want to do . . . *something*.'

Imrin seems torn but he eventually agrees and, before I know it, we are creeping along the corridor, listening for the merest of creaks and watching every red camera light to make sure it doesn't blink while I keep a steady eye on my thinkwatch. We whisper to each other about the individual cameras, memorising where they are so we can add them to Imrin's map.

On this floor, there is only one relatively small area we do not know – the area where the Minister Prime's office is. I had the slightest glimpse when I first encountered Hart, but have not returned since because of the two recording devices above the only corridor leading to the office.

We quicken our pace as we grow in confidence. No one

is around, which only supports Imrin's thinking that there are a lot fewer people here than we've come to think.

There are plenty of doors around the Minister Prime's offices, all of them closed, but with various names on the front such as 'Deputy Minister', 'Home Affairs Minister', 'Foreign Affairs Minister' and 'Defence Minister'. We ignore them all and pass the place where I ran into Hart until we reach a door at the very end of the corridor. I feel my heart start to race again as I spot a scanner identical to the one next to the entrance stairwell which led to the train platform. I take the borodron out of my pocket and check my thinkwatch. 'We've got forty seconds – in or out?'

'There could be anyone inside.'

'Or there could be more stairs that lead outside. We're never going to know if we don't look.'

Imrin stares at me and then the door. I can feel his indecision but somehow I know there is nobody waiting for us, the same way I knew there wouldn't be anyone on the stairs. I press the material against the scanner and step back as it swishes into the air.

I pull Imrin inside and the door slides into place behind us. I check for a camera, but there is nothing except white walls, stretching many metres away from us.

I turn my attention to the rest of the room but Imrin says it before I can: 'Wow . . .'

The three letters can barely describe the wonder as I turn a full circle taking in the entire spectacle. It is the most amazing room I have ever seen; fixed to all four walls are rows of glass-fronted tanks filled with animals of all shapes and sizes. A few I recognise; small dogs, cats and mice, but most I don't.

Imrin pulls me towards the nearest enclosure and we stand in silence watching small green and brown creatures hop across mulched pieces of wood scattered around a pool of water. There is a sheet of glass that means we cannot touch or hear anything but the animals are fascinating, their bulging eyes totally out of proportion to their bodies.

'What are they?' I ask, not expecting an answer.

'They're called frogs,' Imrin says. 'Haven't you ever seen them before?'

'No.'

'I guess if your lake is dried up, you wouldn't have done. They live around water. We have them around the farm – although I've not seen ones this bright. The ones at home are darker.'

I watch them hopping around almost hypnotically in the artificial light before Imrin pulls me towards the next tank. 'What are they?' I ask.

'Tortoises.'

'Do you have them too?'

Imrin shakes his head. 'No, but I've read about them in

this old book we've got. It's about a race between one of these and a hare. Do you know what one of those is?'

'They're like rabbits. We used to chase and catch them in the woods outside Martindale when we were hungry.'

'Who's "we"?'

I realise my mistake. Imrin isn't asking because he's particularly suspicious, he's just interested. I try to think quickly but blurt out the only name other than Opie's I can think of. 'Colt.'

'Oh, your brother?'

'Yes.' I hastily try to change the subject. 'I can't see how one of those could beat a hare in a race. A hare is really quick – he doesn't look as if he's moving.'

Imrin laughs slightly as the tortoise plods across a patch of mottled grass and twigs. It is around the size of my palm with a rounded dome shell and I struggle not to giggle as it looks as if it is smiling.

'It is supposed to be a lesson about not rushing into something. My mum would read it to me and my sisters when we were younger. The hare tears off but gets tired and over-confident, so it stops for a sleep. The tortoise is a lot slower but it keeps plodding away and wins.'

I've never heard the story and I'm not completely convinced. 'What distance were they racing over?'

Imrin laughs and I feel slightly inferior to him. 'I don't think that's the point,' he says, smiling. The tortoise stamps

around its enclosure tearing various leaves from the twigs and merrily chewing away.

The rest of the room is fascinating. Imrin knows almost all of the creatures. He tells me about iguanas, geckos, canaries, parrots and other creatures I have no knowledge of. I'm fascinated by the fish. There are other creatures I do recognise as we make our way around, although the hedgehogs and squirrels seem somewhat strange when they aren't out in the open.

'It must be someone's job to feed them all,' Imrin says, checking his thinkwatch.

It isn't a subtle hint but I take it anyway, making one final stop by the tortoise to see how far it has moved. It is sleeping with its arms and legs inside the shell and a small snout sticking out of the front part. I run my fingers around the enclosure wondering how someone gets in and out. At the top is a catch that looks like a much smaller version of the scanner I swiped to get in but it is a darker colour. For a moment, I think about pressing the borodron into it to see what will happen but I feel Imrin staring disapprovingly at me.

'Not now,' he whispers loud enough for me to hear, before I join him by the door.

It doesn't take long for us to retrace our route back to the corridor and I spend a few minutes helping Imrin fill in the blank spots on his map with our new knowledge of the

cameras, passages and the zoo, as he has christened it. Aside from the offices we ignored, our knowledge of this floor is complete – although the other major areas will be trickier to map: the medical area, dungeons and the King's quarters.

'Did you enjoy that?' I ask, as Imrin says goodnight.

'Not as much as you.'

'It was fun – we should go out again tomorrow.'

'Where are we going to go?'

'I'm not sure, downstairs? Perhaps we can see how close we can get to the medical wing?'

Imrin looks at me in a way I've not see before, as if he is slightly scared. He certainly has doubts about something. 'Do you remember the hare and the tortoise?'

'Your story?'

'Yes. We need to be the tortoise.'

Imrin kisses me on the forehead and then he is gone. For a few minutes, I sit under the blankets thinking about what he is saying. I understand it completely – keep doing what we're doing and wait for an opportunity, rather than rushing into something recklessly. In his story, Lumin is the hare and we're the tortoise, but then we are only ever one King's bad mood away from being forced into something that could potentially see us thrown out of whatever race Imrin thinks we are in altogether.

I am torn between believing he is right and being angry at him for not wanting to get us out of here quickly enough.

The fact we have no plan, except trying to figure out where an exit passage might be, is something I am almost trying to forget in the excitement of thinking I have got somewhere with my camera trick.

I throw the blankets off and hurriedly make my way back to the girls' bedroom, tracing the rough surface of the wall with my hand. By now I know every bump and nook, but I am so focused on Imrin's final words that I have already tripped and fallen to the floor with a painful crunch of my wrist before I realise there is something on the ground close to the exit.

As I try to disentangle my legs from whatever it is, I shriek with surprise as Pietra's voice hisses through the darkness.

24

I feel my heart bursting from my chest as my eyes struggle to adjust in the gloom. All I can hear is Pietra saying my name as I flail and fight. If she is going to take me to Ignacia and put Colt and my mother's lives in danger, then I am certainly going to do her some damage along the way. My wrist cannot take my weight but I shunt myself backwards until my back is against a wall. I then lash out with my foot, kicking hard until I feel it connect with something soft.

Pietra groans in pain as I hurl myself towards the direction of the noise, grabbing at her hair and pushing her face into the ground. The sound of her voice is muffled but I think she is saying the words 'stop' and 'please'. I pull her up and slam her into the wall, holding my arm firmly across her chest, pinning her to the surface.

'What are you doing here?' I hiss, keeping my voice low as we are close to the bedroom door. I feel the drip of something I assume is blood falling from her head and landing on my arm. My other arm is hanging limply next to me, still hurting from the fall.

'I heard you,' she slurs, not sounding entirely with it.

'Who have you told?'

Pietra's head slumps forward, so I lift her back up before releasing some of the pressure on her.

'How many?' I demand more forcefully.

'No one.'

'I could just kill you here and take my chances . . .' I try to sound as threatening as I can. I'm not actually sure that I could, but it sounds good.

Pietra whimpers. 'Really, I haven't told anyone.'

I release my arm and allow her to slip down the wall. 'Then why are you here?'

'I . . . don't know. I was curious. I've heard something happening by your bed a few times. I've checked but you've not been there and then I heard you coming back in a few nights ago. I found the door this evening when I was look-ing for you.'

My breathing is still heavy and I can still only just about make out Pietra's shape in the dark. 'Why are you so concerned about what I'm up to?'

'I . . . I'm not. Well, not like you think, anyway. I was worried.'

'About me?'

'Yes, people keep going missing and I thought maybe someone had come for you in the night.'

I push myself back into a sitting position, massaging my injured wrist. 'Why would it matter to you if I was?'

Pietra starts coughing but I shush her, saying she's going to wake people up. That is assuming she doesn't already have people waiting outside the door for me, of course.

'I'm not the bad person you think I am.'

She sounds like a child as she speaks and it takes me a moment to realise that, despite everything that has happened to us, we are pretty much still children.

'What about Bryony?'

Pietra sniffles and stifles another cough. 'I didn't mean that to happen. I thought I was helping everyone because she was going to get us all in trouble. I didn't want everyone to be punished because she was stealing food. You heard what the Minister Prime said – that we would all be held responsible.'

I barely let her finish before jumping in. 'You did it for yourself – to get yourself in favour with Ignacia and whoever else. You sacrificed Bryony to make yourself look good.'

Pietra is sobbing gently to herself. 'I really didn't.'

'What about the train, then, with poor Wray and Rush. You were picking on him just because he was a Trog.'

'I know . . .'

I find it hard to keep my voice down as all the weeks of frustration and fear pour out. 'Well?'

'It's hard to explain. I don't know where you're from but with my parents and my friends and everyone . . . we all come from this area that's not too bad. Everyone I know is either an Elite or a Member. The Trogs are assigned to work for us; they clean, they follow us around, they do what they're told.'

'And you think that's right?' My voice echoes around the space and I correct myself, whispering the accusation a second time but quieter.

'No . . . well, yes . . . I don't know. That's just how I was brought up – it was all I knew. If your mum or dad . . .'

'I don't have a dad.'

'I'm sorry, that's not what I meant. Look, if your mum spent your whole life telling you that Trogs were beneath you, that they're not really human and that you can do what you want to them, you would probably believe it, wouldn't you?'

'Of course not.'

I say it as firmly as I can but the truth is, with the way she has put it, I can almost understand her reasoning. My mother has brought me up to think that there is no problem hanging around with Opie, even though there was every chance he could have ended up as a Trog. Perhaps that wouldn't have happened if she had spent every day telling me he was beneath me.

'I can only apologise in that case,' Pietra says. 'It's too

late for me to say sorry to Wray now. I didn't know any better.'

'There's still Faith.'

'I know but she won't talk to me – not after Bryony.'

'Do you blame her?'

'Not really.'

For a moment, neither of us says anything but I can hear her panting, struggling for breath.

'Are you okay?' I ask, surprising myself.

'You kicked me in the ribs.'

I still can't bring myself to say sorry. 'What about when you said my ribs were horrible?'

'That was a misunderstanding. I was talking about what they're doing to us – the food, the fighting, all of it. I remember what you looked like when you arrived and what we're all like now. I tried to explain but you were gone.'

She sounds genuine but, of all the people I have told myself not to trust, Pietra is pretty much at the top of the list.

'I heard you talking to Jela,' she says, shuffling in the dark. 'Is it true about the flowers and the two weeks in your village every year?'

'Yes.'

She breathes in deeply, as if smelling the scent of the petals. 'It sounds wonderful. It's nice where I live but not like that. It's in the city, so there are people and clutter and noise. Everything is being rebuilt. It has been going on my whole life.'

I try to stifle a yawn but it gets the better of me and, just for a moment, as she shuffles in the shadows, I fear that Pietra could launch herself at me. Instead, the faint outline I can see of her merely moves sideways a little, trying to get more comfortable.

'What do you want, Pietra?' I am feeling tired and struggling to keep the weariness from my voice.

'I want out.'

'Out of where?'

'Here. Everywhere. I want to go home.'

'Why not ask Ignacia if you can go then?' I immediately regret my sneer as Pietra sniffles again, then replies in between soft sobs. 'I just want you to say that if you're going, you'll take me with you.'

'What makes you think I'm going anywhere?'

'Nothing . . . I don't know. I'm not saying you are. I just don't want to be the next one chosen when the King gets bored again.'

She starts crying, slightly louder, and I'm sure I can hear Jela's name mixed in with the tears. I shush her harshly, saying she will wake everyone else up if she isn't careful.

'If you want people to trust you, you have to earn it,' I say, repeating word for word something I remember my mother telling me years ago.

'I know. What do you want me to do?'

Pietra's offer sounds genuine and I think for a moment before replying. 'Just go back to your bed, go to sleep and forget we ever had this conversation. Don't come anywhere near this end of the room after dark, regardless of what you hear. If anyone else is creating a fuss over by my bed, stop them. Otherwise, don't talk to me. If I need you, I'll ask.'

I speak as sharply as I can, completely serious. Pietra is no use to me at the moment and I certainly don't know if I can trust her. Everything I have seen tells me not to but, as she apologises again and stumbles towards the hidden door, I wonder if there will come a time when I need to call in a favour.

* * *

I don't see Imrin for the next two nights. It isn't completely uncommon for him not to come out but I take my chances and venture to the zoo both nights, walking around on my own looking at the creatures and wondering exactly where they come from and why they are being kept there. My new tortoise friend seems to spend most of its time hiding in its shell, looking at me worriedly as if I am going to make a sudden movement that it doesn't approve of. Each time I see the tortoise, I think of Imrin's warning. I am already fighting against it simply by coming here for no reason other than the fact that I find it relaxing.

I take more time examining the mechanisms above each of the compartments. I try to open the tortoise chamber but the borodron doesn't work, leaving me to guess these are opened with the frequency of the thinkwatch that belongs to whoever is in charge. The one that Porter wears is slightly different to mine and gives him access to areas of the system I cannot get to.

Some of the compartments contain two or three of the same animal, others just a single one on its own. I realise that I know more species than I thought, and I'm able to identify chickens, turkeys, snakes and a few other creatures I have seen around the gully.

Meanwhile, in the evenings, Jela is slowly allowing me to get closer to her. On the day of the next banquet, she is sitting on my bed as I return to the dorm.

'Hello,' I say.

'Hello.'

'How has your day been?'

No answer.

'Do you want me to do something to your hair before we eat?'

Jela angles her head towards the brush on my bed but doesn't say anything. I start running it through her hair, commenting on how long and soft it is, and then separating it into bunches so I can plait it.

'Tell me about your home again,' she says.

By the time Jela has spoken, the room is practically full of the remaining girls. By now there are only nine of us as one by one people go to their jobs and don't return. The ones who are left have all been watching me on and off and go quiet at Jela's words. I realise everyone is listening as I think of the zoo and then begin to speak. 'Do you remember the wildflowers I told you about? Not long after they bloom, lots of butterflies appear. Every time you go out to the meadow, they are fluttering along, zipping up and down by the dying flowers.'

I criss-cross the strands of Jela's hair and look up to see everyone watching me, including Pietra from the far side of the room.

'I have a little brother named Colt. Everyone says he looks like me but I don't think it's true. He's only nine, so it's a few years yet until he has to take the Reckoning. My friend has this little brother too, named Imp. He's only six but he's this gorgeous little guy with blonde hair that's all over the place. Last year my friend and I took Colt and Imp out to the field to see the butterflies. Imp took one look at them and he was tearing off into the field trying to catch one. Colt was completely the opposite though; he couldn't even say "butterfly".'

'What did he call them?'

I am so surprised at Jela's interruption that I almost let her hair go. Instead, I pause just for a moment as I tighten the braid and then wrap a tie around the bottom and place my hands on her hips.

'He tries to say "butterfly", but every time he does, the word "flutterby" comes out. I even talk him through it: "but-ter-fly", but he'll say: "flut-ter-by". I keep making fun of him. Last year, we had some extra butter in our rations but I would never hand it to Colt unless he asked for the "flutter". In the end he got really annoyed and stormed into his room. Then he came back five minutes later and asked if he could have some flutter on his bread. I laughed for so long, I thought my stomach was going to burst.'

Jela giggles gently for the first time since I saw her on the train. 'Did Imp ever catch a butterfly?' Her words seem to light up the room and I hear others laughing gently around us.

'Ha! If you'd ever met him, you'd know he has no chance. He rushed around until he tired himself out and then his big brother had to carry him back to bed.'

Jela doesn't say anything at first but then she slowly turns to face me. 'I'm so sorry they've got you too, Silver. I don't have any of that; I deserve this type of thing but you . . . you have a life.'

It is by far the most she has said since she returned to the room and I feel a lump in my throat as she puts an arm around me. I am desperate not to cry in front of the others but it is the tears on Faith's face that set me off.

Jela hugs me tightly as I hold her, trying to get a grip on myself, but all I can think of is my mum, Colt, Imp, Opie . . . and Imrin. I don't even know how I can think of them in the same place as they represent such different extremes of my life.

After what seems like an age, I separate myself and Jela wipes the leftover tears away from my eyes and whispers a 'thank you' in my ear, before returning to her bed.

Everyone has caught on to the fact that dressing up isn't the best of ideas, so it is perhaps no surprise that when Ignacia comes to escort us she looks at us disapprovingly.

The hall itself is back to its usual appearance for the feast and, as with the past few meals, I eat steadily, focusing on the meat and avoiding anything that will fill me up too fast. Despite my best attempts, I am frustratingly full before the main course is finished. Jela is sitting next to me and for the first time, she seems to be eating relatively well. Not wanting to attract too much attention, I whisper to ask if she is all right. She doesn't answer with words, instead delicately brushing my arm as she reaches for an apple.

As the food is cleared away, we are told to stand as the benches are moved to the sides. I remember Imrin's theory and notice there are only four Kingsmen in the arena, plus one standing behind the King and, I suppose, the Minister Prime.

The boys retreat to one side of the room while everyone

from our dorm sits on the other as the King rises. The girl with the green dress who was taken days before is sitting at his side and, although she doesn't seem as haunted as Jela did, there is clearly something not right as she glares at the King's back while he clears his throat.

'My subjects, my Offerings,' he says in the exact cheerful, authoritative tone he did last time. 'I am still trying to find myself a full-time champion and feel it is time for us all to have a little more . . . *fun*.'

His emphasis on the final word is punctuated by a chuckle that no one joins in with.

'I feel that, after the boys gave us such a show last time, it should probably be the turn of the girls.'

My heart sinks as I do the odds in my head. There are now only nine girls down here, including Jela – and there's no way I'll let her take any further punishment. That means I have a one in eight chance of being chosen – and that's if he picks one girl. If there are two of us, it is one in four.

'Do we have any volunteers?' The King looks hopefully down at us but, unsurprisingly, nobody steps forward. His face falls slightly in annoyance. 'Right then,' he adds, rolling the R. 'In that case, we will have to draw.'

He looks around puzzled until he sees Ignacia, who he waves over and whispers something in her ear. She looks around, part-annoyed, part-frantic until somebody in the rows above the royal box hands her something that looks like paper. After some quick scribbling, she tears the page to bits and then screws them all into tight balls, holding them in her hands and offering them to the King.

He grins unerringly as he selects the first scrap and un-balls it before crisply and joyfully reading the name: 'Pietra Lewis'.

I look sideways as Pietra rises from the bench, clumsily stepping forward and almost tripping over the bottom of her long, plain purple dress. Her eyes are wide with fear and shock at what could happen next. The last time this happened, three boys were killed in front of us.

As I watch her trembling arms, I hear the next name, each syllable echoing through me with more viciousness than the last.

'Silver Blackthorn.'

25

Something strange happens as the King finishes saying my name. It is as if I am hovering somewhere above watching myself. I see everyone's eyes turn to face me as the girls on either side shuffle away to give me room. My legs wobble ever so slightly as I stand and I realise how thin and frail I now am. My shoulders are pointy and jut out at a strange angle, my upper arms lack any of the definition they used to have. My ankles are visible at the bottom of my dress but they look almost like the twigs in the woods outside Martindale.

I look like more of a child than ever.

Around the arena, murmurs are growing and I wonder how Porter is feeling. He has already lost Lumin and now I could be next. And what about Hart? I have been living by his code almost since I arrived here and now the luck of the draw could take me down. I wonder if Imrin is worrying about me in the way Opie would. It's hard to define our relationship but I can't imagine being here without him.

I blink rapidly and suddenly the floating, uneasy sensation is over and I am back in my body. I slowly step forward, desperate not to show how scared I am. My eyes are on the King, wondering if he is going to pick out any other names, but he dismissively waves his hand to send Ignacia scuttling away.

The King beams down at us, his eyes perhaps as happy as I have seen them. 'Aaaah, two lovely ladies . . . what shall we do with you?'

From the main doorway, the Kingsmen start to edge forward. I see their swords bobbing ominously in their belts as I feel Pietra's eyes staring at me. I can't meet them but instead risk a glance across to where the boys are sitting. They are all transfixed. Imrin's arms are rigidly holding onto the bench, eyes wide with fear. As I scan along the line, strangely it is Rush who I feel drawn to. He has somehow managed to maintain much of the size he had when we first met, but his demeanour is completely different. He doesn't have the same intense anger about him; instead he is sitting calmly with his palms apart and fingers touching each other in a way that almost makes it look as if he is praying.

As I finally turn to face Pietra, it dawns on me that perhaps he is.

Pietra's arms are wrapped around herself, hands underneath her armpits as she tries to stop the shudders rippling through her body. She clearly has no confidence she could beat me at anything the King may dream up but then I barely have any more self-belief, given the state of my frail body.

The four Kingsmen are now upon us and I look beyond them towards the door, thinking desperately of Imrin's words. Just four. If one of them gives me his sword, I could turn it back around on him. Would it pierce his armour? I think of the borodron back in the dorm, hidden under the clothes in my wardrobe. It is flexible but as tough as anything I have known. Could I go for his arms? Or reach his head? Could I run for it now and reach the door? If so, where would I go then?

The questions swirl, confusing and disorientating me. Before I know it, one of the Kingsmen is pushing his sword into my hand. I feel the slick material of his gloves brushing my skin as he mutters something I don't take in. His breath smells of wine, his skin of sweat, and then he is gone and there is a weapon in my hand, hanging limply towards the ground.

Something happens to the lighting and it seems brighter but then, as I glance towards Pietra, I wonder if it is just my eyes as I see bright yellow and pink stars along the edges of my vision. It looks as if there is some sort of whiteness majestically haloing Pietra's head. She is struggling to lift the sword, using both hands to grasp it, and it is only then that I realise I can barely raise my sword either. The handle is hard and feels rough in my hand but I clench it tightly, forcing my arm upwards. Slowly it obeys, but the weight of the sword makes me feel unsteady. I stagger from one foot to the other and wonder how I am ever going to be able to lunge or thrust, given the fact I can hardly lift it.

Suddenly, the muttering ebbs away and I peer up to see the King standing again. He is watching as though seeing us for the children we actually are. It is the same way I look at Imp when he has been up to no good – when I want to scold him but instead his grin and dimples leave me smiling. The King is cackling, turning from side to side and looking for support until there is an uneasy stream of laughter from the seats above us too.

'Girls, girls,' he says with a broad grin. 'Of course you don't have to use those unwieldy things; I wouldn't want you to mess up your pretty dresses.'

He nods towards the Kingsmen, who stride towards us and take the weapons. My arm feels flimsy as it drops back to my side, leaving a dull ache in my shoulder.

'Now, what shall we do with you?' The King grabs a tuft of his beard and begins stroking it. It is hard to tell if it is entirely for show or because he is genuinely thinking about what our fate should be. 'So many options,' he adds, prolonging our torment in a way I'm not sure he realises. For him, this is a game.

'Hmmm . . .'

I don't know how long it takes before he starts speaking

because it feels as if I have left my body again. I see Pietra and myself standing a short distance apart in evening gowns already looking defeated. On either side, the other Offerings stare intently at the King, simultaneously terrified, yet relieved their name wasn't chosen.

I do not blame them.

With a stiff, resounding clap of the King's hands, I am myself again, watching the royal box and blinking rapidly, trying to clear the bright haze around my vision.

'I think we will keep it simple tonight,' the King says. 'No bloodshed, well, not much. It is as easy as this; all you have to do is hit each other across the face, one at a time, as hard as you possibly can.'

I meet Pietra's eyes; she is still trembling but is standing slightly straighter in relief that neither of us is apparently going to die tonight.

The King goes to sit but then pulls himself forward. 'No holding back, of course. Anything less than full force and . . . well . . .'

He tails off but the implication is clear. I try to think of the number of people I have ever willingly hit. There was Rush, of course, but that was slightly different because I was defending Wray. All those times rolling around and battling with Opie were nothing other than play-fighting.

'You go first.' Pietra is talking to me, her voice shaking. 'Are you sure?'

'Yes.'

I am almost thankful that I have lost so much weight and muscle because if I had the strength to hammer her as hard as I hit Rush, then I'm not sure she would take it.

'Bend your knees,' I whisper loudly.

Pietra looks at me bewildered.

'Bend your knees but stand firm with your back straight.'

She nods a confused acceptance and does what I instruct. I look up at the King who has a bottle of wine in one hand and a look of such joy on his face that any doubts I may have had about his sanity are instantly vanquished. He isn't simply evil; he has little to no grip on reality.

'Sorry,' I whisper, before lunging forward and punching Pietra in the side of the head with as much force as I can manage, ignoring the pain in my wrist from last night. I try to aim for the hard part just in front of her ear, where her skull is as likely to hurt my hand as I am to seriously harm her. As I feel a crunch in one of my knuckles, I know I have caught it just right, avoiding her jaw, ear or front cheekbone in a way I doubt she will recognise.

Pietra crumples to the floor in any case, both hands cradling her head as she yelps in pain. I am wringing my hand, trying to rid the stinging sensation, but the only sound I can hear is the King's laugh reverberating around the room. He genuinely finds it hilarious and takes another long swig of the wine before throwing the empty bottle towards us and clapping his hands together in glee. Pietra jumps at the sound of the glass smashing but it falls well short of us.

'Are you okay?' I ask.

Slowly, Pietra pulls herself to her feet as I resist the urge to reach out and help. She has one hand close to her ear and is clicking her jaw up and down as if trying to work out if she can actually speak. She mumbles something that sounds like a 'yes' and nods her head.

'Excellent, excellent,' the King booms out. 'I'd rather have her with me than against me, wouldn't you?'

I cannot see who he is speaking to, but it doesn't really matter as I take my own advice, bending my knees slightly and straightening my back ready for Pietra's blow.

'Just do it,' I tell her, making eye contact. She shakes her head, trying to gather her thoughts as I close my eyes and then . . .

My head bounces to the side but it barely feels as if I have been struck. I open my eyes to see Pietra stepping away from me wringing her hand but there isn't even a tingling sensation in my jaw. Imp has hit me harder in the past. Pietra grips her shoulder and grunts an 'ouch' as she takes a step towards the benches but I know she has blown it.

The King is on his feet, furious. 'Stop! You, girl, look at me.' He is glaring at Pietra, eyes bulging as he jabs a finger in her direction. My eyes flick to Pietra who is staring back at the King.

'I'm sorry, I . . . I've never hit anyone before.'

The King is glancing to either side, seemingly for something to throw, before he kicks the banister in front of him in pure rage. The man I once thought was charming and persuasive is but a distant memory. He turns towards the boys' bench and thrusts out his arm again. 'You,' he says, although his gesturing is so erratic, no one knows what he wants. 'Yes, you, get up.'

It takes me a moment to realise what is happening as I see Rush standing and pointing to himself.

'My champion, you, come here and show her how it's done.'

Rush walks towards me, eyes firmly on the ground, but I don't need the hushed hum of voices around the room to let me know that I am in trouble.

Pietra is repeating 'sorry' over and over before one of the girls stands and leads her back to the bench. As I turn around, I see Rush standing over me, his expression blank and fixed. I look to the large, balled fists at his sides as the King bellows at him not to hold back.

I screw my eyes shut as I hear a collective intake of breath.

26

I feel the goosebumps rise on my arm as the chilled rush of the breeze skims across the remains of the lake just outside Martindale. Autumn is nearly upon us and I am hoping the clouds will roll in to treat us with its warm cascade of water.

I have my back to the woods, waiting for the snap of a twig or rustle of undergrowth to disturb me. The soft breeze swishes over me but doesn't disguise the approaching clumsy footsteps. I grin to myself but don't turn, allowing him to get closer as I keep my eyes steady on the wreck of plastic and glass filling the space that once brimmed with water.

A hand touches my shoulder and grunts a 'raargh' of happiness, I jolt my body in mock surprise, then turn around and grab his legs, pushing him to the ground and rolling on top, taking a moment to remember his blonde ruffled hair . . . except Opie's hair isn't blonde any longer. His skin is darker, his hair black, as I stare down at Imrin's grinning features.

Suddenly my eyes are open and I am sitting up in an unfamiliar bed. It is light but I don't remember falling asleep. I blink rapidly trying to clear the grey haze and, as I try to open my mouth, I realise my jaw is locked in place. I clench my teeth together and then slide them sideways across each other, before finally opening my mouth with a grimace of pain.

'Silver.'

It is only at the sound of my name that I realise someone is holding my hand. My fingers clench tightly around theirs but my neck is too sore to turn.

'Are you all right?' a girl's voice adds.

I groan involuntarily, before falling backwards onto the bed and hauling myself sideways.

'Jela?' I croak.

'Yes, are you okay?'

'Where am I?'

'In the medical wing.'

It takes me a moment to process her words, as if she is speaking in a different language and my mind needs that short gap to translate it into something I can understand. I blink my eyes open further to see how bright the room is. Behind Jela, there are large rows of windows, with sunlight cascading through, making the white floor appear as if it is glowing. I try to focus on her but it is hard as the light is so dazzling. Her blonde hair is still in the plait I put in but is looking a little dirtier now and she is wearing the same dress she had on at the banquet. As I remember that, everything else tumbles back into my mind: the King, Pietra, noise, Rush, pain.

'How long have I been here?'

Jela releases my hand momentarily and checks the grey-black face of her thinkwatch, before interlocking her fingers with mine again. There is clamminess between our skin but the sensation of human contact is so reassuring.

'Around sixteen hours or so.'

'You've been with me all night?'

'Yes.'

'Where did you sleep?'

'Right here.'

I look at the chair she is sitting in but it doesn't seem anything other than a plain piece of wood with a low back.

'What happened?'

Jela's fingers twitch slightly and I feel her rough nails gently scratch the back of my hand.

'Do you really want to know?'

'Yes.'

'There was so much noise, just this low hum of people talking to the person next to them that it felt really over-whelming. Pietra was sitting on the floor in front of the bench where we were. Then the big guy . . .'

'. . . Rush.'

'Yes. He sort of looked over towards us and said some-thing but I couldn't hear it. And then he just hit you and you went down. There was this gasp, as if everyone was making the same noise at the same time. The King made this sort of "oooh" sound. I was expecting you to get up, everyone was, but I think you hit your head on the floor.'

Jela stops to wipe her nose with her sleeve and it feels strange for someone I don't really know to feel any sort of sympathy for me.

'The King was clapping and whooping but Rush crouched over you and then called for help.'

'Rush did?'

'Yes. Ignacia was waving at the Kingsmen and then she came down the steps and told one of us to go with you.'

I try to lift myself up again, letting go of Jela's hand as I do so to better support myself. Aside from the glare hurting my eyes, I don't feel too bad. I start to look around the room, which is a lot smaller than I would have thought. There is space for half-a-dozen beds and little else, with a door at either end.

'Which door did we come in through?' I ask. Jela looks at me confused but then nods to the one behind her. 'What's through the other one?'

Jela shakes her head. 'I don't know. That's where the nurse came from.'

'What did they do to me?'

'She injected you with something and wiped away the blood. That was it.'

It dawns on me that through a complete fluke, I have ended up in one of the few places Imrin and I hadn't managed to map.

I want to check through the window but not necessarily with Jela still here. It is dangerous enough that we could be seen as being friendly and, although I want to get her out of here too, I'm not sure it's best to let anyone other than Imrin know what we could be planning. The more people who know, the more leverage the Minister Prime or Ignacia could have if they ever discover what we are up to.

'Are you sure you're all right?' Jela asks.

I realise the way I am trying to take in the room could be unnerving, given the speed with which I am twisting from side to side.

'I'm fine. Thank you for coming with me.'

Jela grips my hand again. 'Can I tell you something about me?'

'Of course.'

She puts her other hand on mine and I look into her weary but smiling eyes. 'When I got on the train, I was with Pietra and the others but my family had only been living in the city for a couple of years.'

'Really?'

I have never known whole families moving into and out of Martindale. I always knew people moved to the big cities after the Reckoning but didn't realise it could be small groups, instead of just one person.

'It wasn't through choice,' Jela replies. 'We used to live in this village that had a stream running through it. There were ten or eleven houses still standing after everything. One of them was the place where my mum had lived her whole life.'

'Why did you have to leave?'

'One morning I was woken up by this hammering on the front door and then Dad was in my room saying I had to pack as much as I could because we were leaving. Kingsmen had come to the village and said we weren't productive enough to be living there.'

'How do you mean?'

Jela shrugs sadly. 'I'm not sure. We would grow our own food and we kept animals. There wasn't much, but between the people that lived there, we had a bit of everything. I suppose they meant that there wasn't much left to hand over when the deliveries came around – but then we almost never took anything, so nobody thought it would be a problem.'

I don't say it but the reasoning now seems obvious given everything we have learned. A small self-sufficient community that doesn't rely on rations or handouts is perhaps as dangerous as anything because, if we were all like that, we would have no need for a King or government. It is no wonder that the Kingsmen eventually put a stop to it.

'What happened to you all?' I ask.

'My parents and I were taken to the city and given this one-room flat to live in next door to all sorts of other people. We were all separated, so I have never seen the others from the village again.'

'How many?'

'There were four of us all the same age. We were all only children but grew up like brothers and sisters. When you were talking about Imp and Colt, it made me think of them.'

'What were their names?'

Jela's entire face changes, the light making her eyes twinkle, her smooth, slightly brown skin stretching tautly into a perfect smile.

'Lola, Muse and Ayowen. There was this huge field full of corn at the back of our house. The day before the Kingsmen came, we had been playing hide and seek in between the stems. Lola lived next door to me and none of us could find her. After a while, it wasn't a game any longer and the rest of us were racing through the field calling her name. Then I heard Ayowen shouting for us instead. He was in the back corner where Lola was curled up with this white foamy liquid coming out of her mouth. I didn't know what to do and was ready to race home but Muse knew instantly.

He heaved her up and was pumping her stomach, then pouring water in her mouth and forcing her to bring it back up. Ayowen and I just looked at each other, not knowing what was going on but then, as if nothing had happened, Lola coughed this black jelly-type stuff up and she was fine.'

I look at Jela, not understanding what happened and wondering why she has told me.

'Lola had found this brown fruit growing in the hedge and taken a bite from it. When Muse pointed at the juice drops on the floor, we could see the leftover core. He called it a tan fruit and said he had eaten some when he was young. It looks like an apple but is squishy and brown. If you eat one, it doesn't kill you but they paralyse you for a while. If there is no one around, you might end up in a position where you swallow your tongue and stop breathing. His dad had saved him and warned him about them. I don't know about the rest of the Realm but they were rare around our village.'

I nod in recognition but I'm still not sure I get the point.

'When I was with the King, I was never allowed to share his meals but he would sometimes throw things my way that he didn't want. Anything green or that looked like a fruit or vegetable would come to me. Usually I would eat it because I was so hungry but this one time he threw a tan fruit towards me.'

I look into her eyes as Imrin's words flash through my mind from when we were talking about the weekly deliveries: '*It is a mixture of foods, most of it we use, some we don't. I'm not even sure I know what it all is*'.

She releases my hand and stands, not adding anything else. 'I'm going to go back to the dorm if you are okay?'

'I am.'

With a smile and a swish of her plaited ponytail, she is gone, her footsteps echoing until the door bangs shut behind her.

I run through Jela's story in my mind again and then slowly haul myself out of the bed, expecting to shiver as my bare feet hit the stone floor. Instead I feel an unnatural warmth. I am slightly unsteady on my feet and hold onto the bed for support, but the moment passes quickly and I pad my way across to the window. Running the full length of the wall is a radiator like the one we have at home – except this one is boiling hot and scalds me with even the faintest of touches. The heat is uncomfortable, something I'm not sure I've ever felt in my life, and it is as I look along the radiator's length that I notice an open window.

Something surges in my chest as I check behind me and then move quickly towards it, thrusting my face into the space and enjoying the cool, refreshing breeze on my skin again. I can smell grass and dew as I breathe and taste the air that reminds me of home.

Opening my eyes, I take in what is below me. Imrin and I believed the medical area was much bigger than it actually is because we knew the main hall was directly underneath it. Instead, it is perhaps a quarter of the size, the hall stretching out in front of me towards the castle wall. From the window is a drop of a couple of metres and then a run across the hall's roof, a jump to the castle wall and then . . . a plummet of around eight or ten metres. It would be too much for anyone's legs to take and the window is too small for me to fit through.

I return to the bed and sit with my legs over the edge, feeling slightly woozy from the walk and trying to focus on the darker corners of the room.

'Too bright?' A female voice comes from somewhere behind me.

I turn quickly, making my dizziness worse, as the silhouette of someone approaches from the door Jela said the nurse came from.

'I suppose . . .' I try to sound more ill than I am. In truth, aside from the slight feeling of disorientation, I don't even have a headache.

I feel a warm hand on my head. 'It's only to be expected after the blow you took.' Her voice sounds genuinely concerned.

'It's hot in here,' I say.

'Yeah.' The nurse doesn't sound too approving and

mumbles something about the heating always being on. I don't catch it all but I'm not sure it's for my benefit anyway.

She looks around the empty room. 'Has your friend gone?'

'We're not really friends,' I say, remembering Hart's instructions and thinking I should play it safe. 'We're just in the same dorm.'

The nurse nods knowingly and then digs into a pocket, taking out two white tablets and handing them to me. 'Here, you take those. It will make you feel better.'

I am wary of swallowing anything without knowing what they are supposed to be, but take them with a smile and ask for water.

'Of course, I'll be right back.'

'Can I come with you?' I ask. 'I want to try walking again.'

The nurse eyes me but then nods and dips her shoulder for me to steady myself on. Together we go to the room at the back. She presses her thinkwatch against a dark sensor, similar to the ones in the zoo, and the door fizzes upwards.

Inside is a smaller room with a single bed pushed up against the far wall and rows of shelves that have piles of small boxes stacked on them.

'The sink's there,' the nurse says, pointing to a small cubby hole on the right.

I use my hands to drink the water, but drop the tablets down the plughole and then quickly wash my face.

The nurse is waiting in the doorway as I turn. 'You're going to have a bit of a black eye but you don't seem too bad, given what happened.'

'Thanks.'

She nods and leads me back to the bed but I tell her I would like to return to the dorm. She tells me I can stay longer if I want but I say I'm feeling a lot better after the medicine she gave me. With a shrug, she says she hopes she doesn't see me soon, which is perhaps the nicest thing any of the adults have said to me since I arrived.

I step out of the main door and make a mental note of the nearby cameras and then deliberately go the wrong way before playing up my forgetfulness in front of a camera just in case anyone is watching, and then retreating back the correct way. As I quickly move past the area where the Minister Prime's office is, I risk a quick glimpse towards the door that hides the zoo and wonder how my tortoise is doing.

As I turn back around, I see the shape of Hart standing in front of me.

I say his name, part in surprise.

'Shh, in here.'

I glance both ways and then follow Hart into one of the side offices Imrin and I ignored on our first night-time visit.

The back wall is decorated with rows of books and the green desk perfectly matches the carpet. As I look around, I feel Hart's hand on my shoulder.

'Silver, pay attention,' he says urgently.

'What?'

'I . . . I thought you were dead. When he hit you, you just fell. Everyone heard your head crack.'

Instinctively, I reach up to the area around my cheek. 'I don't feel too bad.'

Hart nods and then sighs. 'There's something I should have told you when we first spoke . . .'

27

Imrin is so glad to see me in our secret meeting place that night that I have to tell him to quieten down for fear of anyone overhearing us.

'I didn't know if I'd see you at all,' he says, 'let alone so soon. I couldn't ask any of the girls in the kitchen how you were because no one knows we are friends. How do you feel?'

I overplay things a little, sighing and looking for sympathy even though I don't feel too bad. 'I'm fine, just cold.'

Imrin fusses, draping the blankets over me and offering to double them up. I tell him not to be so silly and that he should sit under them too. I want to say that I don't even let my mother look after me as much as he wants to but there is a sweetness about the way he keeps asking if I need anything. Secretly I am enjoying it.

'Rush was really upset yesterday evening.'

'Really?'

'Some of the others were telling him that he had no choice but he was saying he should have refused.'

'The King would have had him killed if he had said no.'

'That's what people were saying but he kept insisting it was wrong.'

'It must be the day for it. When I was in the dorm earlier, Pietra apologised to me in front of everyone. She kept saying she had never hit anyone before and didn't know what she was doing. I told her it was fine and that was the cue for everyone else to join in.'

'So you're all actually talking now?'

'Apparently. All it took was someone twice as big as me to hit me really hard in the head and now we're all friends.'

I laugh gently but Imrin doesn't join in.

'I was really worried . . .'

'What happened after he hit me?'

I have already heard Jela's version but wonder if Imrin has a different perspective.

He swallows before answering. 'It's strange because it seems really hard to remember, even though it was only yesterday. There was noise: people shouting, some clapping, some cheering – but it felt mixed. Not like when Rush won the first game. The King didn't even notice. He was cheering but the Minister Prime wasn't. He swept his hair to one side and whispered something in Ignacia's ear and then pushed her down the steps towards you. As you were being taken out, he was on his feet demanding silence. He got it but it wasn't instant like it usually is. There were still murmurs from the people above us.'

'What did you do?'

'I wanted to come to you but I remembered ages ago when you said we couldn't be friends anywhere other than here. I was almost fighting myself but then Rush was protecting you anyway.'

'You did the right thing.'

'Honestly?'

'We might not be here now if you had come across to me. No one is aware we even know each other, let alone anything else. There's no point in blowing that unless we absolutely have to.'

I rub my head and Imrin fusses again. I assure him I am feeling fine.

'Where are your maps?' I ask.

Imrin scrabbles across to the other side of the passage and fumbles around before flattening out the rolls of paper. It isn't easy to see in the dim light but I talk him through the dimensions of the medical bay, the handful of passages at the front and the nurse's station at the rear. He draws them on and then places one floor's map on top of the other.

'So what's here?' he asks, pointing to a large space.

'I was wondering when you'd realise.' I smile and take the pencil from him, explaining about the roof of the main hall.

'Could either of us fit through the window?'

'No, but it's only glass. We could break it.'

'What about the wall at the far end?'

'We'd need to find a way down; a rope or something similar.'

'What about getting into the medical bay?'

'There's a silver scanner on the wall outside that the borodron should work on. I think the darker ones, like the ones in the zoo, are opened by the frequency in certain people's thinkwatches. There is one in the nurse's station too. I'm pretty sure they are specific to one or two people but the silver ones are for all Kingsmen.'

Imrin looks at his map, then at me. 'So why don't we just go? We can get some sheets, or I can get some rope from the guy I know in textiles. We just need something to break the glass in the medical bay and then we're away.'

'What are we going to do then?'

'I don't know – at least we'll be outside. We can go and do all those things we talked about: live in the woods, hunt animals, grow things, you remember . . .'

I do remember but I know now it is pure fantasy. 'We don't know where we are,' I say. 'Neither of us comes from this area.'

Imrin sounds desperate. 'We'll figure that out.'

I shake my head. 'You were the one who said to be the tortoise.'

'But that was before we found our way out.'

It is only now I realise that he is frantic to get away. Before, everything was led by me and I always assumed it was my idea he was clinging to.

'What about our families?' I ask.

'Our thinkwatches should work again as we get outside, we can warn them.'

I shake my head. 'It could be too late. As soon as we make a break for it, there could be Kingsmen burning down our houses and putting our families in prison.'

Imrin sighs, knowing I am right but still clinging to the hope that we could be out of here within a day.

'What do you want to do?' he asks.

'This is bigger than us now. It isn't just about getting out, or even warning our families.'

Imrin hisses back at me, his voice raised and audible. 'So what is it about?'

I give him a moment to collect himself and then speak slowly and calmly. 'It's about letting everyone in the Realms know what's going on and taking the King down.'

He is staring at me in disbelief. 'You're serious?'

'Yes.'

'That's suicide.'

'It doesn't have to be.'

Imrin tugs one of the blankets towards him, exposing my shoulders. I pull the second one up to cover me but it is not as warm. 'But we're just kids,' he says.

'Exactly.'

He huffs exasperatedly. 'How hard were you hit on the head?'

I reach out to him, trying to hold his hand to tell him it will be fine, but he shrugs me away.

'Im . . .'

He doesn't reply and we sit in silence listening to each other's breathing for what seems like an age.

When he finally speaks, Imrin's whispers are steady again. 'You don't have an older brother, do you?'

'You know I don't.'

'Do you remember when I told you my sisters were all Inters or Members?'

'The first night we met.'

'Yes . . . well, it's not exactly true. My three older sisters are all Elites and no one doubts the younger ones will be too.'

I think back to our very first conversation and the way we ended up speaking about our families. His openness was the main thing which made me trust him. I feel slightly betrayed at the revelation.

'I don't understand why you'd say that.'

Imrin laughs slightly. 'That's because you're the eldest – you have no one to impress. I had to follow them. Anything less than becoming an Elite made me a total failure – but even when I got the result they wanted, it wasn't anything special, it was the minimum they expected.'

'But it doesn't matter to me what you are.'

'I didn't know that then, did I? I wanted to impress you. Everyone I know is completely focused on what you are. There are people where I live that won't even look at you unless you're an Elite. That's why I said I was the first Elite in my family. It sounded good, as if I was something better than I am.'

I remember the way Pietra explained it to me and struggle to know what to say before I finally croak out: 'You're special to me.'

Imrin laughs slightly but it is difficult to tell in the dark if it is genuine or in disbelief. 'Really?'

'Yes.'

I think of Opie back in Martindale and there is a lump in my throat. I find it hard to believe I have somehow ended up in a situation where my feelings are caught between him and Imrin. There was a time when everything I did revolved around seeing Opie but now my life has changed so much, so quickly, that I don't even feel like the person I once was. Will I ever be her again?

Luckily Imrin speaks before I have to. 'When you grow up with so many sisters, it's awkward to be noticed. It's strange because I know my mother wanted a son but my dad loves his little girls, all of them. It's always them . . .

and Imrin, as if I'm some sort of leftover thought. People know us as the family with all the girls – but there's no room for me in that.'

'I'm not sure what you're saying.'

'Just that *this* . . . it's been something that's mine and yours that I don't have to share with anyone else. Now we're so close but it feels as if you're changing our plans. Now, instead of just getting away, you want to do something crazy. If the King was so easy to take down, don't you think someone would have tried it?'

'Maybe but perhaps it's like you said with the guards. No one realises how few there are because we're so busy being isolated and scared.'

'But that was just a guess. There could be Kingsmen everywhere.'

I reach out and grab Imrin's hand, refusing to let him pull it away. 'If we stay here, sooner or later, we're going to die anyway.'

'So let's go!' Imrin is getting louder again, his frustration bubbling over.

'It's not that simple. What about next year's Offerings? Or the year after that? Even if our families are somehow spared, it could be your younger sisters, or Colt, who gets chosen when it's their turn.'

'So what do you suggest?'

'It's like you said – we're just kids, so no one will expect anything from us. The King will probably have something in place because he will expect dissent at some point from the various Kingsmen. He's quelled it before and he'll do it again but what he wouldn't expect is for people like us to cause him a problem.'

'Why?'

'Look at us. The girls have barely talked and we've spent all our time fighting each other. Your lot have at least been working together, but that creates its own problems because one silly mistake will bring you all down. You're so reliant on each other that you can't afford to take big risks.'

'Surely that proves that we should focus on ourselves and get out?'

I shake my head. 'They'll be expecting us to smuggle food, perhaps even make escape attempts, but the one thing they won't imagine is for us to work together.'

In the dimness of the tunnel, I wonder if Imrin has heard as he doesn't reply and I cannot hear him breathing. 'How do you mean?' he finally says.

'Think about it. We have people working everywhere – the kitchens, textiles, the barracks, the admin offices, technology. If the senior Kingsmen were to rise up, they would have to convince almost all the other people in their position because there is only one person per department. We don't need anything like that – we can pick and choose who we think will be the most valuable in each area.'

Imrin sighs again. 'I'm still not sure what you think we can do. We know people who have been placed all around the castle, so what?'

'You'll have to trust me on that for now.'

'Why?'

'Because, before any of that, I need to get into the Minister Prime's office.'

Imrin snorts. 'How? Even with your camera trick, you're never going to get near it without someone spotting you.'

'I'll only need a few minutes.'

'But how are you going to get them?'

I take a deep breath, hoping my persuasive powers are still enough. 'That's where you come in . . .'

28

The next evening, Imrin tells me we are sorted but he still doesn't seem entirely convinced. I'm not sure what I can say to him because it is hard to put myself in his position, especially considering I have kept the truth about Opie from him all this time.

In the morning, I rise early and get dressed, waiting for the automatic lock on the door to disengage. There is a greater sense of togetherness around the dormitory now and although I get a few quizzical looks from some of the girls, nobody asks what I am up to. If we don't know one another's business, then no one can force us to tell on each other. It is one step up from the secrecy of before and the overall atmosphere is a lot better.

As soon as I hear the click, I wrench the door open and head out into the hallways. I don't have to be at the laboratories for over half an hour, so I take a long route, using my camera trick where necessary, until I am standing in the corridor outside the Minister Prime's office.

A voice hisses at me and I turn around, struggling to find its source. 'Silver, over here.'

Hart is blocking the door of the office we were in a few days ago, but he backs inside to allow me through and stands in the doorway looking both ways along the corridor.

'Did you sort something?' he whispers without turning.

'I think so.'

'He's still here.'

'The Minister Prime?'

'Obviously.'

I check my thinkwatch. 'It should have already happened.'

From the back, I see Hart shaking his head. 'Wait here.'

I start to ask how long I can safely remain here until the person working in this office arrives but Hart closes the door with a solid click. I check my thinkwatch again and it is already four minutes past the time when Imrin was supposed to create a diversion.

There are no windows in the room, with a strip light across the ceiling providing the only illumination. The previous time I was here, I was so annoyed at the information Hart had kept from me that I didn't take in any of the surroundings. Now I approach the books and scan along the spines before taking one at random from the shelf. It is heavy and it feels strange to see so many books in the same place. In Martindale, there are only a handful across the whole village, with most of the information we need available through our thinkwatches or thinkpads. I put the book back on the shelf and check my thinkwatch again, cursing Imrin under my breath and wondering what has happened to him.

Trying to stay calm, I look at the thinkpad that has been left on the desk, which flashes to life as it senses my thinkwatch. As the main screen comes up, it asks for authorisation but I press the strip of borodron against the screen and it skips through to a picture of a map. I only know what the outline of Britain looks like because of the Reckoning programmes each year when we get the results.

I try to find Martindale on the map and zoom into roughly the area where I think it might be. It is only when I move in closer that I realise it isn't the place names that are important. Dotted around the map are small clusters of black blotches marked as 'rebels'.

Porter told me there was still fighting going on and although there aren't too many places marked around the country, he is right. I count nine bunches, most of which are close to the castle where we are. That doesn't sound like many but then I don't know how many people are in each group. It could be one person fighting by themselves, or it could be hundreds of people, all wanting to overthrow the King. There isn't even an indication from the markings if they are aware of each other.

With one eye on the door, I slide my thinkwatch along the map, scanning the dots, before shutting the thinkpad down again. The quality of my copies won't be brilliant and I have no idea how I might get to use them but it feels somehow reassuring that there are others out there who also feel the King is unfit to rule.

I check the time again. Imrin should have caused his disturbance over seven minutes ago but just as I am thinking he has failed, the door rattles open and Hart is standing there.

'Quick, the Minister Prime has just gone – he's left his office door unlocked.'

'What did he say?'

'Something about a disturbance in the boys' dorm. He went tearing off with a Kingsman.'

As I leave the office, I note the 'Home Affairs Minister' sign over the top and a small black scanner next to the door.

'Why was that office open?' I ask Hart as we hurry along the corridor. The scanner is the same as the ones from the zoo and medical area that only open for the personal frequency of the correct occupant's thinkwatch.

'I have access because I work for him,' Hart says, holding up his wrist.

'Why did the Minister Prime leave his door open?'

'When there's an urgent problem, he always rushes off without re-engaging the lock. He's done it at least once a week since I started working here.'

I use my thinkwatch to shut down the camera above the

door for ninety seconds and Hart pushes it open. 'None of the other Ministers are due here for fifteen minutes or so but that's not the problem. If he runs there and back and only takes a minute to sort out whatever's going on, that gives you around five minutes maximum, so get on with it.'

Hart pulls the door shut but doesn't click it closed. At first I am distracted by the sheer scale and gluttony of the place. The Minister Prime's office is bigger than the medical bay, with huge paintings on every wall and heavy, expensive rugs spread generously around the floor. A massive thick wooden desk is directly opposite the door; above that is a huge animal's head stuffed and hanging on the wall. I have never seen one for real but I know they are called elephants, and the dead creature's long trunk hangs lifelessly towards the floor. It is both awful and amazing at the same time. At either end of the room are more enormous bookcases, packed with heavy-looking volumes, and there are wooden cabinets pressed up against the far wall.

'Come on,' I mutter to myself as my heart jumps and brings me back to reality. I dash across the room, struggling not to slide on the shiny parts of the floor until I am behind the desk. As I fall into the seat, I check my thinkwatch to see that I have already lost just over a minute of the time Hart has given me.

On the desk are two thinkpads which I turn on and then press the borodron to the screens to make them function, all the while cursing under my breath at the time this has taken. When they are fully operational, I have just three minutes left.

I only have a vague idea of where I am supposed to be looking within the Minister Prime's file system and am operating solely from Hart's partial information. As my eyes flick from one thinkpad to the other, I realise one contains documents about the castle itself, the other seems to hold information on things outside the castle walls. Focusing on the thinkpad with information about the castle, I scan through blueprints, order sheets and masses of personal information on the senior Kingsmen.

If I had the time, it would all be valuable but it isn't completely necessary for what I am trying to do. As I work quickly, I almost miss a list of names, before skipping back to it. It takes me a few seconds to realise it is every Offering since the Reckoning began. It's not what I am looking for but I am transfixed by the length of it: over four hundred people, each of whom has either the department they are working in or the word 'dead' next to their name.

Another check of the thinkwatch and there are under two minutes to go now.

I flick through my thinkwatch and set it to sync, watching the orange hue pulse before pressing it to the thinkpad screen. Each name flashes across the monitor but it seems to happen in slow motion. I see my own name, Pietra's,

Imrin's, Hart's, and Jela's. And then there is a name I don't recognise with 'AWOL' next to it. I want to go back but in the fraction of a second it takes me to register what it has said, it disappears again. When the sync is complete, I check the time again and have a little over one minute left.

Working quicker than before, I use both hands on separate parts of the thinkpad screen, frantically searching for what Hart has promised me is there somewhere.

I jump as I hear a gentle tapping on the wooden door. It echoes around the room, taunting me that time is nearly up but my hands cannot move as quickly as I need them to.

Tap, tap, tap, tap.

I want to shout at Hart, to tell him I know that time is running out, but instead the noise increases both in volume and intensity until the door bursts open and Hart is standing there, out of breath and red in the face.

'He's around the corner. You've got to go now.'

My eyes flick to the screen where I have finally found the information I need. Everything I hope to do rests on what is in front of me; the end game tantalisingly close.

I press my thinkwatch to the screen. 'I need another minute.'

'You don't have a minute!' Hart's aggressive whisper is so full of fear that I almost forget what I am doing. I steady my wrist as I hear footsteps approaching.

'Silver, now.'

I meet Hart's terrified eyes. 'I can't. I've got it.'

'How long?'

'Thirty seconds.'

'Oh no . . .'

The footsteps are so loud I can almost feel them echoing through me. I catch Hart's eyes one more time as his flick towards the cabinets at the back, and then he is gone, charging into the hallway.

I hear raised voices and a cry of 'what were you doing in there' just as the information finishes copying. I clear the screens, but there is no time to shut the thinkpads down before I dive towards one of the wooden cabinets, wrenching the doors open, stepping inside and closing them again just as I hear Hart screaming an anguished 'no'.

29

There is a slim crack where the cabinet doors don't quite meet and I angle myself into the corner, so I can see the office door. The Minister Prime is pinning Hart to the wall by his throat, squeezing with his fingers and pressing his forearm hard into Hart's chest. I remember Porter telling me his real name, Bathix, but the thought makes me shiver. Hart is feebly swinging his legs, before Bathix turns and throws him to the floor then calmly closes the door.

Hart is on all fours coughing loudly and I feel myself wincing as the Minister Prime runs at him, kicking him brutally in the chest. The crack of boot on bone reverberates around the room, leaving Hart gurgling in pain.

'Shut. Up,' Bathix says, punctuating each word, before running a gloved hand through his thin black hair. He turns around and picks up a chair, then places it in the centre of the room next to where Hart is crawling around and sits on it, glaring at him.

'What were you doing in my office?'

Hart mumbles something I can't hear but I'm not sure they're complete words anyway as Bathix stands and kicks him again in the ribs. Hart rolls over in pain, spitting out a flurry of blood, groaning and holding his chest.

Bathix's eyes scan around the room, darting past the cabinet I am in before he notices the thinkpads. He runs out of my view and I hear a clattering of equipment followed by a loud bang. Hart is struggling for breath, his chin drenched with blood as the Minister howls in fury before dashing back into view and pinning Hart to the floor. I can see his knee angled, pressing hard into Hart's chest. Hart whimpers in pain as the bigger man pushes down on ribs that are likely already broken.

'What were you doing in my office?' Bathix's face is only a few centimetres away from Hart's and I can see flecks of spit splattering over him.

Hart's lips are moving but no words are coming out; instead there is a gurgle that becomes a vicious cough. The Minister Prime stands and wipes the splashed speckles of blood from his face, before leaning over and punching Hart across the face. First there is a crunch of fist on jaw and then a second, more sickening, splat as Hart's head bounces off the floor.

Bathix stands over the unconscious teenager and stares towards his desk, unmoving. Underneath him, a puddle of dark blood begins to pool as Hart's head flops to the side. I feel tears in my eyes, knowing his plight is entirely down to me. If I had been quicker and not spent so much time being fascinated by the elephant's head, or taking information I didn't come for, I would have been out of the door and in the laboratories by now and Hart wouldn't be unconscious.

I feel so annoyed at myself and so upset at Hart's predicament that I have to bite my lip to stop myself crying. Bathix is drumming his fingers against the borodron encasing his arms. The steady rhythm reverberates towards me. He turns and strides back to his desk out of my view, from where I hear his muffled voice talking to someone.

I try to hold my breath as much as I can as my mind drifts to my own dilemma. Hiding in the cabinet was the easy part – getting out undetected isn't going to be so simple. There is only one door into the office and, even from where I am, I can see the small dark scanner on the wall, which means that when it is locked properly, not only is the Minister Prime the only person who can get in, he is also the only person who can get out. My thoughts are interrupted as the door bursts open. A Kingsman hurries in and Bathix hisses at him to close the door.

'Am I taking him to medical?' the Kingsman asks.

The Minister lunges across the room. 'Of course you're not taking him to medical, you imbecile.'

'Sorry, Sir.'

'Take him to the dungeons and dump him there with some bread or something.'

'You want me to leave him food?'

'Are you questioning me?' Bathix's tone is of absolute rage and the Kingsman cowers away from him.

'No, Sir.'

'He can't die, not yet, I need to find out exactly what he was doing.'

'Shall I inform the King?'

The Minister steps forward and brutally backhands the officer. 'Don't be a fool. If I wanted the King to know, I would have called him here myself.'

The revelation that the Minister Prime keeps his own secrets startles me as I assumed both he and the King worked together for the same cause. It does make some sort of sense; if Bathix thought Hart had found important information on his thinkpad, the last thing he would want would be for the King to find out he had been careless by leaving his office unlocked. That makes it all the more likely I will not get another chance to access his files again, assuming I can get out of his office in the first place.

The Kingsman straightens his back and apologises once more. For a moment, I think the Minister Prime is going to hit him again but he lowers his arm.

'Just get him out of here, take him downstairs and, whatever you do, keep your mouth shut.'

'Yes, Sir.' The Kingsman hauls Hart up to his feet and then places him over his shoulder before carrying him towards the door. 'I'm going to need a bit of a hand here,' he says, clearly struggling.

'What's wrong with you?' Bathix grunts in annoyance, then crosses the room and opens the door.

'I'm not sure I'm going to be able to carry him all the way to the dungeons.'

'Well, I'm not carrying him.'

'I could call for someone else . . . ?'

'You will not. I'll help you to the stairs and then you're on your own. Throw him down there if you have to.'

The Minister Prime grabs Hart's feet, the Kingsman his head. Together they edge out of the room. I hold my breath, thinking the guard is going to pull the door closed but as he removes a hand, Hart slips and he scrambles to recover as Bathix berates him.

As soon as he disappears from view, I open the cabinet's doors and rush to the exit, skimming around the pool of Hart's blood that has congealed half on the hard floor, half on one of the rugs. I know from Imrin's maps that the stairs are barely thirty seconds away but it will take them slightly longer to get there because of Hart's weight. I count to fifteen and then press the button on my thinkwatch to stop the cameras for the second and final time today. I poke my head around the door to check there is nobody there and then I run for it.

I know I am being reckless, but it almost feels like I have

forgotten Hart's advice – 'be plain and blend in' – as I tear through the passages, dart around the cameras and race to the far end of the castle. I have no idea if anyone has seen me as I arrive breathless at the entrance to the kitchen.

All the rules I have made for myself over the past few weeks are tossed aside as I knock on the door. My heart is pounding, partly because of the running, but mainly because of everything that has happened in the past few minutes. I can't stop thinking of the blood I had to step around. When there is no answer after a few seconds, I knock again, harder the second time. Probably luckily, when the door is opened, Faith is standing there. 'Silver?'

'Is Imrin in there?'

'Imrin?'

'Yes.'

'The Indian guy?'

'Yes.'

She looks at me confused, as if about to ask how I know him, but then she tells me to wait a minute.

When Imrin does appear in his kitchen uniform, he is furious – rightfully so.

'What are you doing here?' he asks, desperately trying not to raise his voice. 'It was your idea never to acknowledge each other.'

'I know. It's Hart, he was hurt and caught and taken to the dungeons. The Minister Prime beat him unconscious.'

I'm not sure what I'm expecting, but Imrin certainly doesn't seem to share the concern I have. 'What do you think we can do? We don't even know what it's like in the dungeons, let alone if there's a way to get him out. Did you get what you needed?'

'Yes, but I'm not going anywhere without Hart.'

Imrin slams his hand into the stone wall. 'What are you on about? It's going to be hard enough making this work as it is. I risked loads for you this morning already. We wedged the dorm's door shut from the inside with this scrap of wood we chipped out from one of the bed frames. When the Minister Prime showed up, he was furious. We were shouting through the door that we couldn't open it as he was bellowing and kicking it. Eventually, I grabbed the wood and pocketed it, then he burst through. He whacked one of the Kingsmen for being weak and then told us all that if he found out any of us were responsible, he would personally rip our arms off.'

I touch him on the shoulder but he shakes me off. 'I can't go without him. It's my fault he's there.'

'You know you're putting everyone at risk?'

'I know.'

'These should be things we're deciding together, not something that you go off on your own to do.'

'Hart is going to die if we don't do something.'

'*We* don't have to do anything – going to the Minister

Prime's office was your idea. We could already have been out through the medical bay.'

'You know why I went to the office.'

Imrin is pacing, exasperated and furious. I have never seen him like this. He takes a deep breath. 'Do you think the King is going to kill him?'

I shake my head. 'It's not the King, it's all the Minister Prime. He doesn't want the King knowing Hart might have been in his office, checking his files.'

Imrin stops walking back and forth and looks towards the door. 'I've got to get back before I'm noticed.'

'I know – but you're going to stick to the plan, aren't you?'

Imrin shrugs and, as I lean forward to try to kiss him, he pulls away, his eyes full of hurt and mistrust.

He opens the door and steps through, before poking his head back around to say one final thing: 'You ask too much, Silver.'

I trudge away thinking through his final statement but it's hard to argue that he's wrong. It should have been our plan, not mine. Instead, I have ploughed ahead doing what I wanted to. He's also right that we could be out of the castle by now. If nothing else, there are enough sheets on the beds in the medical area to hastily put something together which would enable us to lower ourselves half-way down the wall until we can drop the rest. I make my way through the castle until I am at the laboratories but I can remember next to nothing about the rest of the day, except that Porter doesn't make a fuss about me being slightly late.

In the dorm that evening, I lie on my bed trying to think about what I can do with the information I now have. I want to examine the list of Offerings I took from the Minister Prime and find out as much as I can about the person listed as 'AWOL'. Is it someone who escaped? If so what happened to their family and where are they now? As my mind drifts inexorably back to Martindale, I wonder if perhaps Imrin had the right idea – maybe we should have simply made a run for it and chanced the fact our think-watches would come to life outside the castle walls?

I feel tired as the door opens and Ignacia walks in. She tells us not to bother getting changed but to follow her as we are off to the hall again. It is not banquet night and I have only bad memories of the last time this happened, with Lumin humiliated and beaten in front of us. I don't even know if he is dead or alive; Porter has not mentioned him since that day.

Everyone seems to be sharing my unease as we move through the corridors in silence except for our footsteps until we reach the main hall. Inside there is no large table and the area is clear except for a row of benches. The boys are already lined up and we take our places. The Minister

Prime is standing on the lower part of the floor with us, flanked by four Kingsmen. The lights are dim and the seats that stretch above us are as empty as the King's box.

The Minister Prime exchanges a glance and a nod with Ignacia as the hall's doors slam shut and he starts to pace in front of us, speaking crisply. 'Many weeks ago, I reminded you that there are rules we must abide by and I told you that any untoward behaviour must be reported.'

He stops striding and turns to face us, running his eyes along the line. I feel certain he is about to reveal Hart and ask us what we know but instead he begins walking again, his words sharp and over-pronounced.

'Now, before I need to force it, would any of you like to step forward and confess?'

At the far end of the line, among the boys, there is a shuffling but nobody stands. I have the overwhelming feeling that I am looking particularly guilty and can feel a bead of sweat tracing its way down my back and force myself not to shiver. The Minister Prime stops when he is back in the centre, again looking from one end of the line to the other, trying to make eye contact with us all. I match his gaze momentarily before he moves on.

As he reaches the end, his eyes narrow menacingly. 'That was a very, very bad decision one of you just made. Luckily, somebody took my advice and stepped forward to report inappropriate and unpatriotic behaviour.'

I had been thinking Hart was to be paraded but instead the Minister Prime focuses his attention on the boys' benches. His next words make me shudder so badly that the bead of sweat turns into a waterfall.

'Stand up, Imrin Kapoor.'

30

I try not to gasp as I look sideways to see Imrin rising to his feet. His eyes are locked with the Minister Prime's.

'Imrin has a very interesting story to tell,' the Minister says.

I feel a hand on my back and turn to see Pietra's eyes wide. She nods towards the door as if to tell me to go but I turn back to see the stare-off between Imrin and the Minister Prime.

'Would you like to repeat in front of everyone else what you told me earlier?' the Minister Prime says.

My heart is beating so quickly that I feel as if I could collapse. I try to breathe in but something isn't right and I end up struggling for breath. All I can feel is a sinking sensation as Imrin starts to speak, his words slow and deliberate.

'I found a passage that leads out of the boys' dormitory, Sir.'

The Minister Prime purrs a response. 'When did you discover it?'

'A couple of days ago, Sir.'

A lie.

'And what did you do about the tunnel?'

'I followed it, Sir. It leads to a corridor somewhere between the male and female dorms.'

There is a stunned shock along the full length of the bench. Only three people that I'm aware of know about the tunnels: Imrin, Pietra and myself.

'What did you find?'

'A map.'

The Minister Prime spins and claps as a Kingsman steps forward and hands over a roll of paper. I don't need to look twice to know it is the map we created together. He unrolls it, stretching it out for everyone to see. He only has one of the pages – of the floor we are on with the hall, not the one above which includes the recently added medical area.

There are more gasps along the line although, strangely, they seem to be more in admiration than anything else. I hear someone say the word 'camera' quietly before the Minister Prime rips the paper in half and tosses it to the ground.

'Did you have anything to do with the creation of this map?'

'No, Sir. I just found it.'

Another lie. Imrin is surprisingly good at it.

'Why do you think somebody might be making a note of where all the cameras are on this particular floor?'

Imrin coughs but I can tell it is put on. 'I don't know, Sir.'

The Minister Prime laughs heartily. 'Come now, Imrin, an intelligent, honest young man such as yourself – you must have some ideas?'

It is as if the two are putting on a show for everyone, fake-laughing and palling around just to torture me for a little longer. I feel Pietra's hand on my back again but don't turn to face her this time.

Imrin stammers through his reply. 'I guess . . . if someone was trying to escape, they might want to know where all the cameras were . . .'

An accepting nod. 'Why would you want to escape from serving your King?'

'I don't know, Sir.'

He points towards one of the other boys on the bench. 'Would you want to escape?'

'No, er, Sir.'

The Minister Prime jabs his finger towards three more Offerings and everyone responds that they wouldn't want to leave. If I wasn't so scared, the charade would be laughable.

'So, what do we have here?' He holds out his gloved hands and counts on his fingers. 'An attempt to escape, sneaking out of permitted areas, unauthorised materials.

That is quite a list. I suppose the question is who is responsible for all of this?'

Imrin wipes his hands on his trousers but it gives me little comfort that he is sweating too.

'Do you know?' the Minister demands.

'Yes, Sir.'

'How do you know?'

'Because I saw the person. She forced me not to say anything.'

'She?'

'Yes, there is a second tunnel that leads to the girls' dorm.'

The girls are now shuffling uneasily. I can tell that, aside from Pietra, none of them knows about this.

'Did you follow this second tunnel?'

'Not really, Sir. She showed me where she had stored some blankets. I think she snuck out regularly.'

The Minister Prime scratches his chin, glancing along the line at us. I meet his eyes again because I don't know what else to do. Inside it feels as if my stomach has fallen out. There is an emptiness I cannot explain. I feel as if I am drifting again; watching myself from above. I am a scared, small girl who has almost certainly tried to do too much.

From above there is a clang as the door at the back of the royal box opens. The King staggers in holding a bottle of wine in each hand, clearly drunk. Behind him there are two Kingsmen, one of whom seems to be there to hold him up. For the first time, he is wearing something other than his usual robes – what looks like a pair of pyjamas; they are white and ill-fitting, with a crusty-looking red stain on the front.

He fumbles his way to the front of the box and looks down upon us before muttering something inaudible. The Minister Prime seems annoyed to have been cut off mid-flow but bows graciously. 'Welcome, Your Majesty. I was just dealing with the matter at hand.'

The other Kingsmen move from Ignacia and the Minister Prime until two of them are standing behind our bench and the other pair are near the door.

The King mutters something impossible to hear but the Minister Prime ignores him.

'I suppose there are only a couple more questions, Imrin. Firstly, how did she force you?'

Slowly Imrin raises his shirt to reveal the burns, bruises and scars underneath. Ignacia steps towards him to take a closer look. The Minister Prime is unmoved while the King doesn't appear to know what's going on; he is staring up-wards towards the lights.

The Minister Prime nods slowly. 'There can only be one final question: who did that to you?'

I hold my breath and try to imagine him saying any

name that isn't mine but from the moment he stood, I knew what he was doing.

He turns, he trembles, he points, he lies.

'It was her – Silver Blackthorn.'

Everyone turns to face me, but it is Faith's confused expression I notice first, staring as if to ask what's going on. Only Pietra understands but she says nothing. There is no point in both of us getting into trouble, especially considering it is nothing to do with her.

As I am grabbed roughly from behind and pulled to my feet, my eyes lock with Jela's. There is some sort of understanding, but it is mainly sorrow. She knows more than anyone the type of fate that could await me. The Kingsman behind has my hair and yanks me towards him. I hear the ripping sound before I feel the pain. I try not to scream but, perhaps to test my resilience, he slaps me across the back of the head. I manage to shake my head clear, although the Kingsman still has my arms pinned behind me.

'He's lying,' I shout.

The Minister Prime looks to Imrin. 'She says you're a liar, that you made all of this up.'

'I didn't, Sir.'

He rubs his stomach for good measure, as if emphasising how I have somehow hurt him. The Minister Prime nods gently and places a hand on Imrin's shoulder.

'You should all know that we have now blocked these

passages. Any attempt to find or re-enter them will be dealt with extremely harshly.'

He tells Imrin to sit and then turns to the remaining girls on the bench. 'How many of you knew about this?'

I know the answer is only Pietra but silently plead with her not to say anything. The Kingsman is pulling my arms further up my back until they feel as if they are going to be ripped out of their sockets. I try to push myself onto tiptoes to ease the pressure but cannot stop myself from squealing in pain. There is a grunt of enjoyment from behind as his knees connect with the back of mine, forcing me to stumble and increasing the strain on my shoulders.

Nobody steps forward as the Minister Prime looks towards Ignacia and then strides back and forth in front of the girls. 'You're lying. You must know something.'

Another squeeze of my arms, another yelp, more silence from the girls.

The Minister Prime nods acceptingly, a smile slowly spreading across his face. 'In that case, you will all be punished.' He looks up towards the box, where the King is hanging over the edge. 'Your Majesty, I suggest that if you are looking for a champion tomorrow, then it should be an all-female affair.'

'No!'

The words are out of my mouth before I can control myself. The punishment is instant as the Kingsman kicks my legs out from under me. As I begin to fall he lets go of my arms and grabs my hair, hauling me back into a standing position. I try to stop myself crying but it isn't a voluntary thing by now. Instead the sheer pain has tears running uncontrollably down my face.

The King jolts in surprise, possibly because of the noise I made, but it looks as if he has just woken up. He waves his hand, muttering something that sounds like 'fine'.

The girls begin exchanging glances of terror. I feel nothing but guilt as a few of them glare towards me, wondering why I have put them in this situation. I can't explain from the position I am in that I was trying to do something to help everyone.

The second Kingsman grabs one of my arms, with the one who has been torturing me taking my other. The Minister Prime turns to the bench of boys, then back to the girls. 'Men, you will feast tomorrow as a reward for Imrin's brave decisions. Women, you will be locked in your room until tomorrow evening when you will be brought back here for the King to decide what to do with you.'

He turns to me, his smile wide to let me know he is going to milk as much of the moment as he can. With a slight nod, the Kingsman slices through the band of my thinkwatch, sending it clattering to the floor before he stamps on it.

'And you . . . what do you have to say for yourself?'

I look towards the girls on the bench, where they are hugging each other. Faith is in tears, Pietra doesn't know where to look and Jela has her arms wrapped around herself again.

'If you touch them, any of them, I will kill you myself.' I try to sound convincing but my arms and shoulders hurt so much that it is more of a squeal.

The Minister Prime looks into my eyes, perplexed, and then bursts out laughing. 'Are you threatening me?'

I nod before I feel my hair being pulled backwards again and the sharpness of a knife next to my throat. I close my eyes, ready for the blade to slice. The Kingsman's arm is tense but willing, as he asks what he should do next, running the sharp edge across my windpipe.

31

I've heard people say that if you lose one of your senses, then the others become sharper but as I stand with my eyes closed, it feels as if my hearing has gone too. Everyone's words flow into each other until I can barely distinguish between their voices. Somehow, it doesn't seem to matter as I feel the blade removed from my neck and I am half-dragged, half-carried away. Through everything, I keep my eyes clamped shut. I try to ignore the pain in my shoulder and my arms until the sensation becomes almost pleasant. It's hard to describe but it's like my body is focusing so much on the stinging in my shoulder that the rest of me has been freed from feeling anything. Someone hits me low in my back but I don't even flinch and I certainly don't open my eyes. Someone, perhaps the same person, pinches the back of my neck but all I recognise is the material of their gloves; I don't make a sound and I don't open my eyes.

The voices from before quickly disappear with the clang of what I assume is the hall's main door and then everything comes rushing back. Suddenly I can hear every echoing footstep, each sound of a sword blade brushing against borodron. The rhythmic nature is almost soothing as I breathe in to smell my own coppery blood. Somehow even that doesn't faze me. It is as if my body parts have switched off but, at the same time, I am utterly aware of what is happening to me.

Stomp, stomp, stomp. Rattle, rattle, rattle. The sound of a scanner, the swish of a door. Stomp, stomp, stomp. Rattle, rattle, rattle. The sound of a scanner, the clang of a door.

Then the slow pulse of water dripping somewhere close to me.

I open my eyes gradually, allowing them to adjust to the dim singular shaft of overhead light and the overall darkness. As I squint and stare around, the distant corners are too dark, so instead I focus on the space immediately close to me.

Despite the strange mix of old and new that I have grown up in, I'm not sure if I have ever been in a place more ancient than where I am now. The ground is hard stone, with small piles of straw dumped haphazardly around the enclosure I am in. If I were to lie on the floor, the space is perhaps my height and a half wide. On two sides there is a thick stone wall which feels damp to touch and leaves a sticky wet residue on my hand. At the bottom there are small crusted patches where pieces of straw have clung to the water and formed a sort of paste that has dried out and become wet over and over. On the other two sides are thick bars of heavy metal that stretch from the floor to the ceiling and are tightly packed so I can barely reach one of my skeletal arms through.

I can see other cells adjacent and opposite mine. There are perhaps seven or eight in total, with a row of stone steps in the centre that lead to a sliding door, where I can see the faint outline of a borodron scanner that seems utterly out of place compared to the rest of the room.

If Imrin's map was still of any concern, then I would at least now be able to add the dungeon to it.

'Hello?'

A voice resonates around the stone walls but it is much more of a croak than his usual voice.

'Hart?'

'Silver?'

'Yes, it's me. Are you all right?'

In the cell at the far end from me, I can see the faint shape of someone pressed up against the bars. There are at least two cells in between us but I mirror his pose, hoping he can see me.

'What are you doing here?' he asks.

I tell him about the tunnels, the map and Imrin. He sounds stunned by the passageways and says that as far as he knows, nobody discovered the boys' one when he was living there. There is the very real possibility, of course, that the secret exits have been found many times over the years, simply that no one has known what to do with that adjoining corridor and so they have stayed quiet.

'Why did he go to the Minister Prime?' Hart asks, sounding tired.

'I suppose he thought it was the best thing he could do.'

Hart is angry on my behalf. 'For himself. Look at what he's done to everyone else.'

I stay silent as the feeling slowly begins to return to my shoulder, which causes the knock-on effect of the rest of my body starting to feel the aches and bumps from the way the Kingsmen hurt me.

'You know they're going to kill us, don't you?' Hart says.

'Surely we've known that since we found out what being an Offering actually meant?'

'Yes, but they'll do it in front of the others. They'll have us fight each other, force one of us to kill the other just to watch us agonise over it, and then kill the other anyway. I've seen it before.'

I feel a calm I'm not sure I should. In many ways, the way he has described it sounds almost a relief – this will finally be over.

'Your advice about being plain and blending in was perfect,' I say. 'But it was never going to work for me in the end. Imrin told me to be the tortoise but I've always been that hare, racing into things.'

Hart doesn't reply. I know the reference is lost on him but it feels nice to admit to myself.

'It's no way to live, though, is it?' he eventually says. 'I told you what to do despite hating myself for it. Each day you set out to be as unspectacular as you possibly can. You call men you despise "Sir", you do what you're told without question, you turn a blind eye and tell yourself that what you see happening around you isn't what it is. At least you had a go . . .'

Drip, drip, drip.

'You had a go too,' I remind him. 'You told me what was on the Minister Prime's thinkpad and then took the blame for me.'

Hart starts to speak but it turns into a ferocious deep cough that he can't control. I ask if he is okay but I don't think he even hears me. It is minutes before he manages to calm himself again.

'Not much use now, is it?' he finally says.

'Your mum and dad would be proud that you put yourself in the firing line to try to help everyone else.'

Drip, drip, drip.

I wonder if Hart has fallen asleep; his last words sounded tired. As I am trying to bundle the straw together in an attempt to make something faintly approaching a bed, he finally replies.

'What do you think will happen to them?'

It's a question that has no easy answer. What should I say? That Kingsmen could already be on their way now to capture and torture Hart's parents until he tells the truth about what he was doing in the Minister Prime's office?

'I think they'll be just fine.'

It sounds like the right thing to say but I have no idea if he believes that any more than I believe my mother and Colt will be okay. I remember Opie's final promise to me that he would look after them.

'Do you want to hear a story?'

Hart's voice cuts through the rapidly decreasing temperature. I can hear the shiver in his tone, the same one I am feeling through my body. I bundle more straw together in an attempt to make myself warm, stretching into the adjoining cell and pulling through any extra material that I can reach. In the aftermath of everything that has happened, his offer seems beautifully surreal.

'I'd love to.'

'What would you like to hear about?'

'Tell me about home.'

I bury myself in the straw, ignoring the stench of everyone else who has lain in this place before. The thought that Lumin may have been here crosses my mind and perhaps I was hoping he might still be around. Instead, it is just me and Hart.

'I know we were never really friends, but I've known

your mum my whole life,' Hart says, as the mere mention of her brings a lump to my throat that surpasses any pain I am feeling in my shoulder. 'When I was a kid, I was forever getting into scraps and scrapes and damaging my clothes. My mum would shout at me and then call yours over to help. They would sit together, chatting away while my trousers and shirts got stitched back together.'

The straw makes me feel surprisingly cosy and within moments of closing my eyes, I am in Hart's living room in front of the fire listening to our parents gossiping.

'What do they talk about?'

Hart laughs, but that leads into another cough before he continues. 'Mainly about us! Your mum would say how she couldn't keep track of you because you were always off making a nuisance of yourself. She'd ask if I knew anything but we didn't hang around with the same people.'

My back and ribs hurt but I can't stop myself from laughing. 'How old would I have been?'

'Maybe nine or ten? I remember this one time at the end of summer and she came knocking on our door. She asked if any of us had seen you because you'd been out all day. We hadn't but she was looking a little upset, so me and my dad went out to help look for you. We were calling your name but there was no response and then it started raining. It wasn't those little showers we get, but huge thick dollops of the stuff. I remember my dad's face because he looked at me as if to say we were mad being out in this weather. Neither of us wanted to leave your mum though. She was still knocking on doors and then . . . you were just there. You were wandering down the main street soaked to the skin with a huge grin on your face. That white piece of hair of yours was stuck in front of one of your eyes and I remember there was this smudge of dirt on your cheek. Your mum started running . . .'

'I remember . . .'

'And she just grabbed you.'

'She was shouting at me for being late. I'd been in the woods messing around and lost track of time. It got dark really late and it was only then I realised . . .'

'. . . how late it was. I know. But you were so bemused at why she was there. She was hugging you and shouting and I just remember you looking over at me as if to say, "What's going on?"'

'That's pretty much what I was thinking.'

'But that's how I'll always remember you; that drowned girl with the silver streak of hair stuck to her face being simultaneously hugged and shouted at. When I first saw you being shown around the castle, I couldn't quite remember the name but as soon as you told me, I was back on the street that day.'

I try to say thank you but cannot get the words out. The

lump in my throat has grown but my tears are now of love and happiness, rather than pain.

'Silver . . .'

I swallow hard and force back any more tears. 'Yes?'

'If we are made to hurt each other tomorrow, do what you have to. I'm not going to fight back.'

'It won't come to that.'

Drip, drip, drip.

'It might.'

The cold bites across my face, gnawing at my skin as a breeze skims through from somewhere I don't know. I tug at the straw until it is covering every part of me except for my mouth, although my lips are beginning to freeze.

'Trust me,' I say. 'Tomorrow is going to be a bit different to what you think.'

32

The single overhead light is the only one we have and the solitary indication of daytime is a faint glow shimmering through the crack around the door at the top of the stairs. I am so cold that it is almost impossible to move my legs. My arms and shoulders are already stiff from the way the Kingsmen pulled my limbs around and the freezing temperature has only made it worse. I have slept in pitiful fits and starts, jolting awake every few minutes with the drip, drip, drip serving as a constant reminder of where I am.

Nobody comes to see either of us and we spend the day telling each other stories about home. Hart insists he is fine, although his cough is fierce and getting worse. I can see spatters of blood on the floor of his cell through the gloom. Gingerly I walk the few paces from one end of my cell to the other, trying to keep my legs and arms stretched and moving so they do not stiffen up any worse than they already are.

I feel strangely naked without my thinkwatch. It's not just about knowing the time of day, or knowing if I am supposed to be somewhere; it has become a part of life –

the first thing you check each morning and the last thing each evening. Even the relatively new orange face felt somehow right.

Eventually, we hear a clicking sound and the door slides upwards. Light floods the room and three, perhaps four Kingsmen enter the dungeon. The blazing white light from the doorway feels alien to my eyes and I struggle to keep them open as the guards' boots clunk on the floor before the door to my cell is wrenched open and I feel thick fingers clamping around my shoulders and arms. I tell them I'll go willingly but it makes no difference as their podgy digits poke painfully into my bruises.

More stomping, rattling and scanner noises as my eyes gradually become used to being out of the gloom. I hear Hart being dragged behind me and know he is in a far worse state than I am. He is groaning and coughing as the Kingsmen berate him for not moving quickly enough. There is a thud of boot on bone but the pair of guards directing me have such a tight grip that it is impossible for me to turn and see what is happening.

We are taken through to the main hall, which already seems full. In the centre is the banqueting table with the boys sitting on either side and the girls on a separate bench at the far end of the hall. The King is in his royal box already eating, the Minister Prime standing rigidly, watching us enter. The lights are bright and it is impossible to see if there are any people peering down from the seats above.

Hart and I are thrown into a corner at the back of the arena area, with two Kingsmen waiting behind us, hands poised by their swords. There are two more guards by the main door, one by the entrance to the kitchen and another standing behind the King. Six in total, I think to myself, knowing I still haven't seen anything to disprove Imrin's theory. I look towards the bench along the side where Jela, Pietra, Faith and one or two others are peeking at me. I try to read their faces but it is only Pietra who shows anything approaching determination. The others seem defeated and a couple don't even acknowledge I am there.

As for the boys, I see Rush chancing quick glances in our direction, but never for longer than a second or two. I don't blame him. Imrin is sitting at the head of the table, facing the royal box directly. I can see a huge stuffed turkey on the table in front of him and cannot stop my mouth from watering. It is over a day since I last ate and I have no idea how long ago it was that Hart was given food or water.

In the four corners of the room are cameras, each with a flashing red light.

The Minister Prime stretches out his arm for silence, before sitting and allowing the King to take charge. He is certainly in a better state than he was the previous evening;

smiling with the determined twinkle in his eyes that I was so used to seeing on the screen at home.

'My subjects, my Offerings . . . what a day it has been!' He spreads his arms wide and beams manically. Belatedly there is a slow ripple of applause as he points towards Hart and me. 'We have two traitors in our midst. People who think they are superior to you, my subjects.'

He pauses for a response, which he gets with a low booing and stamping of feet, but it feels subdued. The King then points towards the girls. 'We also have those who did not see fit to report unconstitutional behaviour.'

More booing but it feels quieter still. I wonder what Porter is doing in the seats above me. Is he watching? Is he jeering as well?

'We will deal with them later – but first we eat! We drink!'

Cheers that feel genuine – but then it does involve food, so it's perhaps not surprising.

At his cue, the boys around the table in the centre of the room start eating. I see Imrin piling turkey, ham and beef onto his plate, tearing and ripping it from his fork, then picking up extra pieces with his fingers. I don't take my eyes from him, watching him eat potatoes, carrots, fruit, and many other things. I know my stomach would never have managed half of what he has eaten – but with the food directly in front of us, the pain of hunger is suddenly compounded. Hart shuffles close by and one of the Kingsmen kicks him in the back. I try not to move myself, but my stomach is gurgling in protest at the tantalising smells drifting just a few metres from where we are. They could have left us in the dungeon for longer but this is a far better way of torturing us.

As the meal is coming to an end, the King stands again, peering down at the main table. 'My champion,' he says, indicating for Rush to stand. 'Would you take this to our guests?' He throws a thick chunk of meat onto the ground. Rush picks it up and brings it towards us. As he gets closer, he meets my eyes but doesn't have to say a word for me to know he is sorry. He holds the meat towards me but I can see the dark brown skin is covered with dust, sand and grime. It looks disgusting, yet the smell is so overwhelming that I stretch for it without even thinking. My finger has just made contact when a Kingsman steps forward and kicks my arm away. The meat falls to the floor and he stands on it, rotating his foot around a dozen times until it has been mashed firmly into the ground. I can hear the King bellowing with delight and amusement as the Kingsman finally steps back.

The steak is halfway between Hart and me, but it is now in an even worse state, covered with mud and filth, the sand from the floor completely covering it like a yellowy flour. Rush has edged away from us, embarrassed, but Hart and I are watching each other, the thought in both of our minds that we need to eat. He leans forward and picks it up as a low moan of disgust ripples around. He wipes the meat on the remains of his trousers, which are themselves caked in dried blood and grit, before putting it into his mouth and biting.

The King's laughter echoes around the area, if anything getting louder. I can hear him slapping his knees and turn to see him doubled over with tears streaming down his face as he points towards us and asks if everyone has seen.

I turn back to Hart, who is swallowing awkwardly, each throat movement appearing painful. Given that neither of us has had anything to drink in an entire day, it is no surprise. He hands me the mangled steak, which I take and then flick a few of the larger parts of dirt away.

'It could do with a bit of salt,' Hart says.

His timing, combined with our situation, makes me laugh as I take the biggest bite I can manage and then hand the steak back. My amusement seemingly confuses the King to such a degree that his derision stops in an instant. With a click of his stubby fingers, the Kingsman has wrenched the meat from Hart's hand and thrown it across the arena. I finish chewing and swallow what's in my mouth, trying to ignore the tiny flecks of sand which now coat my tongue.

'Maybe a bit of pepper too,' I add.

'Enough!' the King bellows. Any joy has gone from his voice and he sounds close to the edge of insanity once again.

The male Offerings are beckoned to the opposite side of the arena to the girls, as kitchen staff clear the tables until the space in the middle is empty. The King watches the whole operation, shaking with a fury I have no doubt is ready to erupt. Our insolence was the final straw.

Good.

'You,' he screeches, pointing towards me as I feel one of the Kingsmen hauling me to my feet and shunting me into the central area. I can feel everyone's eyes upon me. 'What's your name?'

'Silver Blackthorn.'

He stares at me, his greedy piggy eyes twitching, while I can see smears of food in his beard. In his other hand he has a bottle of wine.

'What's wrong with your hair?'

At first I'm not sure what he means but then it is obvious. I pull my silver streak forwards and then push it back over my head. 'Nothing, I was born like this.'

'Do you know why you're here?'

'Yes.'

'Are you ready to confess to your crimes?'

'Yes.'

He seems surprised as he takes a swig from the bottle. 'Get on with it, then.'

I deliberately look towards the Minister Prime as I reply. 'I confess that I made a map because I wanted to escape.'

'Really?'

The King doesn't seem to know what to make of me but I am still fixed on the Minister Prime. He isn't moving either but I notice his eyes flicker momentarily to the side.

'Yes, really. But I changed my mind before I ever got near to escaping because I had a better idea.'

I speak clearly and slowly, the words rehearsed in my head many times over. There is a hum of confusion around the people above me, who I cannot see. Even the King doesn't appear to know what to say. He stumbles over his words at first, before correcting himself. 'What idea?'

In a flash, I turn my attention back to the King, making sure he is watching me before I reply. 'My idea is to take you down.'

His brow shoots downwards, revealing what I would like to say are worry lines, although his expression is more likely one of confusion. Around me, there is uproar. Many of those unseen are jeering and shouting, although I don't doubt much of it is because they feel they have to, as opposed to them having any great loyalty.

'But you're just a girl?'

'Yes.'

'But . . .'

As the King stumbles, the Minister Prime rises theatrically to his feet and calls for a silence he gets. 'Enough,' he says sharply. 'I suggest we skip the planned search for a champion tonight, Your Highness.'

The King stares from me to him and nods gently.

The Minister Prime indicates towards the boys' bench. 'You.'

I turn to see Imrin pointing at himself in confusion. The Minister Prime makes some sort of sign at the Kingsmen at the front and one of them strides forward and grabs Imrin by the arm, throwing him towards me until we are just a metre apart.

'This farce is over.' The Minister Prime speaks in total contrast to the way he did with Imrin last night. 'Only a fool would believe she coerced you. Look at her.' His eyes narrow as he spits out his next words. 'I've always hated little snitches like you.'

He claps his hands and two Kingsmen approach. I look up to see them throwing two wooden bats onto the ground in between us. As I peer closer, I can see nails and pieces of metal sticking out from the meat of the bat.

'One each,' the Minister Prime orders. 'Now.'

With a shrug, I pick up one of the weapons and weigh it in my hands – it is nothing compared to the sword I held before. Imrin is doing the same and, for the first time, our eyes meet. His face is hard to read but when I see him, all I can remember are the moments we spent sitting under that blanket. He seems like a stranger now, weighing the bat in his hand as I clench the other one.

It feels as if everyone around us is holding their breath because it is so quiet. We both know what is coming.

The Minister Prime is staring at me, his eyes asking if I feel quite so clever now but then his thinkwatch buzzes. He lifts his wrist and shakes his head in annoyance before nodding to the two Kingsmen by the door. They both turn to leave as one of the two Kingsmen who were guarding Hart and me crosses to the main door, where he is joined by the one that was close to the kitchen door.

The Minister Prime scowls at us with another shake of his head. 'Your Highness, I apologise on behalf of these two for any pain they may have caused you with their disrespect.'

I look to the King. He has finished one bottle of wine and is just starting on another.

The Minister Prime turns back towards us. 'As your punishment, you can do whatever you want to each other. You have ten minutes – if there is no winner I'll get the Kingsmen to finish you both off. Whoever wins can come back tomorrow.' His voice is dismissive to the point of boredom, as if I have somehow spoiled his fun.

The Minister Prime claps his hands to signal the countdown has begun. I look at Imrin one final time as a low roar of approval goes up from the seats above us.

33

Imrin is twirling his bat exaggeratedly as we circle each other. I simply hold mine by my side. Already anything up to a minute has passed and we haven't gone near each other. Above us is a low murmur of discontent. I risk a momentary glance towards the Kingsmen, not wanting them to be involved in the way they were when Rush was staying clear of his fight. Imrin's eyes are still focused on me but it is like they are staring through, rather than at, me.

'Remember our window, Imrin?' I say but he doesn't stop edging around me. 'Remember our spot, under the blankets, remember what we said?'

In an instant, he has lunged towards me, swinging exaggeratedly, but I manage to step to one side and out of the way. I think of all the food he has had for strength and feel weaker than ever. Hart told me to do what I had to in order to stay alive and I can't help but hear his words skipping through my mind as I avoid another lunge.

Imrin stumbles a fraction off-balance and I leap forward, swinging quickly and accurately as the wood cracks him over the head.

There is an 'ooh' from above and I hear the King clapping, the booming eclipsing all other noises. I risk a glance upwards to see the Minister Prime sitting impassively. Spurred on, I smash Imrin in the legs as the bat makes a satisfyingly hollow-sounding thwack across his limbs.

The King roars a 'fight back', leaving me in no doubt about who he is backing. I step forward to land another blow. Then, as I swing downwards towards his chest, Imrin moves quickly, flicking the back of my knees and sending me sprawling. His swiftness takes me by surprise as I drop the bat, landing painfully on my wrists.

My stomach is screeching in pain, my head feels dizzy, but I roll to the side as his bat crashes into the ground mere centimetres away from me with a force I never would have guessed Imrin had in him.

'Remember what we said!' I say, but I am scrambling to my feet, not sure Imrin hears me. My eyes flash from the bat on the floor to him as I back away quickly, my arms out wide in submission. 'Imrin, do you remember?'

'Yes.'

I glance over my shoulder but the Kingsmen are close and I know I cannot move much further. Imrin slows his pace, knowing I am cornered as the buzz grows around us. I hear a girl's voice that could be Pietra's, but I can't be sure.

Imrin arches back with the bat but I have been fighting

with Opie for far too long not to know an opportunity when I see one. Springing off my heels, I jolt forward and crash into his legs, using his weight against him as he topples backwards. His bat clatters across the floor as I try to get to my feet but he is holding onto my injured shoulder. I squeal in pain and, even though he releases me, the damage is done as the fire screams through me.

I hit the ground shoulder-first and the whole side of my body goes numb, my vision clouded with grey stars that spring from the bright lights. I try to stand but the effort feels too much as I hear Imrin scrambling. Moments later he is standing above me, bat in hand.

It is as if the whole arena shrinks down to one person as I hear the King cackling and applauding, my ears blocking everyone else out. I hear his words perfectly: 'Finish her.'

My breathing is heavy, my chest tight and my fingers unresponsive as Imrin's silhouette takes a step closer, blocking the light until all I can see is the outline of his arms raised high, ready to strike.

34

Suddenly I hear what I have been waiting for. The King's cheers and demands fade until they are a slur of words that merge into one. I hear confusion all around and scramble onto my front, peering up to the King's box as he sinks into the seat. Half of his face has slumped, drool dripping from his paralysed lips, his eye hanging lazily. There are screams everywhere as the Minister Prime clambers over a barrier and leaps into the royal box, calling for help.

I hear the clatter of Imrin's bat hitting the floor and then his hand heaves me up by my good arm. There are pins and needles in my other and I am exhausted but the adrenaline is now starting to flow and my vision is clear.

'I thought you'd forgotten the routine,' I say.

'I didn't think we were going to need it after last night. I wondered why you kept going on about me remembering. I thought it was just for show.'

Imrin pulls me close and kisses me quickly but we both know it's time to move.

Hart staggers to his feet, as Rush takes the Kingsman next to him by surprise, spearing him with his own sword.

Four of the other boys are by the door, joined by a wild and kicking Faith, where another Kingsman lies bleeding on the ground. His sword is wielded by the largest of the remaining male Offerings, as the group surrounds the only other guard on the ground. Above us, the Minister Prime and the final Kingsman are too concerned with the King to notice what is going on below.

I yell to Pietra, who is racing towards me from the far bench, hand in hand with Jela. She presses something on her thinkwatch and then there is a click and a hum before the lights die. In a fraction of a second, the main doors are open. Imrin leads the way as I wait for Jela and Pietra. Just behind us, Rush is helping Hart, with Faith at the back, bellowing at everyone else to move. More Offerings pile through the door, before Pietra throws me our piece of stolen borodron. I swipe it on the scanner next to the door, sending it fizzing closed behind me. Perfectly in sync, Rush uses his stolen sword to smash the sensor. From the other side of the door, we hear hammering and shouting. We know at best it will only take thirty seconds for any conscious Kingsmen to scramble through the dark into the kitchens and exit that way.

If Imrin is wrong about the number of Kingsmen at the castle we've got no chance – but the corridors are empty. It was a gamble but we were living without hope anyway.

Imrin is terrific, trying to calm a couple of the edgier Offerings before he sets off along the corridor towards the stairs. Hart isn't in a good way and is in the middle of another coughing fit but Rush has one hand hooked around his waist and is practically dragging him up the stairs in the direction Imrin has gone.

'Are you all right?' Pietra asks, placing a hand on my bad arm and then apologising when I wince.

I know we don't have time to be chatting but she seems so worried that I end up replying as we run. 'Some of the lads from the barracks rigged the weapons just in case the King called for them. It's amazing what we figured out when we all started talking to each other.'

Faith tears past us as we hear a crash and the sound of raised voices. Boots are thundering along in the distance, which seems to speed everyone up. Pietra and Jela are surprisingly quick and Imrin is long gone. I try to help a few of the stragglers towards the back but as the echo of the heavy footsteps increases, I am forced to turn and run.

I dash up a set of steps but whoever is after me is not far behind and I almost run into Rush, who is standing at the top. My heart is racing and I can barely speak as my stomach and chest burn with a mixture of hunger and exhaustion. My shoulder is still hurting too.

'Go,' Rush bellows at me as I begin to ask what he's doing.

'Where's Hart?' I say instead.

'The girls have him, now go.'

I want to argue but he is holding the sword across his body aggressively and has both eyes on the exit of the stairwell, his mind already made up. I mumble a 'thanks', which I know will never be enough, and then carry on running until I reach a fork in the corridor. I stand in the centre and turn to watch as the Minister Prime and five other people burst from the top of the steps. One of the Kingsmen is a regular guard, but the other four are wearing the senior uniform. Porter isn't there and I don't recognise any of them.

Rush starts backing towards the direction I went in, the sword still across him defensively as the Minister Prime bellows, asking where we have gone. In a second, he spots me over Rush's shoulder and shrieks in rage. I want to keep running but something makes me stop for long enough to see Rush lunge dangerously towards one of the Kingsmen. Another retaliates immediately, thrusting a dagger under Rush's ribs. His cry ripples through the passages as I set off running again.

I can see Imrin's map perfectly in my mind and dart the long way around the floor until reaching the second set of stairs that lead to the dormitories. As I dash, the shooting, stabbing pains running up and down my arm increase, blending with the emptiness in my stomach, making me feel sick. When I reach the top of the steps and head towards the girls' dormitory, I see coloured stars around the edges of my vision. Bright pinks and yellows that make the corridors feel luminous. Behind me, the Minister Prime is close. I can hear him panting, taunting and calling.

He knows he has me.

I clench my teeth tightly and an anguished wail of agony falls from my lips as I sprint past the dorm, make two quick zigzag turns and then reach the final corridor. It is the place where Imrin and I first introduced ourselves to each other; where we spent hours plotting and planning, talking about the patterns of the fog drifting through the distant trees, laughing, smiling, and living a life that was stolen from us.

The moon illuminates the stone walls with a beautiful white angelic glow. I stop halfway along, the huge window behind me, and turn to face the Minister Prime. His eyes flicker towards the glass, knowing he has me in a dead end, as his lips angle into a cruel, thin smile. Behind him, two of the Head Kingsmen remain. They are both out of breath and one of them has blood running across his arm. They wait against the far wall as the Minister Prime takes one small, slow step towards me.

He speaks slowly and menacingly, each syllable spat with a barely contained fury. 'Where are the others, Miss Black-thorn?'

'Gone.'

'Gone where?'

'Gone through your train tunnel and out the other end.'

His eyes narrow slightly. 'We both know that's not true.'

I smile and nod, taking a step backwards away from him. 'I have no idea then. I guess I got a little lost . . .'

He replies with a lick of his lips. 'Perhaps I will pull your fingers off one by one until you tell me?'

'That sounds painful, *Bathix.*' I try to smile but a fire is flooding through my shoulder now I have stopped moving.

I hear him stumble slightly at the mention of the name I am not supposed to know but he corrects himself instantly with a forced cough. 'So how did you do it all? The animal cages opened in my zoo, so I had to send my Kingsmen to sort it out. The poisoning of the King? The lights going out? I'll find out from you soon enough, but if you tell me now, perhaps I'll be a little more lenient with you?'

He almost sounds genuine but we both know the types of thing he will do to me. I try to test my arm, to see if I can lift it, but I cannot move it at all. I want to laugh, to tell him he isn't fooling me, but the stars in my eyes are beginning to grow larger.

'I was in the dungeon,' I say. 'I didn't even have my thinkwatch. What do you think I could do on my own?'

He nods a snipped acceptance. 'Men are on their way to arrest your mother and your brother right now. They will be here tomorrow and I will make sure you watch me skin them alive before I even lay a finger on you. I'll make sure they know it's your fault; that you brought it upon them.'

'You'll have to find them first.'

The Minister Prime's brow ripples and I can almost see the thoughts colliding in his mind as he realises exactly why the door to his office was open. He is trying to figure out how Hart and I might have been working together; why I wanted to end up in the dungeon; and any number of other things he hadn't thought of, simply because he was incapable of thinking we could work with, instead of against, each other.

'Whatever you've done will be for nothing, you do know that? If your friends have somehow escaped, we will get them back, or we'll kill them. If your families are hiding somewhere, we will find them – and we'll kill them.'

By now, the blur in my eyes is so large that he is simply a hazy black shape. It makes his words sound more vicious; I have no doubt that is exactly what he intends to do.

'You forgot one thing.' I am surprised at how calm my voice sounds.

'What?'

'When you were listing the things you say I'm responsible for, you missed the biggest one. The tan fruit juice in the King's wine, the escape, the zoo cages being opened, the lights, all of those were just sideshows to stop you seeing the obvious.'

I take a step backwards as I hear the Minister Prime stepping forward. 'What did you do?'

'All of the people at home should have had an un-expected broadcast on their screens tonight, courtesy of the cameras around the hall. It's a shame you didn't notice the blinking red lights.'

It wasn't even that hard. On our screen at home, we have seen images from the castle before, so I knew there had to be some way to make the cameras broadcast outside the walls. I can see him trying to roll back in his mind what they will have seen: the King taunting Hart and myself with the meat, forcing Imrin and me to fight, the drunkenness, the ungainly baying for blood, the chaos. It's not the way subjects should see their King.

He sounds panicked, unable to understand what hap-pened. 'How?'

'There are lots of useful frequency codes on your think-pad. How to override the communication block on our thinkwatches, how to broadcast on the one frequency which everyone gets, lists of every Offering. All sorts. Perhaps you should close your door in future?'

The truth is exactly as Imrin explained to me when we started laying out our final plan. The Minister Prime knew it was possible for someone to walk into his office and use their borodron armour – or a stolen scrap – to access his thinkpad. He knew it could happen – but he was filled with the absolute arrogance that no one would dare. When you have that level of delusion, it's no wonder you don't do something as simple as closing a door. All I did was use his broadcasting codes to reprogram the cameras through the system in Porter's office and then Pietra used my think-watch to start them off.

It takes a second to sink in but my final remark is what tips him over the edge. He roars in anger and then I see his dark, hulking shape coming towards me. One half of my body feels like it has given up, but I turn and run in the only direction I can – towards the window. The Minister Prime is a step behind but it makes no difference as I angle my already-numb shoulder towards the dead end and with a grunt of hope, anguish and final exhilaration, I jump through the glass and begin plummeting to the ground.

35

On my thirteenth birthday, Opie and I ventured further into the woods than we ever had before. We had always hung around the edges, making swords out of sticks and playing hide and seek behind the branches and bushes, but the excitement of being that one year older spurred us into going out to the gully to see what lay around the edges.

At first it was thrilling but it wasn't long before I began to feel that sting of fear, a paranoid terror of being lost and not being able to find our way back. Opie laughed it off but I think he was more frightened than me. He lifted me onto his shoulders, allowing me to reach up and grab the lowest branch of a huge oak tree. I climbed, my fingers fumbling along the rough bark as the knife-like stumps scratched and scraped at my bare legs, my sturdy little arms clambering from one tree limb to the next. Eventually I was high enough to see over the tops of the smaller plants. In one direction I saw the crater that was once the lake; in the other was Martindale, peaceful and safe. I was so taken with the beauty of seeing it from the top of the tree that I forgot where I was. I tried to get a better view but in the fraction of a second it took my foot to slide across the dewy leaves, I lost my balance. Something snapped against the back of my head but the one thing I felt before Opie caught me was the incredible, unmatched freedom of falling.

As I drop with fragments of glass glistening around me, I close my eyes and listen to the night. The whistle of the breeze feels like the greatest release I can imagine as I hear the splintering of the glass and the cry of surprise from the Minister Prime. My side hurts so much that I'm not even sure if it is from where I was manhandled the previous night, the way I fell when I was fighting Imrin, or from the window itself. Everything has blended into one stabbing throb of pain.

And then I land.

Not with a bang or a crash, but instead it feels soft and feathery as the sheets from the medical bay beds cushion my fall and I bounce slightly before I feel someone pulling me to my feet. Imrin is out of breath and frantic as the other Offerings drop the sheets and descend on me.

At least four of them ask if I am okay but I ignore the questions.

'Did everyone get out?'

'Not everyone,' Imrin replies. 'There were more Kingsmen, not loads but enough.'

I feel hands on my back and look around to see Jela, Pietra and Faith, concern etched on their faces. Above us, there is another roar of rage. The Minister Prime is standing precariously in the space where the window used to be, staring through the hole I have created, bellowing vengeance.

'Where's Hart?' I ask.

Imrin doesn't answer, instead grabbing my hand as we start running again, scrambling over and around the wrecks of buildings until we reach the tree line that we spent so many hours staring at longingly. Leaning against a tree, his breath spiralling from his mouth in the cold night air, is Hart.

'He needed a head start,' Imrin tells me as we stop momentarily to check he is all right.

Everyone is cold, hungry and tired but somehow we keep moving through the trees, past the remains of villages and towns long gone. On and on we continue, not knowing if we are being followed, somehow fighting our aching limbs until the orange haze of sun slowly begins to rise over the horizon.

I have long since lost any feeling down my right-hand side but Hart is in a worse state than any of us. His chin and chest are speckled with blood from a cough which constantly returns in fits and starts. Imrin is exhausted from helping Hart, and Faith is perhaps the only one who looks as if she could continue for much longer.

I have lost track of how long we have been moving as we cross the remains of what was once a wide six-lane road, jumping across the cracked and crumbling tarmac, until we end up sliding down a bank on the far side. In front of us are the remains of another village – bricks, tiles and endless piles of masonry as far as we can see. The low sun provides no warmth and the moment we stop moving, my teeth begin to chatter. Imrin dashes forward and peers through the collapsed door of the first property, before checking another half-dozen. He waves us over, directing us into the largest of the collapsed houses. Under our feet are broken slabs of concrete and ripped-up patches of carpet. Because of the way the roof has only half-fallen, it provides an almost cave-like environment.

Imrin pushes me into the space first and I count the rest of us in. As well as myself, Imrin, Faith, Jela, Pietra and Hart, there are another four boys and two girls. Of our thirty Offerings, there are just eleven of us – plus Hart.

We are all covered to varying degrees with mud, blood, dust, dirt and grime but there is a sense of achievement and relief. Imrin picks up a broken door and shoves it into the space we climbed through. If someone is going to check every building, we'll be found but from the outside there's no obvious sign of anyone being here.

We huddle together for warmth, making sure we all know each other's names and where we come from. Some-how, it has taken me until now to notice that Bryony got away too. I wonder if she will ever get on with Pietra but, for now, it feels comforting to hear everyone's voices, to know people from all four Realms have worked together to get this far. All I want to do is rest but Pietra stands and lifts her top before unwrapping my mother's purple dress from around her waist and handing it to me. I smell the material and allow it to flow through my fingers, trying to picture Martindale before the questions start.

In one way or another, we have all been responsible for what has happened, although it is only me that knows everything. I ache all over but it is only fair I answer them, given the trust they have put in me.

I tell them how Imrin and I plotted extravagantly in the tunnel outside the dormitories and how our wild ideas eventually became a cohesive plan. Hart helped me into the Minister Prime's office where I stole the list of every Offering along with the frequency codes which allowed me to bypass the block on communications. This meant that I could send a message using my thinkwatch to the relatives of all the Offerings still alive in the castle, telling them to get to safety. One of the boys, Frank, questions this, remembering that my own thinkwatch was cut off – except that I had already switched mine with brave Pietra. No one noticed the orange shade on the face of mine because I levered the front away and pressed specks of dust onto it, making it as dim as possible, before putting it back together. Her black thinkwatch was cut away from my wrist before anyone noticed I wasn't the Elite it was showing me to be. She was the first girl in on the plan; the person who finally got all of the females talking to each other. Without that, we would never have been able to work together.

I tell everyone about the wonder of the zoo hidden within the castle and how Pietra took the cue, using my thinkwatch and the frequencies I found to remotely open the cages – and how she switched off the lights to gain us extra seconds.

I explain how Jela told me about the tan fruit. Faith and Imrin didn't even know what they were at first but put their own lives on the line by covering for each other as they squished the fruit juice from one into a bottle of wine destined for the royal box.

Frank tells me how Imrin got him to rig the weapons, so they were hollow with the metal spikes blunted. They would still have done some serious damage but Imrin and I were never trying to hurt each other. They had also rigged swords to break and canes to snap, just in case different weapons were brought up.

Someone asks how I knew I would have to fight Imrin but I didn't. It could have been Hart, or anyone. If I hadn't have got myself into the dungeon, Hart could have been forgotten about, but it wasn't a huge gamble to think that having the pair of us there would make the Minister Prime and King want to humiliate us. Imrin and I had a routine worked out to cause as little damage as possible but even if it had been someone not in on the plan, the weapons couldn't have caused a great deal of harm. They ask how I knew I wouldn't simply be killed by the King, but the truth is I didn't. It was always going to be a risk and as soon as I had sent the messages, hoping Colt and my mother would understand and get themselves to safety, I was willing to do whatever.

As Imrin cradles me and my eyes begin to close themselves, I tell them about my camera trick and how I reversed it using the codes from the Minister Prime's thinkpad. Instead of giving me ninety seconds to get past them, the cameras started broadcasting across the nation.

One of the boys who worked in textiles – the person who got the borodron in the first place – helped to smuggle out the rope that enabled everyone to get down the wall after escaping through the hospital window. They grabbed sheets from the beds before rushing around to catch me following my diversion. Imrin, who was responsible for so much of the message-passing while I was locked in the dungeon, assures me they didn't harm the nurse.

But the whole plan could have been ruined if it wasn't for Rush's sacrifice. I hung around long enough to make the Minister Prime follow me instead of the other Offerings but Rush was the person who gave us those vital few seconds that allowed us to escape. So, lastly, I tell the others what he did.

As the sun continues to rise, peeping through the gaps in the bricks, none of us knows if people witnessing the brutality inflicted upon the nation's Offerings will change anything.

I rest my head on Imrin's chest and can feel the re-assuring presence of Jela and Pietra nearby. I have no idea where our next meal will come from, no idea where my mother, Colt, Opie, Imp or any of the others' loved ones might be. I don't know if the Minister Prime is after us, or if the King has recovered.

As Pietra presses my thinkwatch back into my hand along with a screwdriver, I wedge the front off and start to wipe away the dust, exposing the gentle orange colour again. I can barely croak an apology for what happened to hers. What I do have is the map taken from the Home Affairs Minister's machine with all the rebel strongholds listed. As soon as we are rested, we will start to plot and plan.

Tonight, the fightback begins – but this morning, as I hear the gentle drumming of rain bouncing from the rubble, we let our battered, bruised and brave bodies sleep.

Afterword

If you're not the type of person who likes movie commentaries or behind-the-scenes stuff, then you should probably stop reading now! But if you'd like to find out about my writing process for the Silver Blackthorn trilogy then keep reading . . .

At some point when I was around ten or eleven years old, I read a book called *The Time Warrior*. It was a *Doctor Who* novelisation written by Terrance Dicks, based on a four-part television serial that aired seven years before I was born. I loved collecting the Target *Doctor Who* books, picking them up in charity shops for ten pence here and twenty pence there. I ended up collecting all 150 or so of them but, for whatever reason, there was a little idea in *The Time Warrior* that always stuck with me.

The story involves a leather-skinned alien named Linx – a Sontaran if you know anything about *Doctor Who* – crashing in Britain of the Middle Ages and hiding in a castle. As he tries to repair his ship, he appeases the castle's owner by providing him with 'magic' weapons, which are really from the future. I don't actually remember much more than that – I've never read the book since and I've not seen the television version –

but the idea of Medieval castles and futuristic technology is always something I thought was pretty cool.

And so we come to Silver Blackthorn. I live in the north-west of England, which can be – and frequently is – pretty grim. It's overcast, wet and windy, a lot of the time. My other series, a more grown-up set of crime books, are set in that grey, grimy world. Perhaps it's no surprise then that I came up with Silver when I was on holiday.

I'd been working full-time and writing the DS Jessica Daniel crime series for around a year when I went away for my first break since I'd started. Working the equivalent of two full-time jobs for twelve months really does take it out of you. I thought I'd have a fortnight's rest, but as soon as I had a bit of a lay down in the sun, Silver's story began flitting through my head – so I started writing again. Over the course of those two weeks, I sketched out by hand the entire plot for the first book over seven pages of notepad paper. Yes, that's what I do on 'holiday'.

AFTERWORD

The following pages contain some of my original notes for the first book in the Silver Blackthorn trilogy. It would've been in a much rougher form than this, but at some point while I was still on holiday, I put everything onto one sheet.

On this first sheet, there are small ideas which became much bigger ideas. For instance, around a third of the way down, it reads: 'Meets prev Offering'. That, of course, refers to Hart – who, in the end, became a big part of *Reckoning*. To a large degree, this is how my notes work. Three words can turn into thousands.

Lower down on the page is an example of the way this planning process works in reverse. It reads: 'Alert over other countries?' At the time, I thought this would be a large development – that Britain would be at war with other nations – but, in the end, I didn't really have anywhere else to go with this idea.

At the top, I've drawn a triangle. At the time, I was thinking of the Reckoning/Offering system as being top-down, like a triangle. There are far fewer Elites than any other rank, so they're at the top. It didn't really work out like that when I started writing, because Trogs are the lowest rank but not the predominant one. The system is more of a diamond-shape.

On the line below, you can see my N, E, S, W doodle, which is how it worked out. Both the Silver trilogy and my crime books include elements about the north/south divide in Britain. I was born in the south but live in the north, so it's probably something with which I have too much of an obsession.

MONARCH   X BEING CHOSEN IS   X DIFFERENCE DRESS, APP
MINISTER PRIME   A HUGE HONOUR-   ELITE, MEMBER, INTER
ALL KIDS TEST @ 16   EVEN THO PPL DON'T KNOW
RANKED △ CLEVER TO NOT.   WHAT EXACTLY IT ENTAILS   TROG

PICKED MORE FROM BOTTOM
ALL "GIVEN" TO KING AS OFFERINGS FROM? WHOSE?
NO-ONE KNOWS WHAT HAPPENS. SOME SAY TRADED OVERSEAS, SOME SAY IT'S AN
HONOUR. OTHERS MORE WARY, THO NOT IN PUBLIC
ALL TELEVISED-CEREMONIAL HANDING OVER.
TEARS, ETC, AS LEAVING
BIG MEAL AT 1ST, KING, QUEEN, MIN PRIME. ALL NICE, THEN KING
KILLS A LAD BECAUSE HE CAN, + TAKES GIRL. JOBS ACC TO RANK
CIVIL WAR WON BY PPL - OPTED FOR MONARCHY. WENT WRONG.
X MEETS PREV OFFERING
X MINISTER PRIME DEPUTY = REBEL
X SCIENTIST
X SMUGGLING FOOD OUT. LOTS WASTE. FOOD TO ANIMALS, THROWN AWAY, ETC
FALLS FOR GUY DISLIKED @ FIRST. KING ORDERED @ END
X LIVE IN WING/UNDER THE PALACE

X MEET ELITE GUY FROM HER DIST 2/3 YRS BK. USED TO BE
ATTRACTIVE. NOW HAGGARD. HE REMEMBERS HER? TELLS
NO WAY OUT

X ESCAPE ATTEMPT SOMEONE GETS CAUGHT, & TAKES BLAME
X SILVER SO-NAMED, HAIR COLOUR EVEN AS BABY
X BLACK MKT - SCRAPS FOOD KITCHEN WORKERS. INFO FROM PPL CLOSE
TO KING, ETC. ALLOWS SILVER TO PLOT
X IMRIN / HART HAS TO BE CAPTURED.
X ALERT OR OTHER COUNTRIES?
X SILVER & IMRIN DEVISE A MAP OF CAMERAS SO IMRIN CAN
↳ STUMBLE ACROSS PRIVATE ZOO.   LOOP THEM.
X WATCHES ARE COMPULSORY & SO NAMED BECAUSE LOOK LIKE
OLD TECH. TELL DAY/TIME, COMMUNICATOR, SCHEDULE.
↳ COMM DISABLED INSIDE PALACE.

X HAS VIRUSES STORED
X PUBLIC/TV EXECUTIONS OF CRIMS ARE POPULAR
↳ INTERVIEWS WITH M-P
X MAKE A FRIEND W/ SOMEONE WHO DIES?
X PUKE & EAT MORE - KING
X FOOD/FRUIT, ETC, SMUGGLED OUT KITCHEN

AFTERWORD

This is the next step of my planning. That first page is a lot of unformed ideas – a few words here or there. Sometimes even just one word, like 'Monarch' at the top of the page. Here, I started plotting things out more or less chapter-to-chapter.

In the top left is the triangle I never ended up using – but the numbers of Elites, Members, Intermediates and Trogs are the same in my initial notes as they are in the book. On the top right was the structure of the overall book. The first act is Silver's realisation of what the system is, the second is the escape from the castle. As it was, the escape ended up being my final act in this book. It's more introduction/realisation/escape.

In my first draft, the book started with Silver being distracted by Opie. I say she is fishing here, but that never made it into the final draft. Also, I hadn't worked out Opie's name – he's just a line. The Reckoning was called the Awakening and the Offerings are called the Chosen. Neither of those made it into the first draft. The notes are still a bit scattered but a lot of the plot points exist in the final book – such as the King skewering someone at a feast.

△ ELITES 16 2B, 2G PER REGION
MEMBERS 8 1B,1G PER REGION
INTECS 4 1B,1G ALL REGIONS
TROGS 2 1B,1G ALT REGIONS

1 REALISATION
2 ESCAPE
3

Ⓧ SILVER IS FISHING. SNAP BEHIND. ___ SNARED. TALKS. READY FOR AWAKENING (TEST)
KNOW HOW USE TEST PADS? USED TO PENCILS. RUMOURS x2 GOING TO
CHEAT. SILVER SAYS ✓ DANG. ___ = YEAH BUT WE ALL WANT TO BE AN
ELITE. + AN OFFERING. THINK YOU'LL BE CHOSEN. SILVER NOT BOTHERED.
___ = SUCH AN HONOUR, SILVER TAUGHT TO READ BY MOTHER. ___
CAN'T REALLY. BIT ABT HUNGRY (MY FISH?)
END TEST. NERVES ON MORNING. DNA TEST IN. KINGSMEN (DESCRIBE)
GRAB x2. KILL? HANG? SHOOT? DRAG AWAY?
↳ TALK ABT PREV OFFERINGS + RUMOURS OF ROLE ✱

Ⓧ MEMORY OF KINGSMEN RUTHLESSNESS. THINK ABT TEST APTITUDE/
PRACTICAL. WHOLE LIFE DEPENDS ON IT COS CHOOSES PROFESSN.
PADS = QUICK RESULTS. TALK ABOUT REGIONS + RESULTS
+ OFFERING NOS. ALL GET RESULT. ___ = TROG. SILVER =
INTER. THAT EVENING, SILVER'S MUM PLEASED. NO TRACE
OF "TROG". ~~KNOW~~ ~~KINGSMEN~~, SILVER CHOSEN. + CHEATS
RESULTS ON TV
PARADED

Ⓧ EXPLAIN CHOSEN = RANDOM. MORNING PARADE + TV OF REGIONS
+ OFFERINGS. SILVER'S FAMILY REWARDED FOOD. TELEVISED
EVERYWHERE. JOURNEY (TRAIN?) TO PALACE. TO QUARTERS
MEET OTHER OFFERINGS. G/B SPLIT. SILVER CATCHES
EYE ELITE BOY OTHER REGION. PARADE KIDS INTO KING'S
HALL. OBV RECOGNISE HIM, BUT EYES STARING & HUNGRY.
FEELS HIM LOOKING. ALL GIRLS ASKED TO DRESS BEST. CLOTHES
IN WARDROBES. DURING MEAL TROG BOY NOISH, DROPS SOMETHING
KING TAKES GUARD'S SWORD & SKEWERS HIM. ⊙ TALK ABT
CAMERAS ⊙

Ⓧ NONCHALANTLY GIVES SWORD TO GUARD, & SITS. SCREAMS/ SHOCK.
SILVER REALISES BEING AN OFFERING = JUST THAT.
IN DORM, GIRLS UPSET, ESP ELITES. SILVER PREV FELT DISDAIN
NOW EMPATHY. HOW 'GET AWAY? DOOR/WINDOWS LOCKED.
MIN PRIME ARRIVES - TELLS 1 GIRL "CHOSEN" BY KING.
DESCRIBE DRESS, ETC. TOMORROW = JOBS. ↳ HORROR.

Ⓧ NEXT DAY. INDUCTION VIDEO. CIVIL WAR RECAP GLORIOUS TRIAL
UNITING NATION. ELITES TECH JOBS, ETC. MORE. SOMEONE GOING
OVERSEE TO. SILVER = ~~TEXTILES~~.
ELECTRONICS
↳ HART

END: MEET REGION'S OFFERING 2 YRS B4. (DESCRIBE EARLIER
CHAPS). HE WAS ATTRACTIVE, ETC. NOW GAUNT + DAMAGED.
HE = NO WAY OUT.

AFTERWORD

At the top of this third notepad page, much of the conversation with Hart is exactly how it happens, some of it word for word. This was always going to be the moment where Silver realises exactly what's going on. Before that, she doesn't really know what to think. The idea of the King's 'public face' is what gave me the ultimate ending of *Reckoning*.

Imrin is introduced on this page in much the same way as in the actual book, although I have him working in electronics rather than textiles. I was unsure about everyone's roles here and didn't really know what sort of jobs would be on offer around the castle. That all came later when I was actually writing. There's also the first aborted escape on here too.

WORKS M-P's OFFICE

ALSO SAYS "KING'S
GAMES NOT STARTED YET"
"NOT A KING'S GAMES?"
"YOU DON'T WANNA KNOW"

Ⓧ HART TELLS SILVER ABT ALL THAT'S HAPPENED. ONLY HIM + 1 FROM
HIS YR OF OFFERINGS. 2/3 FROM LAST YR. KING DOES WHAT
HE WANTS. MOST KILLED FOR FUN. 2 PPL MAD TO FIGHT UNTIL
1 DEAD FOR HIS AMUSEMENT. KILLED EACH OTHER, SO HE
KILLED 1 MORE IN ANNOYANCE. SO IF LUCKY, TRADED ABROAD. NO
WAY OUT. NO COMM TO OUTSIDE WORLD. ~ESCAPE~ IF U RUN
THEY DON'T KILL COS THAT'S EASY WAY OUT. PUBLIC FACE
OF KING = ~SHIT~ SAVIOUR. POPULAR - BUT   U CAN'T THINK UR THE 1ST
HE LIVES IN LUXURY WHILE PPL STARVE.   TO WANT TO ESCAPE.
END: HERE FOR LIFE   ↙ → HART TELLS SILVER DANGEROUS TO
ALSO SAYS SHE'S SAFE FROM TALK. HE IS V. AGITATED. SAYS NOT TO
GAMES COS WORK AS IN TECH   TALK AGAIN.

Ⓧ NOT MUCH FOOD DURING WK - BUT 1 WEEKLY BANQUET. GIRLS
EXPECTED TO DRESS UP. SILVER: BALANCE NOT BEING "PICKED" BY
KING, NOT STANDING OUT AS UGLY/DISPOSABLE. PREV GIRL
PICKED NOT SEEN SINCE. LATER, LOOKING FOR A WAY OUT.
SNEAKS THROUGH (VENT) INTO MAIN CORRIDORS ETC.
DESCRIBE SURROUNDINGS - END: ~BAND~ HAND ON SHOULDER
(IMRIN)   ②SOMEONE CAUGHT TRYING TO SMUGGLE FOOD.

Ⓧ IT IS ~ANOTHER BOY~ (IMRIN) NOTICES. SILVER SEES HE'S MAD SIMILAR
THO UGHTS, EXCHANGE a) BACK STORIES, b) WHAT
HEARD SINCE ARRIVING. TALK ABT DEAD BOY.
WHAT GOING TO DO. ETC? SILVER: WE'RE GOING TO ESCAPE

Ⓧ REALISE W/ ~ELLE BOY~ IMRIN IN ~ELECTRONICS~ TOTTLES ETC, THEY CAN GET A
HANDLE ON EVERYONE'S MOVEMENTS & PLANS.   (3RD PART)
~✗✗~

Ⓧ CONTINUE TO SNEAK OUT, WHILE IGNORING EACH OTHER DURING DAY.
LAST THING WANT TO DO IS ATTRACT ATTN. CONDITIONS STILL AWFUL.
ONLY WAY OUT IS THE SAME WAY IN: A DELIVERY SHUTTLE.
TALK ABT BROKEN INFRASTRUCTURE - LACK OF FUEL.
SO BEGIN TRACKING TIMES, DAYS, SECURITY. RULES OUT EVERYTHING
THAT MIGHT NOT WORK + CAMS UNTIL THEY HAVE A PLAN. PASS NOTES WRITTEN
ON PAPER, ANYTHING. IMRIN ~PROBES~ GETS INTO SECURITY SYSTEM & FINDS OUT
ELECTRONIC DOORS HAVE A WEAKNESS: SILVER STEALS A RIGID FABRIC THING THAT CAN
FIT BETWEEN DOOR/FRAME & MAKE THEM OPEN. SO, CERTAIN TIME, MOVE QUICK, ALL
PLANNING WORKING... UNTIL FIND FAMILIAR FACE IN BK OF SHUTTLE...

Ⓧ IT IS ANOTHER OFFERING. ~TRIBUTE~ SHOCK ON FACE - SAME PLAN. IMRIN ARRIVES, OUT-OF-
BREATH. HE SEES OTHER OFFERING & THEY LEG IT. NO WORDS, RETURN TO DUTIES
UNNOTICED. BANQUET THAT EVENING, NO OFFERING. AFTER, UNVEILED, HANGING.
MIN PRIME: A LESSON TO YOU ALL. - HIS FAMILY HAVE ALSO
BEEN PUNISHED ~(FIELDS)~ BURNED DOWN HOUSE.

AFTERWORD

I don't really know where the idea of the hidden zoo came from on this fourth page. I liked the idea that the castle, and therefore the King, had all these wonderful creatures, Noah's Ark style, and then wasn't bothered about it.

Pietra is rather tactfully called 'girl' here but Silver ending up in the hospital again happens almost exactly like the actual book. After the first quarter of this page, most of the beats of the story are untouched.

The idea next to the 'XX' at the bottom is something to which I didn't quite get. I wanted to show what a 'normal' day was like when you were working in the castle. I couldn't make it work because Silver's day is different to what the others' was like; Porter isn't as horrible to her as some of the other Head Kingsmen. Most of the ideas noted down still crop up, just not how I'd originally thought.

Ⓧ WORRIED GLANCES. SILVER SNEAKS OUT BUT IMRIN
NOT THERE. IS NEXT NIGHT WONDERS IF BEING CLOONED
TO BUT WOULD SURELY HAVE BEEN SNAGGED: ALTHO DORM
MIGHT BE. THEY DISCOUNTED SHUTTLES BEING SEARCHED ON WAY
OUT. IMRIN SHOWS SILVER A MAP HE HAS BEEN CREATING,
SHOWING ALL CAMS + FLOORS. SILVER ADDS TO IT. KNOW
FAMS IN DANGER — BUT ALSO THAT IT'S THAT OR DIE.
IMRIN ASKS WHAT SILVER'S BROTHER WOULD WANT HER TOO.
NEXT NIGHT SHE TELLS HIM SHE CAN LOOP CAMERAS VIA HIS
(WATCH) ONLY GET 90SECS MAX. THEY GO EXPLORING & FIND A SECRET
ZOO. (END: ANIMAL SHE'S ONLY EVER HEARD OF?)
                                    NEVER SEEN
                    SILVER
Ⓧ ~~IMRIN~~ HAS PROGRAMMED HER IS WATCH TOO, SO SHE CAN GO WHERE
SHE WANTS. GOES TO SEE (ANIMAL) EACH NIGHT. REMINDS HER OF HER — CAGED.
1 OF THE GIRLS IN SILVER'S DORM IS A GRASS — CATCHES
HER SNEAKING BK IN.   (TALK ABT HER BEFORE.
                            SHE TELLS ON SOMEONE
                            ELSE FOR HOARDING FOOD)

Ⓧ GIRL TELLS SILVER SHE WANTS OUT — KING'S GAMES SCARING
HER. SILVER & (GIRL?) CHOSEN FOR KING'S GAMES. HAVE TO
HIT EACH OTHER AS HARD AS THEY CAN. SILVER REMEMBERS
HART SAYING SHE WUD BE IMMUNE ... MAYBE THIS A MSG THAT
NO-ONE IS. ALTHO WON'T KILL. (BUILD UP TO "HIT" GAME — SILVER
THINKS SHE CAN'T/WON'T KILL) SILVER GOES 1ST. M-P WARNS
IF KING THINKS HOLDING BK, GO AGAIN. SO PUNCHES (GIRL) AS HARD
AS CAN IN FACE. (GIRL) HITS HER. PAIN. KING SAYS AGAIN COS
NOT HARD ENOUGH. END: BLACKOUT.

Ⓧ REALISES DONE HER A FAVOUR — CAN MAP HOSPITAL. AS RECOVERS
MENTAL MAPS OF IT ALL. NOW HAVE MOST OF PALACE DONE —
KNOW LOCATION CAMS — ONLY A FEW UNKNOWN ROOMS, INCL
KING'S CHAMBERS & M-P'S OFFICE. IMRIN SAYS: WHAT NOW. SILVER
WANTS TO GET INTO M-P'S OFFICE — NO USE JUST ESCAPING IF CAN'T
PROVE WHAT'S HAPPENING.

┌──┐
│XX│ — DESCRIBE A DAY — IE "BOSS", WORKMATES : MAINLY WEAPONS.
└──┘   KING OBSESSED W KINGS
    — EACH WK, KING'S GAMES. PERSON V PERSON. SOME DIE ──→
    — SOME WORKMATES COMPLY COS OF FAMILY / FEAR — ALSO, THEY ARE   BRIT
      ENCOURAGED TO GRASS.   EMPIRE
          IMRIN
    — (NR END ~~SILVER~~ GRASSES ... BUT IT IS TO GET SILVER WHERE SHE
      NEEDS TO BE — NEAR HART IN CELLS)
    — KISS IM/SILVER.

AFTERWORD

The top line of this page is perhaps key to the core message of the books: people can have power without knowing it if they work together. I know that sounds a bit socialist! The point was supposed to be that the King might expect his Kingsmen and Head Kingsmen to betray him, but he'd never expect the people at the bottom of the chain to try.

The ending is sort of here but not really, which gives you the clue that I didn't have the exact finish. Broadly, it's there: 'Run for it' – which pretty much sums up what happens. The intricacies around that came through writing the rest of the book.

Ⓧ "WE'RE JUST KIDS". BUT SILVER KNOWS THATS WHY THEY R
DANGEROUS. KING WOULD EXPECT BETRAYAL FROM PPL CLOSE-
WOT CAN WE DO? A: WE HAVE PPL EVERYWHERE - PPL
SCARED. GIRL WHO GRASSED/ PUNCHED ON-SIDE +
w/ OTHERS ALL WORK DIFF DEPOTS. W/ MAP THEY KNOW AS
HART'S MUCH AS ANYONE. JUST GOTTA TRUST. BREAK INTO M-P's
MB'S OFFICE. LISTS OF OFFERINGS (SCANS INTO "WATCH"(?) HART: HE'S
HERE. HE COVERS FOR SILVER.

END: HART ADRESSED (~~HE DEAD~~) NOT ~~KILLED~~ LOST TO TOWN   M-P POCKET
~~INSTEAD. IN CELLS UNDER QUARTERS~~   WOT SEING

Ⓧ SILVER TERRIFIED OF WHAT MAY HAPPEN TO HART. NOT BEEN KILLED - ALL QUIET.
IMRIN THINKS COJ M-P DUDNT WANT KING TO KNOW. WORD FROM
OTHER OFFERING HE'S IN CELLS: THEY KNOW LAYOUT. SILVER SAYS
GOT TO ACT TONIGHT AT BANQUET.

END - KING: WE HAVE A TRAITOR HERE - SILVER. PRAISES
IMRIN FOR HAVING BRAVERY TO SPEAK OUT.

Ⓧ (SILVER IS WHERE SHE NEEDED TO BE - CELLS TO TALK TO HART -
FBACK?)
        ⌐ KING ANNOUNCES IT IS SILVER ✓ IMRIN -
           (USING STUNT WEAPONS?)

- KING'S GAMES - MIDWAY THRU REALISE CAMS BROADCASTING TO ALL
✓ ANIMAL(S) RELEASED

-                          ALL OFFERINGS HAVE
-                          SET SOMETHING IN MOTION -
-                          SLEEP TAB - FOOD / FAKE WEAPONS / LOUD SIREN / EARPLUGS
- RUN FOR IT

AFTERWORD

Before I started writing *Reckoning*, I wanted to make sure I knew how the world had got to the point at which it started. The first three words on this final page spell out a lot of that – 'Oil ran out'. After that it is general odds and ends. Some of this fed into the main book but some of it doesn't really matter. For example, 'Most of Mid East wiped out' is something to which I never quite got.

When I write, it's entirely electronically. I send myself emails, I write plots in Notepad and back them up on pen drives and through things like Dropbox. This is more or less the only thing I've ever plotted with pen and paper. The only problem was trying to decipher it when I got home – my handwriting is appalling, as you can see.

- OIL RAN OUT
- LONG CIVIL WAR - LOTS DESTRUCTION, ETC
- UNTIL KING STEPPED IN AS "NEW" LEADER & ENDED IT.
- [N] REGION: DUMANG AROUND ELECTRONICS
- ELECTRICITY ON & OFF
- EXCEPT "WATCHES", WHICH RUN OFF A NEW TYPE BATTERY
- SOME COUNTRIES WAR W/ EACH OTHER
- MOST OF MID EAST WIPED OUT - NUKES.
- KING IS MUCH LOVED
- BUT FOOD SHORT, Ø ENG/WAL IN 4 AREAS W $\frac{N}{S}$ E
- E = FISHING, W = FARMING/AG, N = TEXTILES + ELEC DUM, S = DEFENCE / ? FINANCE ?
- TAKE "RECKONING" AT 16 TO DECIDE CAREER. LARGELY ACADEMIC.
- RANKED ELITE/INTER/MEMBER/PROG + GIVEN CAREER REC.
- MINISTER PRIME IS TOP-RANKED OFFICIAL.

AFTERWORD

After all of that, the existence of this series is down to two things: the fact I love *Doctor Who* and the sunshine. The reason it's got this far is, for the most part, down to two people.

Firstly, there is my agent, Nicola. I say 'agent' but it's hard to think of her like that. We talk, text, or email pretty much every day. She was the first person to read the Silver books and instantly set out to get them into your hands.

Secondly is the person who edited these books: Natasha. I have a barely concealed secret that I am awful at being edited, which is the irony of ironies considering that was my day job for a decade. It's not that I mind people tinkering with my words, or that I think I'm always right. It's that I hate looking backwards. I always want to be working on the next project, not bothering myself with things with which I'm done. Most of the time, I can't even remember large amounts of the plot. Frequently, I'll have to re-read something I've written in the editing process and I'll be surprised by the twists because I don't remember writing them. What that means is that when an editor asks me a question about something, I'm as blank as they are. So the editing process for the first Silver book was a long and, for me, frustrating one.

Anyway, the truth is that if it wasn't for Natasha championing the character and the series, and putting up with my complaining, then it wouldn't be in your hands now. For that, we should all send her tweets and emails saying she has good taste. She does.

RENEGADE

the second book in the Silver Blackthorn trilogy

BY KERRY WILKINSON

Silver Blackthorn is on the run.

All she really wants is to be reunited with her family and friends but the time for thinking about herself has passed. Now the fates of eleven other teenagers are in her hands – and they are all looking to her for a plan.

With an entire country searching for the escaped Offerings, Silver is under pressure to keep them all from the clutches of the Minister Prime, King Victor and the Kingsmen. As expectations are piled upon the girl with the silver streak in her hair, she realises that life will never be the same again.

Huge changes are on the horizon and Silver will be forced to face them head on . . .

ISBN 978-1-4472-3531-6